MW00738053

12/1/01

Angels in the Snow

To Sue,

May you always be blessed
to be able to see the
goodness around you.

Whitney Clayton
☺ C W C Jr

Angels in the Snow

by

Whitney Clayton

DORRANCE PUBLISHING CO., INC.
PITTSBURGH, PENNSYLVANIA 15222

All Rights Reserved
Copyright © 2000 by C.Whitney Clayton, Jr.
No part of this book may be reproduced or transmitted
in any form or by any means, electronic or mechanical,
including photocopying, recording, or by any information
storage and retrieval system without permission in
writing by the publisher.

ISBN # 0-8059-4741-8
Printed in the United States of America

First Printing

For information or to order additional books, please write:
Dorrance Publishing Co., Inc.
643 Smithfield Street
Pittsburgh, Pennsylvania 15222
U.S.A.
1-800-788-7654

Dedication

To my daughters Bryn and Leigh.

May you admire Jane.

Acknowledgements

Since this is the first story I've ever written, I have many people to thank. Without all their valuable contributions, I would never have had a story worth publishing. For those who provided me with editorial direction: Pam Boice, Ann Johnson, Michael Valentino (his rewrite taught me so much about proper writing), Patricia Begalla, V. Conti, Jennie Langdon, James Fairfield, and Glenda Baker, thank you all for your expert guidance. I never enjoyed English in school (that's why I went into numbers) and as a result I needed a lot of editorial help. I am grateful to Father Patrick Kelly, Dr. Mary Lewis, my brother Bruce, Charles Connors, Carl Anderson, John Gregorian, and Bruce Schwoegler (WBZ-TV weatherman) to name a few of the many people who provided me with ideas and technical information. As a single male when I wrote *Angels in the Snow*, the catalogs from Chadwick's of Boston, Ltd.® and Victoria's Secret® were extremely helpful with their detailed clothing descriptions. To those who read various drafts: Karen Baker, Alan and Elizabeth Xenakis, Audrey Drummond, Lacy Baker, Father Corbett Walsh, S.J., Nancy Robie, Anne Mastrandrea, Carmen & Sandra Morreale, Dwight & Nancy McWilliams, and my brother Charles: your valuable opinions were greatly appreciated. A special thanks to David Booth who introduced me to Dorrance Publishing Co. and to Dorrance Publishing Company. To the Boston radio station WBMX, specifically disc-jockeys Joe Martelle and Gregg Daniels, for choosing two of my five poems in *Angels in the Snow* as Valentine's Day contest winners (Joe in 1992 with "Angel in the Snow" and Gregg in 1993 with "My Pillow"). You helped me believe my writing would be enjoyed by people who didn't know me. To my childhood friends: Neal O'Boyle, Dwight McWilliams, and Jim Doherty (where are you?) thanks for all the fun kid stuff memories. To my father who never understood why I wanted to write a story (let alone a love story), I wish you had lived long enough to understand. To my dear mother, who during my high school years spent weeks at my bedside in various hospitals praying I'd get better, you are truly my hero to be admired; for you taught me to love and care for others. To my wife Maureen, falling in love with me with each chapter I would let you read, will always be my greatest reward. And finally to my daughters Bryn and Leigh, you have given my life and this story meaning.

PART ONE

Chapter 1

Robert J. McWilliams, III—with his three-piece suit, twenty-five dollar haircut, and patent-leather Italian loafers—looked every inch the high-powered corporate attorney as his heels click-clacked in the weekend-still corridors of Daniels Industries. In the ten years since graduating from Harvard Law, McWilliams had built a reputation as one of the new movers and shakers in Boston's legal community. From the start of Daniels Industries' replacement process for an investment consultant, David Abrams had been his recommended choice.

After a week of business meetings in L.A., Ralph Daniels had set aside Saturday afternoon to meet with and hear the proposals from the two investment consultant finalists. As the fifty-nine-year-old president, chairman, and founder of Daniels Industries, an electronics and manufacturing conglomerate, the ultimate decision of whom that person would be was his.

Returning from walking Abrams out to the front lobby, McWilliams, without knocking, strode back into Daniels's office. "I must say, Ralph, I was quite impressed with Abrams's strategy."

Putting Abrams's proposal on his custom-made, mahogany desk, Daniels looked up and said, "He was persuasive. Got the feeling he likes doing things his way." He sat back in his deep, leather chair, steepled his fingers, and peered over them at the young attorney. "I still want to hear Ms. Melrose's presentation before I decide."

McWilliams glanced at his Rolex. "Hope she's on time. I'm due at the gym by three." Strolling over to a wall unit, he reached for a framed photo of Ralph standing next to the company's communications satellite. The buy-out of the satellite manufacturer was the most recent of the counselor's string of successful negotiations.

There was a firm knock on the door. McWilliams glanced at his watch again and muttered, "Right on time."

Straightening his tie, Ralph Daniels walked over and opened the door. A young woman in a soft yellow jacket dress extended her hand and said, "Good afternoon, Mr. Daniels."

"Nice to see you again, Ms. Melrose. I appreciate your giving up such a beautiful Saturday to meet with me."

"It's quite all right. The birds in my backyard can wait a little longer for their feeders to be hung."

After shaking hands, Daniels led her into the room. "I hope you don't mind," he said, gesturing toward Bob. "I've asked my corporate counsel to sit in on your presentation."

"Name's McWilliams, Robert McWilliams," Bob said, extending his hand without approaching her.

"Jane Melrose." She walked over and shook his hand, trying not to stare at his thick, wavy blond hair and deep blue eyes. "It's a pleasure to meet you," she said, surprised at the slight break in her voice and flutter of her heart.

Bob lowered his pupils, surveying her slim five-foot-six stature. "You seem a bit young to have the experience needed to manage an eight million dollar pension fund. What are your qualifications?"

"Graduated with honors from Notre Dame in '81," she said, ignoring his chauvinism. "Since then I've been with Merrill Lynch— six years in research, the last two as an investment advisor."

"That's a far cry from Mr. Abrams's twenty-five years with Salomon Brothers. He exhibited sensible, mature judgment in his presentation. You just missed him."

Damn, she thought. She had hoped her presentation would be the first. Even more disturbing was the recollection of having passed a smartly dressed man in the parking lot, swinging his briefcase, whistling to himself. She turned from McWilliams and smiled pleasantly at Mr. Daniels. "Are you ready to hear my proposals?"

"I'd like that, Jane," Daniels said, leading the way to his working table in the far corner of his office. "I've been looking forward to hearing your ideas after all the good things my daughter Christine has said about you. She's convinced you're going to make her a wealthy woman."

Walking to the table, Melrose admired a Turkish Hereke silk prayer rug hanging on the wall. With brilliant jewel tones, hand-knotted in intricate detail, it was exquisite. As she sat down, she took a folder out of her black leather briefcase and handed Daniels a professionally bound presentation. "Christine's an aggressive investor," she said.

"Just like her old man," Daniels said, looking up at McWilliams, who had taken his station behind them, arms crossed, feet apart—a centurion guard.

"To start with," Melrose began, "having reviewed your present portfolio, I wouldn't recommend any drastic changes. Most of your investments consist of sound growth stocks and income-bearing bonds. However, I would increase the percentage of equity invest-ments from thirty to forty-five percent. Even though the crash of '87 scared a lot of folks, there are still plenty of good buys out there."

McWilliams's eyes narrowed.

An hour later, she finished. Daniels again steepled his fingers and peered at McWilliams. "What do you think, Bob?"

The young attorney spoke directly to Daniels. "Her background worries me." Looking down at Melrose, he said, "You've been overly involved with utilities. Abrams had a broader approach. For example, he mentioned a company called Unitel Software. Says it's about to take off."

Melrose focused her eyes up on him, taking a moment before answering. "I'm afraid I have no knowledge of Unitel, but I'll be glad to do some research and give you my opinion on it—or any other stock that interests you. I'm always open to new investments." Crossing her legs, she waited for a response.

McWilliams's gaze wandered to Melrose's legs. Then looking away, he walked to the window and peered out. Abruptly he turned and faced her. "Public Service of New Hampshire? You actually like that?"

"Love it," she shot back. "I admit it could be a risk; being in Chapter Eleven, the bonds could become worthless. But the bank-ruptcy judge has ruled that the interest on the first mortgage debt must be paid. And once Seabrook goes on-line, the company's fixed-charge coverage will increase." She paused, expecting a comment.

When none came, she continued. "You can't beat a purchase price in the low seventies and a yield of over twenty percent. It fits in ideally with Mr. Daniels's conservative, yet aggressive, strategy."

McWilliams had started pacing. "That is, if it goes on-line. The NRA may never approve the plant. If you've read the papers lately, you'd know that nuclear power is taking a lot of hits from the environmentalist crowd."

Jane felt a rush of fire surge through her veins. She stood and faced the handsome lawyer. Her eyes demanded attention as she walked toward him. She wouldn't let him break eye contact. Stopping before it was necessary to look up at him, she said, "You know, Bobby, you weren't here last week when Mr. Daniels outlined his investment strategy to me. He didn't mention any political or environmental limitations. His only desire was growth and income." She paused, making sure what she had to say would sink in. "And that's exactly what my plan will provide."

McWilliams's face became taut. His hands clenched at his sides. No one spoke. The clock on Daniels's desk ticked. McWilliams shifted his feet. The silence was filled with tension.

Finally Daniels spoke. "You're right, Jane. That's exactly what I am after—growth and income." Jane thought she saw the outline of a smile forming at the corners of the man's eyes. "And I'm not afraid of taking some risks—as long as there's sound reasoning for such investments." Rising, Daniels glanced at McWilliams and said, "What do you say, Bob?"

Jane recognized the rhetorical nature of the question. She smelled victory. She knew she had reached the older man.

McWilliams hesitated before he spoke. "It looks as if we've found the type of investment consultant we've been looking for." Walking over to Jane, he offered his hand. "Congratulations, Jane, you were well prepared. Despite my spoken reservations, I think you're very knowledgeable. You're definitely a tough competitor. It was your appearance that caught me off guard."

"Thank you, Bob. I've been known to use deception now and then to achieve my goals. I'll let you know what I think about Unitel."

After a short conversation with Daniels, McWilliams excused himself and left the room while Jane collected her papers and stowed them neatly in her briefcase.

"You know," Daniels said, "Bob's right, you are a tough competitor. Where did it come from?"

"Sports. Had a winning record each of my four years of playing soccer at Notre Dame. Made co-captain my senior year. Though, I must admit, it was more for my attitude than my skills."

Daniels nodded. "I'm impressed. I thought I recognized the team player in you, and I always go with the team player. Bob may come across as a bit arrogant, but he's a good team man. He's a lot like I was before I settled down and got married."

She shook Daniels's hand. "Thanks for your confidence. You won't be disappointed."

"There never was any doubt. You put on quite a show. But I'd advise you not to call him Bobby again."

Chapter 2

It was Sunday evening and Jane's apartment was still uncomfortably hot. Sliding down in the refreshing water of the tub, Jane stretched her legs. Lulled by the running water she emitted a long, pleasurable sigh. Relaxed at last, she savored the success of yesterday's presentation and today's installation of her bird feeders.

She felt good. The forecast was for "continued sunny and hot through Wednesday," perfect for her mini-vacation. This year she had decided to take long weekends—a change from last year's trip when she had gone with her mother to visit relatives in Ireland.

When the bubbles reached her chin, she sat up and turned off the faucet. Before settling back, she drew the shower curtain open. Since receiving the curtain three years ago as a gift from Marie, her college roommate and closest friend, she'd spent hours contemplating the romantic scene of a little boy and girl walking together in the snow pulling a sled. In her mind's eye, the boy was Henri von Eeden, who'd been her fantasy dream lover since college. She was the little girl. Details like Henri's blond hair and the curtain boy's brown didn't intrude on her dreams.

Maybe, she mused, just maybe, she was meant for Robert

McWilliams. Hadn't Mr. Daniels said Bob needed to settle down and get married? Well...he had implied it.

She knew exactly what type of man attracted her, and over the years she'd become very particular when it came to dating. *Seldom dating* was more like it. But hadn't all her academic and business accomplishments come from God's help and a strict adherence to a planned course of action?

She would stick to her beliefs about the right man for her. A strategy that so far had brought her nothing but loneliness. But her prayers may finally have been answered. Bob McWilliams had met her requirements. Could their meeting have been God's will?

Cupping a handful of lilac-scented bubbles, she sniffed the delicate fragrance. Then, reaching for her loofa, she began to meticulously massage her body from neck to long, slim legs. By the time she had finished pampering herself, the bubbles had faded and the water chilled.

Settled in bed, lost in her latest book, the phone on the night table jolted her back to reality. A pleasant surprise—Marie, calling from Chicago. "Jane, honey, are you doing okay? Any panic attacks?"

"Marie, whatever on earth are you talking about?"

"What else, girl—you've been thirty for nearly a month now."

Aging in itself wasn't a concern to Jane. It was the ticking of her biological clock that had been causing her many moments of despair. Her dreams of a large family were slipping away. "You should know me better than that. I'm doing just fine. Landed an eight million dollar account yesterday, and I'm off work till Wednesday. I just celebrated with a bubble bath."

"I don't suppose you were admiring a certain house-warming gift I gave you, indulging in a particular fantasy?"

"What if I did?" Jane answered awkwardly, wishing at the moment Marie didn't know her so well. But sharing feelings and dreams with Marie was part of their closeness. "You've got to admit, Henri *was* gorgeous. It would have been so much fun flying down some hill on a sled with my arms wrapped around him, hanging on for dear life."

"Forget Henri," Marie chided. "He was a conceited jerk who was intimidated by intelligent women. You know that as well as I do. Look at the type of woman he married. She was a real bimbo."

"I know, I know. But ever since I was a little girl, I dreamed about a guy like him, and when I first saw him, I felt certain he was the one God intended for me. You and Stanley were falling in love, and it seemed like the perfect time for both of us."

"Your time will come."

Jane twirled a strand of hair. She couldn't keep the news to herself any longer; she had to tell Marie about Bob. "Keep your fingers crossed, because I may have met my dream lover yesterday."

"Really!" Marie's voice rose to a high pitch. "That's wonderful. Tell me all."

"He's the corporate attorney where I got the account. His name's Robert McWilliams, and he's smart, successful, blond, and gorgeous." Poking her feet out from the sheet, Jane began to inspect her hot-pink painted toenails.

"Mmmmm, he sounds perfect."

"He'd better be." Jane picked up the phone and hopped out of bed. Going to her bureau, she picked up a bottle of nail polish. "My mother's acting like she may take it upon herself to find me someone."

"That's how mothers are. How is she these days?"

Back on her bed, Jane cradled the phone with her shoulder and proceeded to touch up her toenails. "She's fine. I'm going out to visit her toward the end of July. You remember my Aunt Sandy, my mother's baby sister? My mother and Aunt Jean, her older sister, are planning a big birthday party for Aunt Sandy."

"In July?" Marie's utter was grievous. After a moment of silence, she said in a solemn voice, "Did you hear about Donna Gildee's husband, Peter?"

"I haven't heard from them since her note in last year's Christmas card."

"He died last week."

"Oh, no!" cried Jane, messing up one of her toenails.

"I know. It's so tragic. I talked to Donna last night. Said it was from complications with his diabetes. She was in no way ready for this."

"Her poor kids. How will she ever be able to raise three children without a father?"

"She has a brother who lives nearby. He's been a big help."

"Thank goodness for family. But it's not the same as having a husband and father. I still don't understand how she could have let herself fall in love with Peter. She knew how serious his condition was. And then to marry him and have children. What was she thinking?"

"Come on, Jane. They were madly in love. You remember how charming he was. Nobody nicer on campus, and that included my Stanley. Believe me, after what Stanley's been through, how's anybody to know how long any of us will live."

"Even so..." The conviction in Jane's voice was unmistakable. Getting out of bed, Jane returned the bottle to the bureau. Jane then eyed her silver and wood crucifix hanging on the wall. She tilted her head back and forth and then reached over and adjusted the crucifix's position.

"That's not how Donna feels. She told me she'd always have her memories of Peter to treasure. I'm going to visit her next month."

"She'll be happy to see you. You two were such good friends. I'll write her a sympathy note tonight, but you be sure to give her my love when you see her."

"I will." Marie paused for a moment and then her voice brightened. "There's a chance I may be out your way in August for a medical equipment convention in Boston. I'm trying to convince my boss I should attend. I can't afford to let the competition get ahead of me. I'll let you know of my plans."

"There's no stopping you, Marie. You'll be the top sales woman yet.

"Honey, with my weary bones, I deserve to be at the top."

"It'd be great to see you. I treasure our get-togethers and having intimate chats..."

After the call, Jane wrote the promised sympathy note, then settled down in bed and turned off the light. After her prayers, she thought about Donna's unfortunate situation until she drifted off to sleep.

It was nearly dawn when her sleep became disturbed and restless. "No! You're wrong!" she yelled, jerking up to a sitting position. Awakened by a bad dream, she looked around the room with a deep sense of loneliness. The hope of the last two days that Bob was the man of her dreams had been wiped away. Overwhelmed once again by her feelings of despair, she began to sob.

Her phone conversation with Marie must have caused the

12

nightmare. The dream was a variant of frequent dreams, which ultimately came to the same dreaded conclusion. It had begun with her being brought out onto the stage of a large auditorium in front of hundreds of eligible men, and she had to choose the one she wanted. She was led to a small room where, one by one, the men came in for her inspection. Yet with every man she found some flaw and kept declining them. Finally when she asked for the next candidate, her mother said, "I'm sorry darling, but there are no more men for you to choose from."

Chapter 3

Seeking solitude, Jane stepped softly into the stillness of Sacred Heart Church. She knew she was early for Monday's nine o'clock Mass, but this morning—especially this morning—she wanted to avoid drawing attention to herself. Tissue in hand, she dabbed under her sunglasses and wiped away a lingering tear.

She wore a white blazer over a pink dress that hung to mid-calf. Her shoulder-length hair had been haphazardly fastened in a ponytail. Down the right aisle was her usual pew, adjacent to the Twelfth Station of the Cross. Kneeling there, she slipped the sunglasses into her pocket and clasped her hands, gazing beyond the altar to the figure of Jesus on the cross and its message of pain, suffering, and ultimate glory—a message which didn't seem to pertain to her, Jane Melrose. At least not the glory.

Her location in the middle of the pew guaranteed privacy and was indicative of her desire for obscurity. On this quiet morning, the young woman kneeling in the pew epitomized solitude—the solitude of the lonely and troubled.

She continued her gaze. Questioning her feelings—feelings of faltering, of faithlessness—she made a tight sign of the cross, a personal quirk, and began to pray. "Oh, God, please God, I'm so lonely. Please give me the strength, the hope—help me find the person I'm to marry. I truly believe you've made man and woman to be together as one. I so desperately want to share my life with another—to be part of Your plan and purpose of life. But after all these years of looking and praying, everything feels so futile. I'm lost. I feel like I'm drifting away from You. I've always counted on You constantly being with me. Without You and Your approval, God, how will I know the man I'm to marry? Please Lord, help me."

When Father Kiley finished reading the Gospel, he surveyed the typically sparse weekday congregation, then said, "When I got up this morning and looked out my window, I was struck by how the little things we take for granted are actually great gifts from God. After I thanked Him for the clear blue sky and green grass, I thought how sad it must be for people who don't feel as if God is in their lives.

"I think all of us have had a time when we've felt this way. Some may feel this way now. There may be events in your life that make you doubt Him." Father Kiley paused, as if to allow each parishioner time to recall any such event. Then he went on. "If you find yourself wavering, think again. In today's Gospel, we heard a section of Paul's second letter to Timothy. That reading holds as much truth now as it did back in Paul's time. Just as the Church finds its strength in its two-thousand-year-old roots, you must go back to your spiritual roots. It's there you will find the wonders of God's love for you and the strength that love gives you."

Absorbing Father Kiley's words, Jane drifted back in time. As a child she had thanked God for every good thing that happened to her, no matter how small. She'd been sure God was listening to her every wish and prayer. She wondered now what had happened to that belief. How, when had it started slipping further and further away until now, this morning, she felt He had abandoned her?

By the end of Mass, she knew Father Kiley was right. She would renew her faith, her childhood faith.

When Jane had finished telling God of her renewal, the church was empty. She walked down the center aisle to where Father Kiley was standing. Turning toward her, he said, "Isn't it a beautiful morning, Jane?"

She reached for his hand. "Thanks to you, Father, I know it will be. The feelings of sadness I woke up with this morning are gone."

Father Kiley lifted his hands to his chest—a gesture of prayer. "I'm glad the word of God has touched you." As they strolled out of the church, he told her, "Remember, Jane, I'm always here for you. But what I think you need now is some fresh air. Enjoy this wonderful summer-like day God has given us."

"Thanks, Father, I will. I'm going for a walk to the grocery store. It will give me a chance to see the many flowers in bloom and hear the birds singing."

Leaving Father Kiley, she headed down the steps. As she walked slowly, her mind drifted back. Eleven years ago, at Notre Dame, she'd thought she'd found her dream lover. She'd been practicing with her soccer team when she first saw him playing lacrosse on the adjacent field. With his blond hair flowing, he jogged, and then with a burst of speed, he broke free from his defender. Racing toward the goal, he took a pass without breaking stride. Evading the final defender, he swooped in on the goalie and rocketed his shot into the net.

Her Adonis, Henri von Eeden, was a junior left winger for the varsity team. How her heart had pounded when she saw him walk into her Contemporary American History class the following semester. She knew it was destiny when she was chosen to debate him on the effect of Ford's pardon of Nixon.

Even though she had out-performed him in the debate, she was sure he would like her. But he never asked her out, despite all of her efforts. The following year he got engaged to a woman he had known less than a year. It was then that Jane crawled into a shell for emotional protection.

Today though she knew that the kind of man who made her heart race was as she had always believed: someone like Henri...Bob McWilliams, perhaps...

When she returned from her mental meanderings, she was walking in a neighborhood of lovely houses, many with colorful flower gardens. She had always loved flowers, and now she delighted in this plethora of color and texture. Responding to the warm morning sun, the portulaca's rose like blossoms in pinks, yellows, and oranges were opened wide for the busy honey bees. On the side of someone else's yard, there was an immense rhododendron shrub engulfed in bouquets of deep red blossoms.

Foot traffic seemed scarce, which she found surprising for such a lovely morning. Since college she had felt uneasy walking alone and always paid close attention to those around her.

A few blocks from the grocery store, she pulled her shopping list from her pocket. Distracted by the squealing of little children, she looked up. A boy about four, waving a butterfly net, careened around the corner of a large Victorian house with a neatly manicured lawn. He was in pursuit of a little girl who, laughing in delight, yelled, "I'm a butterfly! I'm a butterfly!"

After they'd disappeared around the corner of the house, Jane directed her attention to the front walk—old dark brown bricks in a herringbone pattern were edged with two rows of alternating red and white geraniums. Red and white impatiens echoed the color theme in circular beds around three mature black maple trees. The contrasting colors were set off by dark, fresh bark mulch and well-defined edgings.

Not watching where she was walking, her left foot stepped awkwardly in a sidewalk crack. Her ankle crumpled, and she pitched forward. But before she hit the pavement, a man's arm reached out and caught her.

"Are you okay?" the man asked, helping to steady her. Shaken, she stared at him as he picked up her sunglasses. When he handed them back to her, he looked deeply into her eyes. "You could have been hurt."

"Yes..." Her voice faltered. "But I guess I'm all right." Still a bit flustered, she asked, "Wh-where did you come from? I didn't see you..."

"I came from Marlborough."

Marlborough, the next town over, was not the answer she expected. She was positive there was no one near her before she stumbled.

"It's such a nice day for a walk," he said. He had a way of keeping eye contact that made her uneasy. Like he understood her every thought. She wanted to look away. "Is there something bothering you?" he asked. "I know crying eyes when I see them and you've been crying." His own eyes seemed to roam over her as if he was on a voyage of exploration. He appeared to pay particular attention to her naked fingers.

Jane turned from him—embarrassed, unsure, vulnerable. "I'm fa-fine now...Thanks again for catching me." She turned to move away.

He pressed the conversation. "I've always dreamed of a beautiful woman falling for me, but I never really believed it'd happen, especially the way you just did." His voice was cheerful and pleasant. Then he gave her the strangest look she'd ever seen: a cross between a wry grin and an animated smirk. After the expression faded, she focused on him. A rather ordinary man—slender, over six feet, the first signs of thinning, brown hair. He seemed to be only a few years older than she. He wore a purple jersey and a pair of shorts hardly proper for public wear. Definitely not her type.

"I'm sorry to disappoint you, but I didn't fall for you. I stumbled because I wasn't watching where I was going."

She started to back away from him. He scooped up the shopping list she had dropped. "Look," he said, handing her the list. "I realize I'm not as pretty as those flowers you were admiring, but even a beautiful woman like you could be a bit more grateful, don't you think? After all, you won't be young and gorgeous forever."

Jane looked at him. Was he serious? She tossed her head and started down the sidewalk. Somehow she wasn't surprised when he fell in step beside her. Before she could complain, he flashed his strange look again.

This guy was so odd.

"Mind if I walk along? In case your ankle goes again."

With her head high, she continued looking straight ahead. "It's a free country."

"So what store are you going to? How can you eat that stuff anyway?" Glancing at him, her eyebrows knitted. "You know, the things on your shopping list. Carrots and grapefruit, sure, but rice cakes, sprouts, chick peas, and yogurt?"

This time she didn't leave it up to her eyebrows. "How could you have seen all that...so quickly?"

He just grinned. Now his silly flirtation had lost what little charm it had, and his observations were making her uncomfortable.

"You know, I'm really a nice guy when you get to know me. Even my mother still tells me that." Jane's lack of response didn't seem to bother him. "Can I ask you something?" he added.

A little curious, she turned her head toward him. "Never having been married, and with no sisters, I want to know if you can really buy bras and panties in a grocery store, or are you one of those people who buys edible underwear?"

Jane halted and glared at him. He just grinned. A grin like he was waiting in excited anticipation for her to open a surprise Christmas present. "Are you sick or just perverted?" she demanded. "What are you talking about?"

"Your list. They're on your list."

She quickly glanced at the list and immediately felt mortified. There at the bottom, under ice cream, she had written bras and panties. Speechless, she tried walking faster, but she couldn't lose him.

At the food market, she turned to him. "Look. I appreciate your concern. But we're here now and my ankle is fine, so good-bye."

"But you don't even know my name." His tone was almost plaintive. She resisted the smart answer which was forming in her brain.

"My name is John Avery. What's yours?"

She let out a heavy sigh. "Jane."

"That's it? Just Jane?"

"That's right. Plain Jane." She didn't bother to veil her sarcasm.

"Well, you're anything but plain, Jane. The lady without a last name. I hope you don't mind, but I feel like going into this store, too. I might need something." She stared at him, wishing he would realize just how bothersome he was. Why didn't he get the message?

Inside he got a shopping cart. "I'll help you..." Snatching the cart from him, she hustled away without a backward glance. "Well, at least let me get the ice cream," he called out.

Raising her voice, she snapped back, "You don't know what kind I like."

"Oh yes I do. Your beautiful face and gorgeous green eyes tell all." And off he went.

For sure all eyes were on her. She lowered her head and retreated down the vegetable aisle. Her face burned like a hot mask.

Alone, she composed herself. Soon a smile, reluctant yet determined, crept over her face. Somewhere deep within her, somewhere she didn't even recognize, she had enjoyed his flattery.

Jane was almost finished shopping when she spotted John Avery striding toward her, smiling, tossing a package from hand to hand like a hot potato. As she watched him, she cringed. God, those shorts. But she couldn't help noticing his legs—long and trim, covered with fine dark hair, with well-defined muscles. She'd never liked men with hairy bodies, she hurriedly told herself.

Despite herself she asked, "So what did you get?"

"Black raspberry. Brigham's black raspberry. Nothing better on a hot, sunny day. A lovely woman and black-raspberry ice cream. You know, the kind you want to swirl around on your tongue. The kind that makes your taste buds explode." He ran his tongue around inside his lips.

She felt that warm mask on her face again and turned away. "I wouldn't have chosen it," she said, "but it'll do."

John walked beside her as she headed for the checkout counter. "Where do you think they keep the edible underwear?"

Jane ignored him.

A man with a store manager title on his name tag, turned down their aisle. "Well, I guess I'll have to ask the manager," John said, approaching him.

Jane, not wanting to hang around, hurried away.

"I have gas," John informed the manager, "and I wondered if you carry a product called Beano?"

"Yes, we do. It's in aisle five."

Package in hand, John went up to Jane at the checkout line.

"What's that?" she asked.

"Beano Drops," he said, showing her the package. "They help eliminate the problem of gas. I told the manager you wanted them but were too embarrassed to ask."

Jane's mouth dropped. She whipped her sunglasses off. "I shop here all the time, and I don't appreciate your going around embarrassing me. Now, get away from me!"

John moved to the shorter, express-checkout lane. Standing in line, Jane, compelled by some unknown reason—protective curiosity, she rationalized—looked at John. He spotted her surreptitious glance and immediately responded with that ridiculous look. Worried that he'd misinterpret her intrigue, she quickly turned away.

With his purchase safely hidden in a bag, John went over and stood at the end of Jane's checkout counter. After she had written a check for her purchases, he said, "Let me carry the bags for you. I'm still worried about your ankle."

"I've really had enough of you. And I certainly don't want a whacko like you to know where I live."

"But I already know who you are and where you live."

21

"You do not!"

"Your name's Jane Melrose, and you live at 1017 Kent Road."

Stepping back, a shuddering chill swept through Jane's body. "How..." her voice trembled. "How do you know that?"

"Relax. I'm not a rapist stalking you. I saw it on your check."

She simply glared.

"Look Jane, I'm just a guy who's attracted to you and concerned about your ankle...really. I know I'm a little goofy, but I'm quite harmless."

Sure, she thought. *Jack the Ripper probably said that as he pulled out his knife.* She looked at John, only to see that silly expression again. The look had a way of disarming her, and her resistance faded.

Picking up her bags, John said, "Come on. Show me the way to 1017 Kent Road. We can talk on the way, and you can get to know me better. I really am a nice guy."

"Yeah, yeah," she said, looking at his childlike grin. "Your mother tells you that. I know." Despite herself, when her eyes connected with his own ever inquisitive yet friendly ones, her stoic expression thawed.

With a look of euphoria, he walked out of the store with Jane at his side. "You almost smiled at me back there. Does that mean you're beginning to like me?"

"Of course not." Her tone was serious and controlled. Looking around, she made sure nobody but John could hear her. "You don't know me well at all—it was a gas pain."

John doubled over in laughter. Expressionless, Jane watched his uncontrolled public display. In a muffled voice, she said, "I don't have laughing gas."

Jane thought John's continuous waves of laughter would never end. But finally, still chuckling, John managed to catch his breath. "Those were good ones," he told her. "You have real spunk."

Passing a flower shop, John stopped and looked in. "That reminds me...Wait here, I'll be right back."

Right, she thought as she stood there waiting. *You think I'd run off when you have all my groceries?*

He returned, put down the bags and presented her with a corsage—a single short-stemmed pink rose. "Matches your dress," he said, pinning the rose to the lapel of her blazer. "There." He stepped back to admire her. "You brighten up the day."

She glanced nervously around, her blush matching the rose. "I don't wear flowers any old day."

"It's not any old day. It's the day we met." There was the weird look again.

Jane studied him intently. "Is there something wrong with your face, a twitch or something?"

He looked puzzled.

"Surely you know what I mean. The half smile with the dimple and the blinking eye?"

"Oh, that. I'm not blinking, I'm winking. I like to think of it as my sophisticated, sensuous look. Actually it comes naturally when I look at you. It's the way you make me feel."

Jane rolled her eyes. "Believe me, it's anything but sophisticated or sensuous."

"Oh, my heart." John grabbed his chest. "You'll see. Someday you'll come to appreciate that look."

"You're impossible," she said, shaking her head. "Do you have a driver's license? I'd like to make sure you're who you say you are."

He pulled out his wallet and handed her his I.D.

She studied it. John Avery, 20 Providence Road, Marlborough, MA. Born December 1, 1948. She looked at him. "You're only forty. I figured you to be older." She handed it back. "Bad picture, John."

"Coming from Miss Congeniality, I take that as a compliment. Do I pass your security check, or do I need to send you some written references?"

"Okay, John Avery," she said, beginning to walk. "Who are you and why are you special?"

"Me? I'm not special. However, I will try my best to make you feel special."

As they walked, he capsuled his life for her. About to enter college, he had developed a serious kidney disease and had since suffered two relapses. Because of an insurance mess-up with the second one—*prior condition*, the insurance company claimed after he had changed to a higher-paying job—he was still paying off old medical bills, more than a hundred thousand dollars worth. He now worked as an accountant for a large floral nursery. Part of his job, however, the part he liked best, was tending the plants. He was starting a two-week vacation and flying to North Carolina on Wednesday to visit his parents.

Spotting a soda can in front of Jane, he stepped ahead and kicked it away. It clanked and bounced onto the side of the street. "In my free time I do volunteer work for the Samaritans, a suicide hotline." Almost as an aside, he added, "I write poetry, too."

With her interest now piqued, she asked, "Any published?"

"No, nobody would enjoy them but me. I write morose stuff that deals with my issues. Besides, a Boston continuing adult education instructor, Ricky Riccio, said my style was outdated and not very good."

As he talked he continued to study her, moving slightly in front of her and walking backwards, looking at her from that angle. Then he'd walk from one side to the other for different angles. She was getting exhausted just watching him speed up, slow down, and go from side to side. But she became really uncomfortable when he dropped behind her.

"Do you mind?" she said, spinning around to confront him. "I really don't like it when you get behind me like that."

Ignoring her plea, he said, "You know, you have pretty ankles and calves. I'm not a leg man, but you must have nice legs. Of course with that long dress, I can't really tell. I can only imagine. Then again they may be flabby with lots of cellulite. Maybe even hairier than mine."

As he came back in step beside her, Jane hoped the look she shot him conveyed her disgust. The guy was like a chameleon, only he changed personalities. One minute she warmed to him, the next she hated his guts.

"If you're not a leg man, what kind are you?"

"Well, I guess it'd have to be eyes. But it's more than eyes—it also includes the facial structure. It's hard to explain, but I know what I like when I see it." She caught his stare. "That's why I look at you so much. I'm trying to figure out what it is about you that makes me feel the way I do."

Blushing again, Jane looked away. Luckily she saw her next-door neighbor, Mrs. White, rocking on her porch with her knitting. Jane waved. "Hi, Mrs. White. Isn't it a beautiful morning?"

"Oh, hi, Jane. Yes, it's a lovely day," Mrs. White said, scrutinizing John.

24

"This is John Avery from Marlborough."

Mrs. White set her knitting aside. "Nice to meet you, Mr. Avery."

Before Jane could move on, John had asked Mrs. White about her knitting. Jane had her reason for introducing John to Mrs. White, but starting a friendly conversation wasn't it, so she cut in.

"I'm sorry we can't stay and talk. I have some ice cream that must get into the freezer."

As they left, John said, "She seems like a very friendly lady."

At her own front walk, Jane announced, "Here we are. It's a nice quiet duplex. My landlord lives in the other apartment. He's a retired police officer, and his wife's an elementary school teacher. Now, I'll ask you in for ice cream as long as you don't misunderstand my intentions, which are to thank you for your help and for being so concerned about me. But that's as far as it goes, so I don't want you to even *think* about touching me. To be on the safe side, I told Mrs. White your name and where you live, and I know my landlord has a gun." Jane knew that her landlord had gone to the Cape for the week to prepare his cottage for the summer, but John didn't need to know that.

Looking at John, smiling, she said formally, "So, John Avery, would you like to come in and have some black-raspberry ice cream?"

"With such a friendly invitation, how could I refuse? Yes, I'd be delighted to join you for some black-raspberry ice cream, Jane Melrose. And, as always, I'll be on my best behavior."

"Whatever *that* may be," Jane said under her breath as they headed for the door.

Chapter 4

Entering the apartment, Jane gestured to a clear space on the counter in the cramped kitchen, barely big enough for two people. Leaving John, she went into the bedroom to hang up her blazer. When she returned, her eyes were no longer obscured by sunglasses. With John handing her each grocery item, she neatly put them away.

Once they were done, John walked into the living room and looked out the sliding glass door to the patio. Beyond the concrete patio, the lawn stretched about forty feet to a wall of lilacs, which with the taller maples beyond them, made other houses barely visible.

At the far corners of the patio, two eight-foot metal posts stood in freshly poured concrete. Swaying on a thick strand of wire stretched between the posts were two bird feeders.

"I see someone recently put in the posts for the bird feeders," John said.

"I put them in myself. Do you like it? I thought I did a good job, but the birds aren't impressed. Haven't seen one yet."

"Well, *I'm* impressed. And if I were a bird, this backyard would be my choice to hang out in. Unless of course, you serve lousy food."

"I know what to feed birds," she snapped. It was so easy to get annoyed with him. "Thistle for the songbirds and a mixed variety for the others. I even spread some seed on the grass for the ground feeders."

"Do you want me to go outside and announce lunch time?"

Her eyes rolled, exasperated at his continued outlandish behavior.

"How about if I only lip sync it. What type of bird do you want?"

Without waiting for her answer, he unlocked the door and went to the center of the lawn. Jane watched as he looked skyward, making nonsensical contortions with his mouth while turning in a full circle. She had to contain a giggle—there seemed to be no limit to the lengths he would go to make a fool of himself.

"Well, that should do it." He brushed his hands together for a job well done. "They'll be arriving any time now."

Back inside the apartment, they stood at the patio door, waiting. Jane felt more foolish by the second. Then just as she started to turn away, a mourning dove swooped down and fluttered to a gentle landing near one of the posts. Bobbing its head as it walked, it started feeding.

"I don't believe it! If nothing else," Jane said, slowly spacing the words, "you're lucky."

Flushed and grinning in victory, John eyed the lilacs. "I bet those lilacs were really beautiful a couple of weeks ago."

"You're right." There was a noticeable softness to her voice. "Every day I'd get fresh cuttings. I love being greeted by the fragrance of lilacs when I come home."

After a discussion about lilacs, John meandered to a bookcase in the corner, then past a desk to scan another bookcase. Glancing at the desk, a *Wall Street Journal* was opened to a stock page; a company circled in red had a note next to it: "Call Wayne for latest S.E.C filings." He looked around. "You certainly are a neat person, or were you expecting me?"

"Ha. If I had known you were going to follow me around all day, I'd have never gone out. Yes, I *am* organized. And neat. Something wrong with that?"

"Not at all. I have good intentions of being neat myself, but my execution is somewhat lacking. My apartment's a mess."

"Why doesn't that surprise me?"

The sarcasm bounced easily off him. "Did you call Wayne?"

"Yes, I did. As if that's any of your business."

Grinning, he asked, "What does the rest of the apartment look like?"

"The rest is personal."

"Well, if I'm going to eat ice cream, I have to wash my hands." He raised his hands and wiggled his fingers. "My mother always told me to wash my hands before I eat."

Jane pointed to the bathroom door. From the hallway, she kept a distrustful eye on her visitor. "You have an attractive bathroom as far as bathrooms go," John called out. "I really like the snow scene on your shower curtain with the little boy and girl dragging their sled behind them after making the angels in the snow. Which towel should I use?"

"The small one. I'm surprised you recognize the snow angels."

"You're looking at an expert angel maker."

"Well, la-de-da. Anyone with a messy apartment certainly couldn't make better angels than me."

"We'll see," John said, coming out of the bathroom, but instead of following Jane to the living room, he crossed the hallway and entered her bedroom. "I've never known anyone who kept a bedroom this tidy unless they're expecting guests. Now I've met the exception." He gazed at the orderly, frilly, pastel pinkness of the room.

"Get out of there!" Jane yelled. "You have a nerve!"

"What's the matter? There's nothing embarrassing to see. I think it's interesting how people keep their bedrooms. You can tell a lot about a person by that."

"As you can see, all I have is a bureau and a single bed. Now get out."

"Does that mean you're a virgin?"

Speechless, she glared at him—fists clenched.

"Okay, I'm going," he said, glancing down at the night table.

Once Jane had him safely back in the living room and looking out the patio door, she went into the kitchen.

"How much ice cream would you like? And do you want it in a dish or a sugar cone?" She waved the scoop.

"I'll have two scoops, and a sugar cone would be great."

With her dish of ice cream in hand, she gave John his cone. John chose to sit on the chair across from the end of the couch near the patio where she sat.

An uneasy tension came over Jane as she contemplated John's erotic description at the grocery store of his tongue touching the cold ice cream. Trying to avoid his eyes, she watched in fascination. What was he thinking as he looked at her with that silly grin? Licking her spoon, she winced as she watched him stick his tongue out again against the tip of the ice cream. But this time he turned the cone, and his tongue slowly and expertly slid across the entire mound. She felt his eyes slowly working their way from her feet to her face. What was he thinking that caused him to smile with pleasure as his tongue went back into his mouth?

In her nervousness, Jane found herself gulping her ice cream. Realizing John must have noticed her less than dignified eating, she forced herself to slow down. As she watched the twirl of his tongue, she became increasingly uncomfortable until she put her dish down on the coffee table and adjusted her dress.

Overwhelmed by his persistent smile, she folded her hands across her lap, arms obscuring the front of her body. How she wished it were wintertime so she could cover herself with the afghan she kept on the couch.

John had only a few remaining bites of his cone when she reached for her dish. She was curious to know what he experienced when his tongue probed the cold smooth surface. He was busy watching the mourning dove, so she felt safe to experiment.

Lifting the spoon to her mouth, she stuck her tongue out, pressing it deep inside the cool, refreshing mound. Her lips wiped the spoon clean. While she was absorbing the full sensation of swirling the ice cream in her mouth, her eyes went to John's legs and shorts. In no time her imagination was taking her on an unfamiliar but vivid journey...

"Your tongue looked really nice."

Jane's sudden return to reality was disastrous. She gasped, then swallowed the wrong way and choked. Tears ran down her cheek as she continued choking. Finally she managed to take some deep breaths.

"Good to the last drop, wasn't it?" he said, after her recovery.

"As I told you before," she answered, still bright red from choking and being caught, "black raspberry wouldn't have been my choice."

John knew there was more to this woman than just pretty eyes. He liked how she leaned back against the couch, as if to give the impression she was calm in handling his unorthodox behavior. "So, are you ready to go shopping for your other items?"

"No way. I'll do it another time."

John stood up and picked up Jane's dish from the coffee table, then went into the kitchen. "Come on," he called out as he rinsed the dish. "It'll give us something to do while we talk some more. I hate staying in on such a nice day. I won't bother you while you shop, I promise."

Jane considered it. She didn't want to just sit and talk. The way he gazed into her eyes was really unnerving. She had planned on going to the lingerie store, and it'd be a good way to get him out of the apartment. "All right, as long as you leave me alone while I go in the store."

"Whatever you say."

Stepping out into the bright sunshine, Jane reached for her sunglasses. "Hasn't the weather been great the last few days?" she said, steering any conversation away from herself.

"Well, after all the cold and rain this spring, it's about time. Business was booming at the nursery last weekend."

Silence fell between them, giving John time to assess the situation. *Let's be realistic,* he told himself. *Except for her eyes, she's not your type. Never go out with a woman who's smarter than you.*

"Look at those pink and purple lupines," he said, pointing to a garden across the street. "It's rare to see them that thick. I find them to be temperamental plants."

"They are pretty, aren't they."

"The way their spires point heavenward in such wonderful colors makes them so majestic."

John became silent once again. Looking down at the cracked concrete sidewalk, his attention wandered. *Step on a crack, break your mother's back,* he said to himself. Altering his stride, he made sure he didn't step on a crack.

His mind turned to another woman, Amy, the one real commitment of his life. But Amy had left him—*why?* The persistent questions and lingering hurt, along with his financial mess, had kept him from forming new relationships. *What you need is a simple friendship,* he told himself. *Jane's easy enough to talk with and has great reactions to your foolishness.* He stepped forward to get her attention. "So what size bra do you wear?"

She stopped abruptly. "I should have known. I can't believe I agreed to do this with you."

31

"What's the big deal? I have a fifteen-and-a-half neck, thirty-three-inch waist, and thirty-two-inch leg inseam. What difference does it make? Or are you the type of woman who buys a 36C bra just to impress a guy, only to exchange it later for a smaller size?"

"No, I'm not that type of woman. It's not an appropriate question."

"Well then, don't tell me."

An awkward silence fell between them. Birds chirped and the sun shone brightly. They walked past some nice homes with pretty gardens. Then out of nowhere he blurted, "I've only made love to one woman. Her name was Amy. I thought we were going to get married. We had gone out for three years and talked about getting married. But one day she called me, and from out of the blue, told me it was all over. That was fifteen years ago. I guess I'm still trying to recover."

Jane was dumbfounded. "Why are you telling me all this?"

"I thought it only fair. I had asked you if you were a virgin, so you should know about *me*. So...*are* you?"

"Why do you keep asking me? It's none of your business."

"I'm interested in people's behavior and their reasons for doing things. And by your behavior, I think you might be a virgin. I admire a woman who can withstand social pressure and curiosity and chooses to remain a virgin for something she values—like her religious beliefs. But if she stayed a virgin solely for some messed up psychological reasons or fear of pregnancy, I'd consider that a less than noble reason. She could end up dealing with the same problems after she got married. I just wondered where you stood."

Jane didn't reply, and he didn't push the subject. During the remaining distance to the store, they didn't speak. At the store, she said, "You promised not to bother me, so wait out here."

Left outside, John began pacing back and forth, occasionally stopping to peek through the window. He wondered what the passing shoppers were thinking. Perhaps they thought of him as a puppy dog, obediently waiting for its master. Or worse, a sex pervert, who enjoyed standing in front of lingerie stores. Suddenly feeling too uncomfortable, he entered the store. It didn't take long to spot Jane and her cold, hard look.

A fiftyish saleslady, who was apparently used to perplexed male shoppers, approached him. "May I help you?"

"Yes, I'd like a very sensuous bra for a gift."

"Do you have anything special in mind, and what size should it be?"

"I'm not sure. Could you suggest something?"

She turned and pulled down a box. Unwrapping the tissue, she revealed a fine lace bra with an embroidered rose design. "This is imported from France. A lovely item...now about the size..."

"Well, she's about the size of that woman," he said, pointing to Jane, who by this time had her back turned to them.

"It's difficult to guess what size she is, especially with that blazer," the saleslady said.

"Actually it is *for* her. I just met her, and she won't tell me her size. For all I know, *she* may really be a *he*. Wouldn't that be a hoot." John laughed more to himself than to the saleslady. "I'll try asking her one more time."

John hoped the saleslady couldn't hear Jane's response, but he was sure she must have seen how irate Jane became. He chuckled to himself as he returned to the saleslady. "Well, I don't know if you heard, but she's apparently not too pleased with my idea. She said she doesn't want a gift from me because she doesn't even like me. I'll tell you what. When she pays for her purchase, you'll know what size she is. Then I'll buy this style bra in her size." That settled, John retreated to the window and waited patiently.

After Jane paid for her purchases, it didn't take long for her to realize John's ruse. "I don't believe what you're doing!"

John noted that despite her voiced displeasure, Jane waited for him to purchase the bra. John gave Jane his weird smile and wink, and after paying the saleslady he took his package. When Jane started to leave, John turned to the saleslady and said, "By the way. Do you sell edible underwear?"

Jane's neck shrunk into her collar as she quickened her pace for the exit.

"I'm sorry, we don't," said the saleslady. "I think you'd have to order something like that from a catalogue."

"Well, thanks anyway." John then lowered his voice. "I think she likes me."

Rushing to catch up with the quickly retreating Jane, John opened the package to look at the tag, satisfying his curiosity.

In silence they headed back to her apartment. Soon however something else came to John. Something else unexpected to outrage her. She had such wonderful reactions to his unconventional friendliness. "That certainly was a nice saleslady. I think I'll give her all my business."

"I'm sure you will," Jane said, shaking her head.

John grinned at her disgusted look, and his chuckle seemed to only add to her frustration.

She stopped abruptly and faced him. In a firm voice, she said, "You're sick. I can't imagine any sane woman getting seriously involved with you. It's no wonder you're still single. What type of woman are you attracted to, anyway?"

"Well, that's easy enough," John said, resuming his leisurely stride. "I've spent over twenty years thinking about it. The first requirement is that she be tall, between five- seven and five-eleven. I don't want to bend over far when we kiss. I especially don't like the idea of being with a short woman whose nose only comes up to my armpits. I'd find it very disconcerting. She should be slim, but not sickly thin. Her hair definitely has to be dark brunette to go along with clear, mysterious brown eyes. She should have larger than average breasts. She'd be wild and outgoing to counteract my shyness when I'm in a group of people. She'd be sexually uninhibited, the type of person who'd do an aerobics tape with me wearing only a camisole and tap pants. With a playfulness to distract me while we're working out, so that we'd take a whole morning to do a half-hour tape. I'd like her to be impressed with my knowledge and be pleasantly surprised by what I can do."

"In other words, she shouldn't be very bright," Jane said, with a grimace.

"If that's how you wish to look at it." John smiled. "Since I believe that personality traits are influenced by birth order, she should be the oldest sibling, so as to offset my personality as the baby of the family. Also, I don't want her to have more than one earring hole in each ear. I believe that when a woman wears two or more earrings in one ear, she's displaying feelings of insecurity about who she is. Beyond that I don't think I'm looking for anything particular in a woman."

"Thank goodness I don't match many of your requirements," Jane said, amazed at some of his prerequisites.

"I've noticed that, too. That's why it's so much fun to talk to you.

34

You're not my type, but you'd make a good friend. As a friend, I wouldn't have to worry about impressing you. I can be who I really am when I'm with you."

Jane looked at him coldly. "Why don't I feel honored? Maybe it's because I'm constantly being victimized by your *not* trying to impress me."

"Hey. You can be the same way with me. It's only fair."

As they continued toward Jane's apartment, John took a deep breath and asked, "May I see you tomorrow? I'd like to get together again before I go down to North Carolina to visit my folks."

Jane was surprised at his request and didn't quite know how to reply. She kept on walking as she thought it over. She had mixed feelings. He had been exasperating at times—causing more frustration in one day than any previous entire relationship—but at other times he was interesting and fun.

She glanced at him and was greeted with his now familiar weird look. She stifled a laugh. Somewhere in the far corners of her fragile and disappointed heart, she sensed sincerity in his friendship. A strange, kooky kind of sincerity.

"I was planning to walk to the park tomorrow and feed the ducks," she said. "If you'd like to join me, we could do that together."

"That sounds like fun."

"I'll fix a picnic. Why don't you come over at 10:30? I better give you my telephone number in case something comes up. It's unlisted."

"I already know it."

Jane's body went cold. Once again he knew something about her she didn't expect. Not wanting to reveal her concern, she casually said, "Oh? And just what *is* my number?"

"It's 555-8437. If you have something to write with, I'll jot mine on this bag."

Reluctantly she pulled a pen from her blazer pocket. This man had found out things about her in one day that few knew, and it made her feel very uneasy. Giving him the pen, she hoped he didn't notice her hand trembling. "How do you know my number?"

After he wrote on the paper bag he grinned at her and said offhandedly, "I saw it when I was in your bedroom."

As they neared her apartment, Jane's worry went from how much John knew about her to the awkwardness of saying good-bye. She wouldn't allow him inside again, even if he used some excuse to do so. And she certainly wouldn't let him get close enough to kiss her good-bye.

By the time they reached Mrs. White's, Jane's head was pounding. She began to concentrate on what she'd say when they got to her door.

At her walkway, John stopped. "Well, I guess this is it. Here, this is for you." He handed her the bag containing the bra. "I hope you enjoy it. If it's the wrong size, I'm sure you can return it. I'll see you in the morning."

Jane thanked him and took the bag, then watched in bewildered relief as he turned and walked away. She couldn't believe what had happened—he was leaving on his own, before she had even expected it. What needless worry, she told herself as she watched him walk up the street. *Oh, those shorts,* the proper woman in her thought. But she couldn't quite hold back an audible sigh as she gazed at his slender hips. She shocked herself with another thought—*oh, those buns.*

When he reached Mrs. White's, John turned and gave a little wave. She smiled and waved back. Something inside her kept her standing there as he receded from sight. It was as if she expected to see him disappear into thin air, just the way he had come into her life. But he didn't. He turned the corner, and a house blocked her view.

As she entered her apartment, her apprehension returned, causing the hairs on the back of her neck to stand on end. Perhaps she'd made a mistake about tomorrow.

Chapter 5

The next morning at 10:30 sharp, John pulled in to the driveway, convertible top down. A faded Red Sox cap protected his head of thinning hair. He reached to the passenger seat for a baby-shoe-box-sized package wrapped in silver foil.

Jane greeted him at the door with a friendly enough smile. "Good morning." She stepped past him to see his car. "Sporty car. I like the color."

"It's metallic dark moss green."

"Bucket seats and four on the floor. Nice. So, you drive a Ford."

"Actually to get the full effect, you have to say it's a '67 Ford Fairlane GT convertible."

Eyeing the chrome numbers on the front fender, she asked, "What's the 351 for?"

"That's the size of the engine in cubic inches."

"Does that mean it's fast?"

"Well, let's say it uses a lot of gas, and I could wear out a year's worth of tire tread just accelerating from a stoplight if I wanted to."

"It's in great condition. You must take care of it. Like you would a wife, I suppose?"

The expected kooky answer didn't come. Instead he seemed to give her question serious thought. "Since I've never had a wife, I don't really know. But I'd like to think so."

"So you'd give *her* a wash every week, too, huh?" There was a noticeable friskiness to Jane's demeanor.

Amused, John wasn't about to let such an opportunity slip by. "Every week I'd get into the tub or shower with her. I'd meticulously wash her, not missing a single spot. And, as an added treat, once a month I'd stretch her clean, naked body out on the bed. After pouring exotic oils on her, I'd work them in with my fingers, using a slow, circular motion. My hands wouldn't be satisfied until every inch of her skin became silky smooth."

Jane's own flushed body flowed with fire. He had taken the conversation totally beyond her control. Feeling awkward, she looked at the package in John's hand. He handed it to her shyly.

"How nice. I wonder what it could be." She lifted it to her ear and gave it a shake. Knowing him, she was afraid to guess.

"Careful or you'll break it."

Curious, she unwrapped the package and discovered a yellow-rose corsage tucked inside. A little surprised, she looked up at John, seeing a smile that evoked her sympathy. She knew he wanted to please her, but she had told him yesterday she wasn't the type to wear a corsage for no reason at all.

"It's very pretty," she said politely. He must be so desperate, she thought. She had only asked him to join her at the park to feed the ducks, but he's acting like they were off to a prom.

"I guess it doesn't go with your pink top."

"That's okay. It's the thought that counts." She turned, saying, "I just have to finish up in the kitchen. I fixed a lunch for us and something to feed the ducks. We can walk to the park. Okay?"

"Then I'll put the car top up in case it rains."

In her apartment, Jane took out the corsage. Admiring it, she lifted it to her nose, savoring its sweet fragrance.

When she eventually came back out, John beamed. "You look really lovely." She had changed her outfit. A loose, green, V-neck tee revealed her slender figure, and the yellow shorts, though mid-thigh, revealed long, slim legs. She was wearing the corsage. John took the tote bag she was carrying and peeked inside at the paper bags and blanket. "So what do we have to eat?"

"For the ducks there's stale bread; for us there's some fruit, rice cakes, and homemade lemonade."

"Yuk," he said, grimacing. "Do you think the ducks would mind if I traded my rice cakes for their stale bread?"

Jane gave a half-hearted swing at him and laughed. "Yes, they would mind."

Once again John moved from side to side of her as they talked. Yesterday it had irritated her; today his goofiness seemed not so strange.

Off to the side of the park, a pond glistened in the morning sun. Jane led the way along the water's edge until they reached a grassy slope, rimmed by stately oaks. She stopped in the shade and announced, "This is the nicest spot in the whole park for a picnic."

Spreading the blanket, they dropped down on opposite sides. John wrapped his arms around his knees and admired Jane's profile as she gazed at the shimmering pond. "So, this is where you came as a kid?"

"As far back as I can remember." She turned and faced him. For the first time since knowing her, she appeared relaxed. Happiness seemed to radiate from her eyes. Thinking about how he was actually sitting on a blanket with her talking, his stomach knotted. She was so beautiful. "My parents would pack a picnic dinner and bring us here. My sister Cathy and I used to feed the ducks and walk around the pond looking for frogs. Only when the mosquitoes came out in force would it be time to go home."

John looked out to where two ducks splashed and skimmed the water. With wings flapping and shrill squawks, they chased each other. Jane looked at John. He appeared calm and thoughtful. Looking back at her, he said, "It'd be very easy for me to find inner peace here."

"That's one of the reasons I still come here. It connects me with something."

"I know what you mean. When I feel the need to get in touch with myself, I either walk around my old neighborhood or along a beach. Listening to the rhythms of the surf is so soothing." Sliding down on his side, he pillowed his head on the palm of his hand. "Do you like beaches?"

"It's been a long time since I've been to one. I don't enjoy lying in the sun, baking. I do swim, though. When I was a kid, we had Sunday trips to Nahant Beach. After we got home from Mass, we'd pack up and spend the whole day. I remember my parents always brought the Sunday paper." She paused, her mind going back, then started to chuckle.

"What is it?"

Suddenly uncomfortable, she said, "Oh, it's nothing, really."

"Tell me. I'd like to know what makes you laugh."

Trying to downplay an important part of her childhood, she told him. "Back when I was still learning to read, I'd bring my book of Bible stories to the beach. I'd sit on the blanket with a hat on, a sweatshirt to protect my scrawny body, and a towel across my knobby knees..."

"The ugly duckling before she became the beautiful swan," John interrupted, followed by his weird smile.

"Will you stop that."

"Well, you are beautiful. Why not accept the truth?"

Jane rolled her eyes. "Now you've made me forget what I was saying."

"Your knobby knees."

"Don't you forget anything?"

"Actually I have a lousy memory, but I try to remember what's important. Like you. So go on with your story."

"That's it, really. I spent my Sundays on the beach reading Bible stories. I guess you can say that God and I became close at the beach."

"Yeah. I can picture you at the beach reading Bible stories."

His stare made her uncomfortable, so she continued talking. "My sister Cathy, on the other hand, became very close with the boys at the beach. She'd wear the skimpiest bikini Mother would allow, and made a ritual of applying suntan lotion. She made sure that everyone noticed her." Jane sighed as her memory roamed. "She was really nice, but she had such an enormous need for attention."

"You said 'was' and 'had.'"

Jane looked down at the blanket. "Cathy died ten years ago. She was driving with a friend on a mountain road in Italy one night. It was just south of Bolzano. The police said she missed a sharp curve. Both were killed."

"I'm sorry." John knew he was fortunate. Being blessed not to have had to experience the loss of a parent or sibling. He watched in silence as Jane hugged her knees and stared at the pond. She was lost in thought, and he wanted to bring her back. "Tell me more about your family."

She remained mute, continuing to gaze. Then she said, "My mother has moved back to Pittsburgh where she grew up. She wanted to be closer to her two sisters. I visit her once in a while, but you might not know how mothers can be with single daughters. The more time I spend with her, the more she tells me how I should live."

"What about your father?"

"He died eleven years ago—bad heart. They seem to run in his family. He was an attorney and spent most of his practice helping kids in trouble. We were lucky he wanted to give us what a family needs most—himself. We spent a lot of time together."

"Your father's death must have been a great loss for all of you."

"We were devastated. Especially Cathy. He was always closer to her. She was four years older than me and very beautiful. He took a lot of pride in that. In fact after she graduated from high school, he encouraged her to go to New York to try modeling. He kept a scrapbook of all her pictures. Cathy's the one who got me interested in my career."

John gave her a quizzical look.

"She became so successful as an international model that she asked me to help manage her financial affairs. She made a fortune. But she'd spend it all on things like cars, clothes, and travel."

"Ah, so your neatness and organization reared their ugly heads when you were younger."

"That wasn't it," she said, throwing the piece of grass she was fidgeting with at him. "It was because I did so well at school. Especially math. My father always told Cathy how beautiful she was, while telling me at least I had brains. I used to be jealous of her beauty. He never told me that I was his good-looking daughter. When I was in high school, I would cry myself to sleep praying to God to make me as pretty as Cathy. I even told God that I'd trade my intelligence just to be attractive."

"Your father was wrong. Any woman as lovely as you must have been pretty as a girl, too. Besides, no matter how beautiful he thought Cathy was, he should have let you know you were equally so in your own way."

"It wouldn't have made any difference, because in my freshman

41

year of college I stopped all those wishes. Cathy and I were home for Thanksgiving, and I could tell something was really bothering her. She swore me to secrecy and told me that the previous summer she had been raped. Not just once, but twice. Twice in a period of only three months. Can you believe it?"

Although it was impossible to fully understand the specific trauma and lingering damage Cathy or anyone in that situation had to live with, John felt a rush of sympathy. Sadness flowed through him in knowing another person had to endure such an inexcusable violation.

"The first was when she was working in Los Angeles. She was walking to her room at a motel where she was staying, and had passed an innocent-looking man getting a soda from a Coke machine. He came up behind her, put a knife to her back, and forced her into her room. He taped her mouth shut and beat her with his fist. They never caught him."

A woman pushing a stroller stopped by the edge of the pond. Kneeling by the seated child, she pointed at the ducks and alternated looks from the swimming ducks to the child. John paid little attention to the woman. Instead he concentrated on what Jane was telling him. He knew when to be a careful listener. That's one of the reasons why he was successful as a Samaritan.

"The second time was a date rape. She was at an art show reception in Paris and met a really charming man whom some of the other models knew. He offered to drive her to a post-reception party, but he didn't take her there. Instead he tricked her into going to his apartment where he proceeded to force himself upon her. He told her that nobody would believe she hadn't consented, so she might as well relax and enjoy it.

"So, I decided that it wasn't worth being beautiful. I also became very cautious around strange men. At least God had blessed me with the enjoyment of reading. I spend a lot of time safely tucked away at home, lost in one book or another."

Jane looked down at the blanket, lost in another bout of painful memories. She ran her hand over and over the blanket's rumpled surface, trying to smooth the blanket and her life. "I think that after those rapes and our father's death, Cathy started to live a lifestyle with a death wish. She had lost so much of her life in so short a time, she just couldn't handle it."

With empathy John watched her trembling lips and glistening eyes. What she had revealed explained so much about her. From the pond there was a uproar from the ducks. The woman with the stroller was leaving without throwing them any bread.

"Cathy certainly paid a heavy price for living in the fast lane," he said, "as well as for her need for constant reassurance of self-worth through her appearance. From the little I know about you, I think we have both chosen lives that are not very exciting but are, at least for us, comfortable and secure."

John allowed her time to gather her thoughts before lightening the mood. "Do you hear that duck quacking over there? Do you know what he's saying?"

Jane looked up and chuckled. "I've mastered many things, but duck talk isn't one of them."

"Well, I have, and he's saying—impatiently, I might add—'Hey, stop all that gabbing and feed me.' So I suggest we feed him before he starts bad mouthing us." John stood up. "I'll let you find the duck food. With the menu you've prepared, I'm still not sure what to feed them."

At the water's edge they threw bread to the squawking duck—who was instantly joined by others—and watched as they all swam around gobbling up every piece. Then they walked along the shore, and a third of the way around came to a stream where the pond drained to lower ground. John led the way downstream, looking for a spot where they could jump across. Spying two rocks sticking up midstream, he suggested they jump from one rock to the next. Without hesitation he demonstrated his idea.

"I'm not going to do that." She wasn't sure why she felt apprehensive. As a child, she used to jump across those rocks all the time when searching for frogs and tadpoles. "What if I miss and fall in?"

"You won't fall in. I'll catch you."

"Are you sure?"

"Well, you might get a little wet, but I wouldn't let you go in over your head."

"That's a big comfort. The stream's only a foot deep at most."

"Just grab my hand."

With a shriek, Jane leapt from one rock to the other, the shriek peaking each time a foot landed. John grabbed her hand and helped her to a safe landing. As soon as she regained her balance, he released her hand.

Straightening up next to him, she boasted, "I knew that if you made it, I could too. I just don't like to take needless chances." She looked down at the hand that had helped her to safety.

As they resumed their walk, Jane kept thinking about her new friend's behavior toward her. She wondered why he didn't try to touch her, except when he had to—and even then he released her as soon as possible. She couldn't help comparing him to the other men she had dated. Usually by the second date—which this might as well be, after all the time they had spent together yesterday—other men would have been trying, without success, to maneuver her into bed. Yet John was satisfied with only looking at her and talking. But there was something nagging at her—for some unexplainable reason she liked those fleeting moments he had touched her.

She decided it was time to take control of the situation. "Let's go back and eat our lunch."

When they reached the rocks she stopped, and, as she hoped, John promptly jumped to the other side. Like a damsel in distress, she said, "Grab my hand and make sure I don't slip."

He gripped her hand obediently as she leapt confidently across. This time she didn't let go of him. "I told you I could do it." Smiling to herself, she began walking toward the pond, holding his hand.

John made no effort to release her. His hand felt relaxed and comfortable, as if holding on to her was totally natural. He'd swing his arm occasionally, causing hers to sway along with his. Whenever he moved to one side or the other to investigate something of interest, he'd pull her along with him.

She deliberately loitered. Soon she felt the sensation of his warm fingertips gently caressing the back of her hand. Her mind was telling her she was crazy, but her body knew she was experiencing much more than just another person's hand holding hers.

John looked at their swinging arms and said casually, "Those rocks must have been handy to jump across back when you were looking for frogs."

Jane flushed and did her best to answer nonchalantly. "I suppose so."

Back on their far sides of the blanket, they ate lunch. Munching on a pear, he asked her, "How do you keep so fit?"

"Oh, you mean my 'flabby legs'?" She gripped a muscular but trim thigh. "I've always been athletic. Played soccer in college. Now I have to settle for a workout two or three times a week at a women's fitness center."

"Maybe if I worked out I could get rid of this," he said, grabbing a handful of flesh at the side of his waist. "But I'm told that love handles make a man a better catch."

Jane let out a laugh. "You don't know as much about women as you think you do."

After lunch John rolled onto his back and watched the puffy white clouds meander across the sky. "Do you ever see pictures in the shapes clouds make?"

Lying down, Jane gazed up at the sky. "Can't say I do." Her voice took on a mock-professional tone. "What fascinates me is how the air temperature causes the moisture in the atmosphere to condense and makes clouds at different altitudes. See that narrow band of thin, white cloud cover? Those are cirrus clouds. Actually cirrus clouds are ice crystals that form high above the ground—maybe as much as ten miles high."

John looked over at her and grinned. "I knew you were too smart for me."

"Ever notice that one type of cloud moves in one direction while others might move in another direction? That's because the winds at the earth's surface may be different from those of the jet stream in the upper atmosphere." She looked at John. "I bet I'm boring you."

John rolled over on his elbow to admire her. "I'd never be bored with you."

For the next few hours, they talked about whatever came to mind as if they were childhood friends. Jane knew he wasn't the type of man she would ever contemplate marrying, but she did enjoy his companionship. Her soul-deadening loneliness was easing its grip.

John sat up, hugged his knees and said, "It's been a long time since I've felt like this."

Tentatively, she asked, "Like *this*?"

"Yeah, peaceful, content...wanting to look at my soul."

Jane's silent smile was as much an agreement as words would have been.

"Did you know," he continued, "that astronomers say there are as

45

many stars in space as there are grains of sand in the oceans? There have been times I'd sit at the beach sifting sand, imagining I was one of them—a lonely star traveling through space. Ever feel like that?"

Jane stifled a laugh. "Honestly, no. I guess my feet are more earth-bound than yours. The closest feelings I have to yours would be that I've lost my way in life. I'm not following the path God intended for me." She lay back and stared wistfully at the clouds. "Ever dream of getting married?"

"I don't think of the actual *act* of getting married, if that's what you mean. But I always thought I'd be married someday. Yet the reality of being so deep in debt and getting older makes it very unlikely now."

"I dream about my wedding day a lot," she confessed. "It's going to be special because I believe God wants to bless my marriage in a meaningful way. My husband will be a tall, strong man—an Adonis really. Not the type to go bald, his blond hair will blow in the wind. He'll be some sort of philanthropist because he cares so much about others. I dream about him night and day."

"He sounds like quite the guy!"

Ignoring the quip, she said, "But what makes my dreams so special is that I've always felt that Jesus will be there to take part in the sacrament. I don't know why, but I know He will be there."

"Ah, there is nothing like a little girl and her dreams of marriage. The way we each think about it must be one of the many differences between males and females. I just expected that at some point I'd be married but *you* dream about some elaborate way for it to happen. That's probably why it's the bride's responsibility to plan the wedding day."

Jane didn't respond. Instead she stared at him, doubting the feelings that were intruding on her consciousness. Noticing her stare, John made his weird look.

Caught off guard, Jane let out a loud snicker. "Why do you keep doing that?"

"I told you already. It's the way you make me feel. Ever since I was a little boy, I've realized, whenever I've become really happy I get this urge."

"You're so strange. What do your parents think of it?"

Jane expected a kooky answer. But John became lost in reflective silence. She noticed his eyes began to glisten as if tears were going to form. Finally he said, "My mother says she misses it."

The sadness in his voice penetrated her. She tried to comprehend his mother's pain—did she miss spending time with her son, or was it that John had stopped making that look?

An uneasy silence grew, neither knowing what to say. From the other side of the pond came a loud commotion of squawking ducks as two little boys and a young woman threw out bits of bread. And in the distance there were the sounds of happy children at play.

As she turned from John, Jane feared to say the words stuck in her throat. But a deeper power now drove her to reveal one of her innermost convictions. "I'm a virgin because I believe God wants a man and woman to wait until they're married in His eyes."

John didn't respond. Instead he contemplated her revelation. He knew she must have just shared a most vulnerable part of her psyche, and he studied her intently. She avoided his eyes by looking out at the ducks as they frantically searched out floating chunks of bread. "I kind of figured you were," he said at last.

Jane jerked her head and sat up erect. With facial muscles tight, she glared at him. "I don't like being made fun of."

Surprised by her reaction, he defended himself. "I'd never make fun of you about something like that. You're a woman to be admired and respected, Jane Melrose."

She looked deep into his eyes. She needed to know if he was truly sincere or just making fun of her.

Seconds passed like hours as they earnestly gazed at each other. John's warm, gentle gaze tried to assure her he could be believed and trusted. His friendly smile gradually brightened, and it wasn't long before Jane's stoic look softened. Noticing a glimmer of a smile, he couldn't hold himself back any longer. He gave her his weird look again.

With that, all their pent-up emotions spilled out in a flood of giddy laughter. Before long, feeling safe and relaxed, they continued to share their individual thoughts and beliefs, while above them the clouds thickened and darkened. At a distant rumble of thunder, they decided to pack up and leave.

John picked up the tote and started walking back. Jane stood for a moment, disappointed he hadn't taken her hand. She quickly caught up but made no attempt to reach for his hand. After all, she told herself, he was only a friend. She couldn't let him misinterpret her actions.

The first drops of rain started to fall just as they turned down Kent Road. Jane started to run, laughing as she shouted, "We're being attacked by the cumulonimbus."

John also started to run, trying to keep up with the expert sprinter. As the bombardment of king-sized drops became heavier, their laughter got louder and their pace quickened. Finally when they reached the apartment, Jane panted, "Would you like to come in? I can offer you some water or juice."

"What, no black-raspberry ice cream? Or are you keeping it all for yourself?"

Jane blushed at the mention of the ice cream. This morning, on impulse, she had eaten it for breakfast. Rather, she made love to it—eyeing each spoonful before lifting it to her mouth, closing her eyes and savoring the initial sensation. Then pressing her lips together around the spoon, she had pulled the spoon slowly from her mouth twisting her tongue around the cold, soft mound. Before taking the next spoonful, she ran the cold tip of her tongue across her warm, parted lips while visualizing John doing the same.

Remembering his question, she blurted, "I ate it this morning."

"Well then, I guess juice will have to do."

Inside Jane poured the fruit juice and took the glasses into the living room. John had settled in the middle of the couch. She sat down at the end to his right. At first neither said anything as they listened to the rumble of thunder.

"Do you like kids?" Jane asked rhetorically. "When I get married, I'm going to have five kids—three boys and two girls. The first little boy is going to be named Neal, and he'll have a sister named Mary. I'll have to decide with my husband on the other names. I think a family should have lots of kids. How many would you like?"

"Me? I don't know. Babies mean dirty diapers, sleepless nights. They spit up on you. I'm not sure I could cope." His eyes sought hers. "But on the other hand, they are cute, and I would have fun with them. Besides, then I'd have a chance to clone a kid just like me." He seemed bemused by the thought.

Jane shrieked when a bright flash was followed instantly by a deafening thunderclap. "I'd better not sit near you," Jane said, laughing from fright. "You seem to upset God."

"God isn't upset with me, silly. She's agreeing," John said as he reached over and gently shook Jane's head to get rid of her nonsense. Then, instead of removing his hand, he worked his fingertips into her hair. She closed her eyes and sat perfectly still. His fingers traced small circles along the nape of her neck. In a widening circle, they slid behind one ear and over toward the other.

When he returned to the back of her neck, she murmured, "That feels good." Becoming rag-doll limp, she leaned back while her head slumped forward, chin on chest. He removed the clips holding her hair and the soft, ash-blonde tresses tumbled to her shoulders. Slowly he combed the silky strands through his fingers. Then his fingertips returned to massaging her scalp, bringing deep sighs in response.

Letting go of her, John reached down and took off his sneakers. He lay down with his head on the pillow at the end of the couch, his feet dangled to the floor beside her. "We'll be more comfortable if you lie on my stomach."

In an instant a multitude of conflicting thoughts flashed through Jane. The initial thoughts, the ones that caused the numbing chill, were of fear. To be in his arms would risk her physical safety—a possible rape victim. Even if he could be trusted, she wasn't attracted to him romantically.

He made it sound so simple and innocent, "We'll be more comfortable..." as if it was no big deal. For some unexplained reason, positive rationalizations were taking over. It's natural for friends to hug and comfort each other, and that's all that this would be. Besides, if she laid on him and rested her head on his shoulder, he wouldn't be in a position to kiss her lips like he would have been when he was sitting next to her.

Without a word, she took off her sneakers and rested herself on top of him. She placed her head on his chest near a shoulder and snuggled into a cozy position.

His fingertips went back to work. Soon he was memorizing the shape of her head and noting her reactions to his different touches. His fingers with neatly trimmed fingernails worked their way down and caressed the soft skin on her neck, causing Jane to moan, "That feels good, too."

With his hand at the base of her skull, he commented, "Did you know that the bone back here comes to a point?"

What an inept Don Juan, Jane thought. She caught herself—that's not what she wanted him to be. But curious, she lifted her body and felt her head. Sure enough there was a protuberance.

John rubbed the back of his head. "My head's not pointed like yours."

Putting her hand behind his skull, she felt its natural roundness. She laid back down on his chest before commenting, "Can I help it if you have an underdeveloped head?"

Ignoring her comment, he went back to his massage. Jane had no trouble succumbing to his soothing touch. But again he interrupted, "Do you know you have a mole right here?" He rubbed his finger near the crown of her head. "You realize don't you, that if you go bald, it'll be noticeable?"

Jane bolted upright. "What charm school taught you your technique? Stop pointing out my faults."

"I'm not finding fault, I'm discovering you."

"Well, don't or I'll ask you to leave." Her crankiness was genuine.

"Okay, if that's what you want."

"Yes, that's the way I want it," Jane answered, collapsing down again in frustration. She didn't realize how much he was learning and remembering about her, even things she didn't know about herself.

John lifted her hair in his fingers and watched it cascade down. He brushed away what had fallen on her face so he could see her expressions. While he ran his fingers through her hair near her ears, Jane closed her eyes and said, "I can hear your heart beating. Lying here, listening to your heart beat while your hands stroke my hair, is very calming."

"You're the one who's calming. I can't remember a time in my life when I've felt so peaceful." Moving the hair away from her right ear, he traced it with a finger. Then he leaned over and delicately blew his warm breath into her ear.

A tingling sensation went directly from her ear to the center of her brain, causing her to twist and giggle. "That tickles."

John put his fingers under her chin and started wiggling them back and forth, asking, "How about this, does this tickle too?"

Squirming in uncontrolled laughter, she yelled, "Yes. Stop it! I can't stand it."

Without hesitation John removed his hand.

Placing his hand on her shoulder, his fingertips moved downwards toward her waist, gently kneading her back. He wanted to discover all there was to know about her body.

Jane again found herself praising him. "That's much nicer."

For the next half hour, John concentrated on her reactions, learning her preferences. He worked his hands carefully over her entire back, neck, and head. Soon he knew which touch on which spot brought out the most contented moan or sigh. Once he was sure of a special spot, he'd move on to discover additional ones, only to return to those spots he had originally found. He wanted to make sure he remembered where they were and what Jane's reactions would be.

Jane sighed. "How did you learn to massage a back this way? Nobody's ever made me feel like this before."

"I don't think it's something I've learned. I've taken the time to care. With you I really want to care."

"Do you realize that I'm crushing my rose lying on you like this," Jane said, saddened that the pretty corsage was being ruined.

"Oh, is *that* what's been pressing on me? And all this time I was hoping it was your breast."

John could almost feel the fire in her eyes as she dug her elbows into his stomach and pounded his shoulder. "You are so crass."

He laughed and pulled her, resisting, back down so she couldn't hit him again. "You certainly are a lively one. I don't think I've ever met anybody who appreciated my humor as much as you do. If it makes you feel any better, I'll try to pretend you don't have any breasts."

Jane tried to relax yet again, thinking about his sense of humor—which she didn't enjoy—and his touch—which she did.

Thinking of something else to say, John readied his arms and legs. "I don't know what I'll pretend they are, but I better think of something quickly." Laughing, he immediately wrapped his arms and legs around her, holding on firmly to prevent her determined struggle for freedom.

"Let me go!" she shouted. "I don't want you holding me."

"Truce," John gasped when he finally stopped laughing. "I promise I'll be good."

Jane stopped her squirming. "You'd better."

They settled down and relaxed, allowing the calmness both felt to flow between them as their bodies curved together. His fingers came to life again and casually traced her bra strap along her back and shoulders. After ten minutes of this soothing motion, John said reluctantly, "I've got to go now."

Jane lifted her head and looked sleepily into his eyes. "Do you have to?"

"It's getting late, and we both need our beauty sleep. You have to go to work tomorrow, and I have to get ready for my trip."

As she watched him slip on his sneakers, she wondered at the uniqueness of their simple cuddling. She realized how much she wanted him to kiss her before he left. She had never felt like this. Never before had she innocently rested on someone's body, while he was content to just rub her back. But she was afraid he might misinterpret her intentions. Intentions she wasn't sure of herself.

After tying his shoes, John looked at her and smiled. Expecting him to get up and leave, she wasn't sure how to react when he lifted a hand to her forehead and slowly brushed his fingers across her face. From her eyebrows, he continued his journey to her nose and then down its side to her cheek and chin. When he traced his fingers across her lower lip, it was as though his fingers caused an electric surge. The tingle was unrelenting, as he continued to lightly touch her lower lip and then the upper. She sat frozen—lips quivering—not wanting to break the spell. They remained looking at each other; her heart pounded. Feeling such tension, Jane had to restrain herself from screaming out: *What are you waiting for? Kiss me.*

John broke the hush. "You're so beautiful, and your body is so soft to touch." Slowly his face approached hers. Jane said not a word. Just as she was about to close her eyes, expecting his kiss, he started to rub his nose against hers. Feeling his warm soft skin against hers made her heart pound as if it would burst.

As he kept rubbing his nose back and forth, she couldn't conceal her desire. She closed her eyes, moistened her puckered lips, and waited. Then, like a thunderbolt striking, his moist lips pressed against hers. Her whole body jolted to his touch. Then it was over almost as quickly as it had started. But he kissed her again—longer and harder. Her body felt trapped in a whirlpool, her head light and dizzy. Again his lips pulled away, leaving hers still wanting, even after they had returned for a third and fourth time.

Breaking the spell, John said shakily, "You trapped me. I wasn't going to kiss you tonight. I was only going to rub my nose against yours. But your lips were so inviting, how could I refuse?"

"I didn't trap you. And my lips weren't inviting you. Besides, how did I know you only wanted to rub your nose against mine? What did you expect me to do?"

Retreating, John stood up and reached out his hands. Smiling, he reassured her, "I expect you to always be yourself. I think you're wonderful." Taking her hand, he helped her up. At the door, they embraced, melting into each other's arms. "I had a wonderful day with you, Jane Melrose. I hope you have a good day at work tomorrow."

Unwrapping his arms, he opened the door and stepped outside. As he reached his car, Jane called out, "Have a safe trip."

"I'll call you in a couple of days." His last glance at the slim figure silhouetted in the night touched him as he got into his car and started the engine. Her hand was at her heart, clutching the rose.

Chapter 6

"So we'll meet tomorrow for lunch," suggested Bob. It was late Thursday afternoon, and Bob McWilliams had called Jane in response to her fax to Ralph Daniels about Unitel Software.

"I'm really looking forward to it," Jane said, eyeing the dozen red roses in a makeshift vase on her desk.

"Let's make it at the Bay Tower Room, say 12:30." From the thirty-third floor, the Bay Tower Room, one of downtown Boston's premier restaurants, afforded a magnificent panoramic view of Boston Harbor.

"Do you always go to such lengths to make a person feel like part of the team?"

"Only when they're as pretty as you."

When the phone call was over, she reached under her desk for the florist box.

"Leaving early today?" Wayne Jensen asked from the desk behind hers. The best that could be said about Wayne was that he was an impeccably dressed, hard-working investment consultant. "Sounds like you have to prepare for tomorrow's heavy date." The leer in his voice reminded her of how obnoxious he could be.

A serious knee injury four years ago had put an end to his glamorous life as an Aspen ski instructor and bartender. Giving up turtlenecks and ski bunnies, he'd bought designer suits and moved East to put his finance degree to work. Wayne's short stature did nothing to lessen his belief that he was the answer to every woman's dreams. For more than six months, Jane had suffered from his advances. Then she had accidentally learned that his semi-monthly, Tuesday afternoon business meetings were actually Hair Club for Men sessions. At least toward Jane, with her knowledge of his hair replacement, Wayne's demeanor had changed overnight. For the two years since then, they'd had a mutually beneficial business relationship.

"Sorry to disappoint you, Wayne, but there's nothing to prepare for. I just don't feel like burning the midnight oil tonight to make the big bucks like you do." She carefully inspected each rose as she placed them in the long box.

With the box cradled under her arm, she headed for the exit, relieved to escape the day-long inquisition. Tossing a look over her shoulder, she said, "Goodnight, Wayne. Good prospecting."

At home she meticulously arranged the roses in a vase and set them in the center of her dining room table.

After a meal of broiled chicken breast, new potatoes, and a garden salad, she cleaned up and headed for the bedroom. On the way she picked up the vase. She carefully placed it center stage on her bedroom bureau. Again she fussed with the arrangement until she was fully satisfied.

Smiling inwardly, she selected a nightgown. Tonight she shunned her usual plain cotton pajamas for the sensuous nightgown her Aunt Sandy had given her a year ago. It was still in the gift-wrapped box. She undressed and slipped it on. Peach colored and ankle length, it was a light cotton knit in an English floral and ribbon print. The slightly scooped neckline, trimmed in lace with a peach satin bow centered above her breasts, made her feel special. At the dresser mirror, she reached back, undid her barrette, and brushed her hair to a golden shine. Putting the brush down, she raised a hand, and slowly combed her fingers through her hair. Pondering its significance, she watched it, silk-like, drift down.

Admiring the roses again, she whispered softly, "Thank you, God." In sheer happiness she lifted her arms and did one of her childhood ballerina-like twirls.

Her bedtime ritual was completed by 7:30. Getting into bed, she arranged the phone for easier access and picked up her book. As the evening wore on, her concentration dwindled, and her eyes drifted from the roses to the phone. By ten o'clock she gave up. Once again she fell asleep with a feeling of emptiness.

The jarring ring made her jump. Forgetting her planned strategy, she immediately grabbed the phone. "Hello."

"Hi, Jane? It's John Avery."

"Oh, hi." She tried not to sound groggy. "What a surprise."

"I hope I'm not calling too late. My parents took me out to dinner."

"No, it's all right." Turning on the light, she sat up and fixed the pillow behind her.

"You seem to be great therapy. Ever since I met you, I've had really good feelings about myself."

"I'm glad. I enjoyed the time we spent together also, except when you were embarrassing me, that is. Speaking of which, please don't send me any more flowers. Yesterday's arrangement was bad enough, but after today's roses, everybody in my office is talking."

"They're all impressed, huh?"

"No, they like to gossip. Besides, you can't possibly afford them."

"It's too late. When I told my boss, Mr. Farris, about you, he promised to take good care of you while I'm away. You should expect something every day. What can I say, I'm like a second son to him."

Jane let out a long sigh of anguish. "I don't believe it."

"It's pretty good, huh?"

"No, it's terrible. Will you ever stop embarrassing me?"

"I doubt it. We look at life differently. You should loosen up some."

"I'm loose enough. I like my life just the way it is. So, why are you and Mr. Farris so close?" Jane asked to change the subject.

"Well," John dragged the word out and paused. "I was twenty-five when I met him. I was in the hospital receiving treatment for a relapse of my kidney problem, and Steve, Mr. Farris' nineteen-year-old son, was my roommate. Steve was very sick with leukemia and complained about how unfair life was. Whenever his family came to visit him, he'd make them feel guilty. His mother, bless her soul, came in every afternoon and sat at his bedside. I could see what he was doing because I had done much the same the first time I was hospitalized for my kidney problem.

"We talked a lot and shared our feelings about death, and he seemed to accept the fact he was going to die. I asked him why he wanted to make his parents feel so bad, especially his mother.

"I told him to just tell them what he had told me—tell them how scared of dying he was. But also to tell them how much he loved them and that their being at his side was what he wanted most of all."

"That was really nice of you."

"Well, it must have worked because he called his parents and they immediately came to the hospital. After an emotional reconciliation, his parents arranged to take him home. He had to have around-the-clock nursing. But his final days were spent at home with his family at his side."

John was quiet for a moment, remembering. After recalling the dream he'd had after learning of Steve's death and a quick thought to God, he said, "Ever since then the Farrises have taken me in. Not really as Steve's replacement, but as a way of saying thanks."

"You must be very special to them."

"I'm glad I was able to do it, but I don't think it was anything special. All I did was talk to Steve and listen to him speak about his true feelings. We all spend too much time hiding our feelings, not letting on what we really think or desire."

There was a long silence as John allowed Jane time to comment. When she didn't respond, he said, "Let's not talk about illness any more; let's talk about you."

"There's nothing to say."

"Sure there is. You can tell me what you're wearing."

"Aha, the truth comes out. This is an obscene phone call."

John chuckled. "Not unless you're standing there naked. I guess I'd like to visualize you lying on your bed by the window wearing a pretty nightgown. With the lights off, the moon would be shining down on your wonderful silky hair spread out on the pillow."

"You do have quite an imagination, but I'm sorry to disappoint you. I still have my work clothes on and my hair is pinned up. But I'll look out the window to see if the moon is shining." She put the receiver down and went over to the window. Opening the shade, she saw John's yellow rose from the picnic sitting on the windowsill. She carefully picked it up and went back to the phone. "I can see it; it's almost full. Let me turn my light off."

With the bedside lamp off, she arranged her pillow. Holding the rose to her heart, she looked over at the bureau and saw the moonlight shining on the vase of red roses. Then, as the moonlight shone on her smiling face, her hair fanning out over the pillow, she picked up the phone. "Hi, I'm back."

"Thank goodness. I was starting to miss you."

"Let's not flirt now. Remember, you said you didn't have to impress me."

"Me, flirt? You must be having delusions of grandeur."

"What is it about you that makes you so irritating? Can't we enjoy the moon and have a pleasant conversation. Like, did you know that June's full moon is known as the strawberry moon? And last month's full moon was the flower moon?"

"Well, I can't say I did. But I *have* heard of the harvest moon," he added, not wanting her to think he was a complete idiot.

"That's the September full moon. Each full moon has a name. October's the hunter's moon. The only other one that I think is romantic is February's. That's the snow moon."

"It's hard to imagine," John said wistfully. "I'm a thousand miles away from you, and yet we're looking at the same beautiful moon. I wish you were here lying beside me. Then we could talk in the moonlight, and I'd be able to feel the warmth and calmness that flows from you."

"Cuddling up in your arms in the moonlight. That'd be romantic. To be able to hear your heart beating again would be so relaxing. I'm sure it'd put me right to sleep," Jane heard herself say.

"I wouldn't fall asleep unless I knew you were safe and comfortable. Then I'd know I'd be lucky enough to wake up, and the first thing I'd see would be you lying next to me."

"Ummmm, that sounds nice, too. But remember, we are only friends."

"I remember. That's all I've been thinking about since I've been down here. It seems funny, but you make it feel so natural for a woman to be my closest friend. I have never...."

59

❀ ❀ ❀

Jane studied herself in the ladies' room mirror. The little black dress and French braid would definitely catch Bob's attention. Ready to make her entrance, the thought of how a white corsage would make her look special crossed her mind.

Bob hadn't arrived yet, but the maitre d' went out of his way to accommodate her. "I've a special table waiting for you and Monsieur Bob," he said in his heavy French accent, leading her through the dining room.

On a clear day the view would have been spectacular. But with today's rain, only a thick, gray mist was visible. Nursing a glass of wine, she waited with pleasant anticipation.

It wasn't long before she saw Bob enter the room. Filled with excitement, she was about to stand when he bent over to talk to a group of men at a nearby table. It was no wonder everyone took notice of him. He made a striking presence, with his wavy blond hair and broad shoulders, impeccably dressed in his gray pinstripe Armani suit.

"I trust Pierre took good care of you?" he asked, finally sitting down across from her.

"He couldn't have been more gracious. Judging from the fuss he made over me, he must really care for you."

"I did some important legal work for his family a few years back." Bob looked away and acknowledged a man sitting a few tables over who had gestured to him.

"What are you drinking?" he asked, lifting her glass.

"The house rosé."

Bob raised an arm. Immediately a waiter rushed to his side. "Take this back and bring a bottle of Chateau Lafite-Rothschild."

Jane was wide eyed. "This *is* a business lunch, isn't it?"

"In business as in pleasure, I'm a firm believer in going first class." The glint of his piercing blue eyes was mesmerizing.

After lunch they lingered over coffee. Jane felt comfortable sitting with Bob McWilliams. He wasn't like John, who studied and made note of her every move. Between an easy flow of business and personal conversations, Bob was busy instructing waiters and being interrupted by various acquaintances passing their table. It seemed to Jane

60

he knew everyone who was anyone in the city. He emanated a magnetic, fast-paced aura which attracted people to him.

"I understand from Ralph you played soccer in college," he said, lifting his coffee cup. "I was a lacrosse man myself. Unfortunately I was sidelined my senior year with a knee injury."

Yes, she said to herself, trying to control an ecstatic smile—it seemed all the pieces of her dreams were finally falling into place. "Is that so? What position did you play?" She was noticing an attractive man approaching Bob from behind.

Slapping Bob on the shoulder, the man said, "You old rogue, you. Who's this beautiful woman you're keeping captive?"

"Dustin." Bob stood and grasped the man's hand in one motion. "When did they let you out of jail?"

"It's only a lunchtime furlough, I'm afraid."

For the next ten minutes and with an occasional exchange of barbs, they caught up with each other's lives. Dustin, she quickly learned, had been a law school classmate of Bob's and was now the County District Attorney. Law school wasn't the only thing she found out they had in common. Both had been named in the current issue of *Boston Monthly* as one of Boston's top twenty-five most eligible bachelors.

Even more interesting to Jane, Dustin let it slip that Bob was currently involved with another woman. Bob was quick to inform her that they were in the process of a mutual dissolution, brought on by her decision to accept an end-of-the-month job transfer to Chicago.

By the time Jane had to leave to go back to her office, she thought about Bob being a free man by July. Until then she'd try to think of as many reasons as possible to have business meetings with him.

Chapter 7

Jane paced around her apartment. Stopping, she checked herself in the mirror. She glanced again at her watch, saw it was nearly ten. John Avery had returned home last night, and she had taken the day off to spend it with him. Any minute he'd pick her up to take her to his childhood hometown. All morning she had tried to rationalize their relationship, telling herself he was only a casual and kooky friend. She knew he was far from her ideal, but she couldn't overcome this irrational schoolgirl anticipation.

The doorbell's ring sent her heart pounding, and without thinking, she greeted him with a hug. It seemed so natural, but she hoped it wasn't misleading.

"Mmmm," she heard him murmur as their bodies molded into one. "I've been thinking about this moment for days. How about you?"

"Oh, just you never mind what I've been thinking," she chided, dropping her arms to avoid his inquisitive, brown eyes.

Before releasing her, he pressed a quick kiss to her responsive lips. "Can you believe it's been ten days since we've seen each other?"

She led the way into the living room. "With you calling every night, it hardly seemed like you were away. I can't imagine what your parents must think. What will they say when they get their phone bill?"

"They were so happy to see me in such good spirits. Over the years they've come to expect a mopey, gloomy me." He sat next to her on the couch and stroked her knee. "They said the phone bill would be the best investment they ever made. They'd like to meet you."

"I'd like to meet them, too. Then I'd know who to blame for your wacky ways. I'm still amazed that we found things to talk about for two hours every night." With her eyes on his, she absently ran her fingers over his hand.

"It's easy when there's so much to learn about each other. I'm just glad you were home when I called, especially after you told me how often you have business meetings at night."

"You were lucky, I guess," she said, thinking about the scrambling she had done to rearrange her schedule.

"Will you show me the peach nightgown with the satin bow that you told me about?"

Jane's eyes tilted heavenward. He certainly hadn't lost his bizarre and outrageous ways.

"I take that as a no?"

"That's right. Friends, remember?" she said, removing his hand from her knee. "It's time for our trip down your memory lane."

"Well, you'd better get something for your hair. I've got the top down."

John pulled over to the side of the road and turned the ignition off. "We should get out here," he said, pointing to the road ahead with a dead end sign. "There's no place to park down there." Then he pointed out the passenger's window to a golf course. "That was my backyard for over twenty years."

"You must have loved it when your father asked you to cut the lawn," Jane teased, opening her door.

They walked along the edge of the golf course down a hill toward the house. "That's where Timothy lived," he said, pointing to a large, brown house across the street. "He was my best friend. We were both three when he moved in."

Passing a white ranch, he pointed to another large, brown house. "And that's where I lived until I was twenty-three." Eyes darting, he

64

absorbed the scene. "It's pretty much the same. Some trees have been cut down and those over there are new, but basically it's how I remember it."

"How often do you come back here?"

"About once a year, I guess. I just walk around."

"Is that how long it takes you to find a woman to go out with you?" With a big grin, she jabbed him in the ribs. "Touché!"

"No, it's not. And I'll have you know only you and Amy have been here. It's as if a bell goes off inside, telling me to come back here. It gives me peace of mind."

John scanned the view from the house to the hilly terrain of the golf course and back. "I could really bore you with all my memories. Almost every spot around here has an important meaning to my life."

"You wouldn't bore me." Jane reached for his hand. "I'd like to know what your memories are like."

They walked quietly together to a partially buried two-foot-high rock. This had been his perch to watch the weekend golfers. The memories were too numerous, but the silly kid stuff was the best. "When Tim and I were little, we used to go out after rainstorms and have puddle days. We'd get our boots on and go run and jump through all the puddles. During the winter, we'd check out how solid the ice was by jumping up and down on it to see if it would break. If it was solid enough, we'd run and slide across it." John chuckled at the memory. "Puddle jumping had its risks. We'd have to be careful, because some of the puddles were over our boots. Tim always had boots you'd wear over stocking feet, and they'd go up to his knees. Unfortunately my mother always bought me boots that went over shoes and that style must have been about four inches shorter. Even though we were careful, we were always coming home with our feet soaking wet." He paused for a moment and added, "Gosh, that was fun. There are times now I get the urge when I see a puddle. I guess you never forget the good stuff in life."

The house was unusual in that the front faced the white house and not the road. Walking past the house, Jane noticed John staring at a house beyond some trees on another road. It was a cold, lifeless stare. He'd had the same unnatural look earlier when they'd driven past that house. She wondered if there was some lurking dark memory of the neighborhood bully connected to that house.

65

Turning back to his childhood home, he pointed to a set of second-floor windows. His lighthearted grin returned. "Those were my bedroom windows. From there I could see everything important in my life—like this backyard and our gardens. In the summer, I could watch the golfers." Jane listened intently as he enthusiastically relived his youth.

"Winter snowstorms were like a winter wonderland. I used to go sledding, tobogganing, and skiing on the hills. I loved to play in the snow, and I sure had a big enough area to play in. Now you know where I learned to make such great angels in the snow." He poked his index finger into her stomach to get his point across.

Emitting a squeal, she grabbed at his hand.

With his hand restrained by hers, he continued. "Along the far side of the golf course is the trolley line to Boston. I'd sit by my window and watch and listen to them go clanking by. At night it was fun to lie at the foot of my bed and watch their lights. Sometimes I could see the sparks as the power rod bounced along the cable."

As if on cue, there was the sound of a trolley, and John turned to the right. "Here comes one now, heading into Boston. They've replaced the tracks and these new cars are a lot quieter, but the memories are still there."

They stood quietly and watched the trolley snake its way past the trees and hills. Jane enjoyed the reminiscing; somehow it seemed to touch her own life, connecting their nostalgia.

"See that building beyond the tracks?" John asked, pointing to the left at an old, two-story, brick structure with a lot of windows. "That's where I went to grade school. During the winter, if we'd had a big snowstorm at night, I'd wake up early and look out at the school. If there weren't any big puffs of black smoke coming out of the chimney, I'd know there'd be no school that day. But my mother would listen to the radio announcement anyway, just to make sure."

Jane was attentive as he revealed these cherished remembrances. She didn't want to take lightly the responsibility he had given her as he unfolded his life story.

Looking out at the golf course, John pointed toward a hill. "Do you see that fence up there? It used to be an old rusty thing made out of chicken wire. I'll always remember a Friday night back when I was in high school. Another friend of mine, Jim, and I were drinking beer.

He was on the gymnastics team, and that night he decided to do back flips. He couldn't understand why he kept landing on his head. He'd get back on his feet explaining, 'No, no. I can do it this time', and then land on his head again. We were laughing so hard. He only stopped trying when we both rolled helplessly on the ground in laughter.

"Later that night we were walking along that fence for some reason. Without warning I fell through a rust-weakened section and rolled head over heels all the way down that gravel hillside, laughing all the way. It must be forty feet to the bottom. I couldn't believe how bad I looked when I got home. My face was dirty and cut up, but I didn't feel a thing. I was too busy laughing." He chuckled as he related the story to Jane. She smiled, enjoying his happiness.

The laughter subsided, and a solemn look crept across John's face. "You know, Jim was the only person I ever drank with. It's been over twenty years since I've had a drink. I sure miss him—not for the drinking, but for the camaraderie, the friendship."

"Where is he now?"

John looked up at the sky as if lost in thought for a few, long seconds. When he finally spoke his voice was a monotone. "He didn't go to college like the rest of us. He enlisted in the army and became a Green Beret. They sent him over to Viet Nam. He was out on a night patrol when he tripped a booby trap and a grenade killed him."

He stared back up at the sky, biting his lower lip. It was as if he had gone back in time and reflected on what it was like back then. Then he shook his head. "Those were crazy days to grow up in."

Moving behind Jane, he wrapped his arms around her waist without speaking. Soon there was another memory. "See that mound? That's where I kissed a girl for the first time. I was fifteen. It was an early summer night, and we were walking home from a movie. I managed to get up the nerve to kiss her, but I missed her lips when I closed my eyes. I think my mouth landed on her cheek next to her nose. I'm still a lousy kisser." He grinned and shrugged.

Smiling back, Jane said, "At least you've improved your aim."

John only smiled weakly. Lifting his hands, he wiggled his fingers before her. His eyes twinkled now, brightening a broad smile. "It's with my hands and fingers I best express my feelings."

Jane let out an impish chuckle. "Is that a threat or a promise?"

The expected retort didn't come. John became serious. "With you...." then he paused. The silence became awkward. "Forget I ever brought it up," he mumbled, and looked away.

Jane moved to face him. "What's wrong? Tell me. Please."

He stood not saying a word—trying to gather courage. Finally he reached for her hands. "Passion with a woman is so special to me. That's why I've only allowed myself to hold your hand and give you a few quick kisses. I was only hoping for a friend. I can't believe I've known you for less than two weeks."

"What do you mean?" Now there was no mirth in her voice.

He hesitated, then looked into her eyes. "You've become the most important person in my life...and it scares me." He quickly turned away. His heart pounded, fearing rejection.

Feeling uneasy, Jane thought it best to lighten the mood. She shook him gently, saying, "That's what's so special about friendships. Besides you don't have to be scared of me. I won't bite you."

If John heard her, he did not react. His eyes were focused on that house.

"Do you see that house?"

She turned to where he pointed—to *that* house beyond the trees.

"When I was thirteen the man who lived there sexually molested me in that house." Jane froze in shock. "The first time was on a hot summer's night. I was so naive. I had no idea what sex was about, or what he was doing. I can't believe I just let him do what he did."

Jane's mind whirled in turmoil. The gut-wrenching feelings of fright and pity she had experienced in Cathy's room rushed back and crystallized. She had thought rape was something only women had to fear, not a boy. How could she have known that someone as goofy as John harbored such pain? She stood speechless, deeply caring, but not knowing how to express her concern.

"There was never any penetration, just masturbation. I was so scared, and when it was over I ran home to my room and cried all night. I've never told my parents. How do you tell your parents something like that?"

Jane caressed his face. "Oh, John. I'm so sorry."

"I wrote a poem about it. It was good therapy. I've never been good at reciting my poetry from memory, but this one is etched in my brain. Would you like to hear it?"

"Only if you'd like me to."

"I titled it, 'What Does This Mean.'"

He began reciting the poem, all the while staring at that house. Jane listened, alternating her gaze from John's eyes to that house.

"It was in my thirteenth year, the summer of '62,
A time of boyhood innocence, a victim of a taboo.
Asked to weed the garden by the huge man next door,
The night he paid me, he wanted something more.
Saying, 'Come upstairs while I get my wallet.
Do you want to know if you've become a man yet?
Take off your pants and come sit on the bed'.
"WHAT DOES THIS MEAN?

"Nervous and not knowing, how could I have been aware?
Sitting next to him, he pulled down my underwear.
Unable to say anything, I became so dutiful.
He wrapped his large hand around my penis and started to pull.
He kept pulling, faster and faster, but nothing resulted.
'Think about playing with other boys' penises', he exulted.

"WHAT DOES THIS MEAN?

"He told me an excitement like this should get me erect and
    large.
But I was being brutally violated, for which he felt no regard.
He kept pulling as fast as he could, but why should that gratify?
Then saying he'd show me what he meant, he unzipped his fly.
Forced to put my hand in his pants, I pulled out his thick, hard
    cock.
Told to squeeze and quickly move my hand, I was in a state of
    shock.

"WHAT DOES THIS MEAN?

"He tired of pulling on me and took over my chore.
Suddenly from his cock something squirted to the floor.
Quickly, I put on my pants to get away from his id.

He told me, 'Make sure you don't tell anybody about what you
    just did'.
Numb by what had happened, I ran all the way home,
Directly to my room, I cried all alone.

"WHAT DOES THIS MEAN?

"Unsubsiding fright kept me from my sleep.
Again I went to the bathroom and took another peep.
Holding back tears I passed my parents' bedroom.
I had good parents, doing what was right, I presume.
In a neighborhood like ours, who'd think it necessary to be
    informed.
My sore penis grotesquely misshapen in puffiness, was I perma-
    nently deformed?

"WHAT DOES THIS MEAN?

"So many times later, I'd pass by that house,
Terrified that I'd fall prey again to that louse.
Again and again he entrapped me, even when I was on the look-
    out.
Why didn't I just run, scream, or let out a shout?
He was a pillar of the community, from one of those Ivy League
    schools.
How ironic, he was elected to the School Committee, oh, what
    fools.

"WHAT DOES THIS MEAN?

It was the summer of '62,
And some things you can never undo."

They held each other quietly as the poignancy of the poem lingered. Jane put her head on his chest to conceal her tears. After a long
pause, as though talking to himself, he said, "You know why I wrote
that poem? One night while I was doing an overnight shift on the
phones for Samaritans, I got a call from a fourteen-year-old girl. She

was crying hysterically. She had just been raped about two hours earlier and was all alone because her mother was working an overnight shift.

"She had been walking home from the library and took a shortcut through a hospital parking lot. Two men jumped out of a van and dragged her inside. When they were done, they just dumped her out. Once she got home, she was too scared to call her mother because she wasn't supposed to have left the house. A child, all alone, scared out of her mind—she had no one to comfort her in her time of despair. She had to call a stranger on the phone. I don't know why she called a suicide hotline, but I tried my best to console and befriend her. She called throughout the night, and by morning she had decided to tell her mother and to go to the hospital because of the bleeding.

"I cry when I think of that girl and what she endured. I can feel the death her soul must have experienced knowing that something very important and precious had been stolen forever from her."

Jane thought of Cathy's ordeal and the curves of the road on the Italian mountainside. Had *that* been Cathy's way of coping with her own special loss?

John shook himself as if to shake off his tragic mindset. "Enough of that. We can discuss it further some other time. There's more happiness in my memories here than I can tell you in one day. I'd rather have you know the goodness around here which makes up the foundation of who I am."

Jane wiped her tears and smiled at him—a smile that acknowledged how she cherished and accepted his unconditional trust and friendship.

He took her hand. "Let me tell you about the gardens," he said. They strolled along the road until they had a better view of the backyard. "We had flowers growing from the corner near the garage all the way down to the bottom of the yard. And our vegetable garden was over there," he said, indicating a far corner.

"I used to know where every perennial was, and each year, long before the snows were gone, I'd be out searching for any spring bulbs poking out of the ground. I loved to anticipate the flowers. We had snowdrops, crocuses, daffodils, tulips—all the early spring flowers. Later on there'd be lily-of-the-valley, poppies, peonies, iris—so many others." Pointing to the upper side garden, he said, "I would pick lily-

71

of-the-valley and lie there on the grass, with my dog, Hooffy, drinking in the fragrance.".".

"Hooffy?" said Jane, followed by laughter.

"Yeah. It was the name of my oldest brother's imaginary friend." John couldn't stop now; he wanted to tell her everything. "There used to be an apple tree over there, and there's the Chinese cherry tree we planted the year Kennedy became president. Over here we had butterfly bushes. All the butterflies would be attracted to the wonderful, fragrant nectar, and they'd flutter around from one blossom to another. Whenever I see butterflies and flowers, I see living proof that there's a God. A beautiful gift from God to our planet Earth."

Hands joined, they took a long walk around the edge of the golf course. Two hours later on their way back to the car, Jane pointed to a shady area under a grove of trees. "Do you have any memories of that spot?"

John looked at the trees. "None that I can think of."

"Good. Let's sit there on the grass and maybe you'll think of one." When they reached the grove of oak trees, Jane plopped down and leaned on an elbow. "So, what happened here? You said you had memories of every spot around here."

"I think you've found the one place where nothing special has happened."

Jane smiled and said, "Oh, is that so?" She leaned over to her startled friend and said softly, "I'm going to have to change that."

She pressed her lips hard against his, maneuvering her body on top of him. She slipped her hands behind his head to control where and how his lips met hers. He responded eagerly, wrapping his arms tightly around her. She shifted her weight, causing their bodies to roll, lips intact, until John was on top. His hand stroked her face as their breathing became more pronounced. But Jane wanted to stay in control, to be the memory maker, so she jerked her left arm and shoulder up, forcing their bodies into another half revolution. On top again, she raised her head and their lips parted. "Friends are allowed to kiss," she said, giving him a sweet smile.

"You must be a very good friend, because that was definitely a very good kiss."

"Let me warn you," Jane said, getting up, "don't get any other ideas, because that's as far as friends go. Do you understand?"

Standing, John brushed off his legs. "Hey, with kisses like that, who needs anything else?"

At the car, John looked back at the grove of trees. "You sure know how to create a great memory." He gave her his weird look.

"That was my intention." She leaned forward and tenderly kissed the dimple on his cheek.

Driving around the area, he continued showing her all the different places that had affected him as a youngster. Then they stopped for dinner at the first McDonald's he'd ever eaten in, back in his early teens.

With an eighty-degree temperature and high clouds blocking the sun, it was a lovely evening to drive with the top down. The rush-hour traffic had thinned to just a few cars, and John drove leisurely below the forty-five mile-per-hour speed limit.

At a stoplight, a black car, its radio blasting, pulled up alongside them. John looked over at the three college kid occupants. The passenger in the backseat yelled out, "Nice car. Wanna race?"

When John turned away, the kids began a flurry of taunts. As the lights turned green, John looked over and said, "You kids think you're good, don't you?"

The black TransAm with New York plates squealed away, while both passengers leaned out, presenting John with the one-finger salute. Refusing to be angered, John eased away from the stop light.

"Why did you say that?" Jane asked, sounding perturbed.

"Come on. They were harmless. Just a lot of talk. Besides, have you ever drag raced before?"

"Of course not. Why?"

As they slowed down for the next set of lights, John told her, "Anticipation. Always know how far ahead you can go before you have to stop. That's if you expect to have a real race."

He glanced in the rear-view mirror, then turned to the black car alongside him again. Reversing his cap, he said to the kids, "So, you think you know how to drive that thing?"

The kids whooped and yelled, "He's going to race. All right! We're going to wipe your ass, old man."

John ignored them as he adjusted his car seat forward. Jane looked astonished. "What are you doing?"

"There's one thing about racing—it sure gets the adrenaline flowing." He glided the stick shift from first gear through fourth, reassuring his nerves with the feel of the car.

Conditions had to be just right before he'd commit, plus he didn't want to get stopped for speeding. The greatest danger would be a speed trap. However, everything looked okay ahead. The road was straight for over a mile with no stoplights. The lights seemed endless at this usually busy intersection. John knew there'd be a green left-turn arrow first. The kids in the other car were shouting obscenities while the driver kept revving the engine in an immature, non-verbal challenge. Adrenaline charged, John now moved the stick shift between first and second.

While the green arrow was on, only one car crossed in front of them. After a reassuring final check in the rear-view mirrors, John made his decision. He gripped the stick shift tightly and waited in first gear. Maintaining total concentration on the light, he lifted his left foot until he felt the gear ready to engage.

The moment the light turned green, he floored the gas pedal. The engine responded with a powerful roar. A split second later he popped the clutch. The car's front heaved up a foot as the back wheels dug into the pavement. With the engine's tremendous power, the tires engaged the road, and with the utmost friction, squealed agonizingly. Both cars screamed as they shot forward, leaving behind a trail of white exhaust and black tire treads.

The tires on John's Ford squealed the entire thirty feet it traveled in first gear. At twenty-five miles per hour, he knew from the sound and feel that it was time to shift. He slammed in the clutch and whipped the stick shift down into second, not bothering to take his foot off the gas pedal. He had a one-third car-length's lead as he popped the clutch into second gear. The tires continued to scream and squeal. Eyes focused entirely on the road ahead, John relied on his acute sense of feel and sound to determine how the car was performing. Finally the wheels stopped squealing, but the engine's roar didn't abate as the car continued accelerating down the road.

At forty-five miles per hour it was time to shift. Again the wheels protested as the gears engaged. He now held more than a full car length's lead over the TransAm, and the accelerator was still pressed firmly to the floor. His lead had widened to over two car lengths by the time they reached sixty-five miles per hour and had shifted into fourth.

All this time Jane remained gripped in her seat, scared out of her mind. Unable to breathe properly, she prayed they wouldn't crash. *For sure,* she thought, *a tire would blow or the engine would explode under such pressure.* Never before had she heard such a sustained roar from an auto's engine, or such force of wind rushing through the open car. The road, trees, and telephone poles flashed by in a blur.

The lead continued to widen as they flew down the road. Jane took a terrified glance at the speedometer and saw it advance from seventy to seventy-five miles per hour. Looking back at the TransAm, she saw that it was at least four lengths behind. Now they were up to eighty-five miles per hour. Thankfully no cars were in front of them. She prayed that this wild ride would end safely.

When they had reached ninety miles per hour with a five car length lead, John finally removed his foot from the gas pedal. The TransAm shot past them still accelerating. The two passengers stuck their heads out of the window and yelled, but their words were lost in the rush of air.

John eased on the brakes until they were traveling at the legal forty-five miles per hour. He looked over at the petrified Jane and asked, "Do you think they were stupid or just crazy?"

Trembling, she still clutched the seat. "I think you're all stupid. I've never been so scared in my life."

"I told you it would get the adrenaline flowing!" John chuckled. "I think *they* were stupid. *I'm* only crazy. They didn't even know when it was over and time to slow down."

"And you think you did?"

Back home, Jane drew the drapes across the patio door. Turning around, she found John, sneakers off, lying on the couch. "Come, lie down with me."

"I'm not sure you deserve it."

"Oh, come on. I was only showing off for you. I'm sorry I scared you."

"I'll cuddle with you only if you promise never to race your car like that again. With or without me."

"Okay, I promise."

75

"You don't think I'm serious, but I am. I was so afraid something would happen. We could have crashed, been killed even. Did you stop to think about *that*?" She was angry and wanted to chastise him. "It's not worth it, John."

He held out his arms. "I'm sorry. I really am. I won't do that again—with or without you."

Pleased he had relented, apparently contrite, she accepted the comfort of his arms.

"Now you know what I was like as a kid," he told her. "After some of the crazy things Tim and I did, we'd go to the Arch Street Church in Boston for confession. We figured city priests would be more lenient with us. That, and we didn't really trust our parish priest not to tell our parents."

"Pray tell, what did you two do to create such a need?"

"Some other time. Right now I only want to hold you and relax." He reached up and unclipped her hair.

"Remember," she warned, "we're just friends."

"Of course. How could I forget? Would you move up a little on me so you can put your forehead on mine?"

"What?" She looked perplexed. "Why would you want me to do that?"

"I don't know. I just think it'd be nice."

Reluctantly, she did as he asked. Moving up until they were face to face, she gently placed her forehead on his. After a few minutes of lying quietly, he said in a sad voice, "You don't have to do it any more."

"You sure?"

He nodded.

Noticing the sudden mood change, she scrunched lower and placed her head back on his chest. While she tried to figure out what had happened to upset him, she heard him say, "I don't think we should see each other more than once a week."

She raised her head—too quickly, she feared. "Why?"

"Well, when you think about it, that's plenty of time for friends. I have an inconvenient work schedule and then there's my work with the Samaritans. You have a busy work week, too, complete with night meetings. Besides, you need time to read, and I need time for my poetry."

She settled her head back on his chest as he ran his fingers through her hair. She knew exactly where to place her head to hear the gentle rhythmic thumping of his heart. "Are you upset because I keep insisting that we just be friends?"

"Of course not. Besides, a friendship is all I can handle. With my messed up life anything else is an impossibility."

He stroked her cheek with the back of his hand. Brushing some strands of hair from her face, he said, "But friends are allowed to talk on the phone."

Noticing an upbeat tone, she asked, "And how often should friends call?"

"I think good friends should call every day they're able."

"No more two hour conversations," she warned.

"Only if there's that much to talk about." He raised his head to kiss her waiting lips. With the ground rules established, neither felt the need for further conversation.

They lapsed into sweet contentment as John massaged her back and neck. Soon she was being lulled to sleep by his casual strokes along the contours of her back. That is until one of those innocent strokes down her back returned up inside her jersey.

The touch of his warm hand against her bare skin sent conflicting shock waves throughout her body. Her heart raced; shivers of pleasure ran up her spine. But her mind flashed a protective warning, and she lifted her head to stare directly into his eyes. "What do you think you're doing?"

"Rubbing your back. Why?"

She wasn't going to fall for his wide-eyed act of innocence. "Don't get any ideas. Remember, we're only friends."

Having set him straight, she put her head back down and savored the touch of his hand. Ever so gently, John fondled the sensitive skin of her back, and ever so slightly he expanded his area of exploration.

When his hand reached the side of her rib cage, Jane feared the worst. "What did I tell you?"

Mischievously, he answered, "What am I doing wrong? What are you worried about?"

She knew directness was her best defense. "You wanting to feel my breasts."

John laughed at her. "Not me. Remember, last week I said I was going to pretend you didn't have any? What you should have worried about was this," and he wiggled his fingers deep into the side of her ribs.

The unexpectedness of John's tickle attack caught Jane off guard. Laughing uncontrollably, she twisted and squirmed to avoid his relentless fingers. Unable to free herself, she yelled, "Stop it! I can't stand it."

John removed his hand from her ribs. Trying to catch her breath, she scolded him, "I don't believe you did that. We could have fallen and gotten hurt."

"Never."

"How can you be so sure?"

"Because I would have protected you, like this." Holding her securely with his left arm, he hooked his leg around her and suddenly tilted their bodies over the edge of the couch. Jane let out a shriek as she tried to grasp for something to hold. Rolling off the couch, they headed for the floor.

John reached out with his right arm and leg and broke their fall. With a thump, they landed safely on the carpet with John on top. Jane's shriek turned into giddy laughter.

"Did you get hurt?"

"No," she said emphatically. "But I could have."

A silence fell as John gazed deeply into each Jane's eyes. He had never known such happiness. Running his palm over her cheek, he felt the softness of her skin. She was incredibly beautiful. "Mmmmmm," he murmured. "Now I have you where I want you. I need lots of room to do what I have in mind."

Eyes wide, she asked coquettishly, "And what is that?"

"First, I'm going to kiss you." With parted lips he explored her face, from her eyebrows to her nose to her cheeks until he discovered the ultimate prize, her warm, soft lips. They became lost in the timeless intoxication of sweetness and passion. Afterwards he asked in a husky voice, "Where did you learn to kiss like that?"

"I had a very affectionate teddy bear when I was a little girl." She hoped the offhand quip would distract him from the thumping of her heart and what must have been a flushed face.

"Lucky teddy bear, sharing your kisses and your bed."

"My teddy bear was very special to me."

"And I'm not?"

"Not like my teddy."

"Where is he now?"

"He's gone to teddy bear heaven. It happened when I was in college."

"Bummer." John frowned. "What was the cause of his demise?"

"I think he went to the college laundry rolled up in my sheets. He never came back."

"What a terrible way to go."

"You don't have to remind me," Jane said, in a lowered voice, looking away.

After a few moments of silence, John's face lit up. "With such a child care background, I'd worry about you tossing your baby out with the bath water."

Jane started pounding John's back. "I wouldn't do that. I'll be an excellent mother. I don't like your attitude." She pushed him off of her and then climbed on top of him.

"Well, is this any better?" he asked. He clasped her body in a tight embrace, and they rolled across the floor. Jane shrieked in laughter until they came to a stop on the other side of the room.

"I'll show you what's better," she said, rolling them back across the room until John groaned in dizziness.

"Poor baby," Jane teased. "I hope you've learned not to mess with me. Remember that hill by the pond. I was the family hill-rolling champ."

"Well, you may have me this time," he moaned. "But you're not so tough. I'll keep track of who gets whom the most, just so we'll know who the boss really is."

Chapter 8

Flustered, John wracked his brain, trying to make a word from his jumbled letter tiles. Suddenly a Cheshire cat grin wiped away his frown. "Boy, you're going to love this one," he gloated, as he placed three tiles on the Scrabble board. "Your *WREATH* now becomes my *WREATHE*," he said, arranging the word *HEM*. "The *M* lands on a double-letter square, so I get eleven for *HEM* and twelve for *WREATHE*."

Enthusiasm renewed, he reached for the pencil and recorded the score. "That's a total of twenty-three. You're only 184 to my 142 now. I've cut your lead to forty-two points. That's less than a third of what you won the first game by."

Sticking to the agreement with Jane, John had seen Jane only twice during the past three weeks. Two weeks prior, he had planned for them to play miniature golf, but because of bad weather, he had rented the movie *Old Yeller* instead. He had wanted to share a meaningful part of his childhood with her. He explained that when Old Yeller had to be shot, it had been really traumatic for him. But he had left the movie with a feeling of optimism, because the ending showed Old Yeller's puppy. He knew that Old Yeller's spirit would continue through the puppy.

Jane managed to survive the hokey movie. She couldn't understand how John, a grown man, could be so unrealistic and childlike in his perception of life. However, she did like what the father had told his son after Old Yeller's death—look around for something good to take the place of the bad.

The following week, hoping to educate John with a more mature treatment of life and death, Jane took him to see the movie *Beaches*. This week they had planned to go for a walk, but since it was raining again, they decided to stay in and play Scrabble.

As soon as Jane had taken her first turn, John knew he'd have been better off walking in the rain. But now he was confident luck was on his side. "And not only that, I made it so you can't get the triple word score."

"Ahem," coughed Jane, to quiet him down. "Don't be too sure of that." Picking up two of her tiles, she placed the letters *A* and *T* on the board. "The *T* would make your *HEM* my *THEM*."

"Well," John stammered, realizing his oversight, "*AT* will only give you thirty-three points."

"Is that all?" Jane said playfully, enjoying what she was about to do. "I wonder what I'll get if I do it this way?" She plucked the rest of her tiles from the rack and nonchalantly arranged them.

"*MOZETTA?*" John reached for the dictionary. "I'll bet *AHEM* isn't even a real word."

"I think you'll find mozetta to be a hooded cape worn by bishops, and ahem is an expression of doubt or attention." Now she was wearing the Cheshire grin as he thumbed determinedly through the dictionary. After a desperate but futile search to prove her wrong, he closed the book with a loud slap. "How do you know the word mozetta? I've been going to church ten years longer than you, and I've never heard of it."

"Must be a female thing, or...I'm just smarter than you."

As he grumbled, she said enthusiastically, "Let's see. The triple word going down gives me twenty-seven, and I also get the triple word going across." Uncovering the *Z* to reveal a double-letter score, she said in delight, "Oh, what do you know. I get to double my ten points for the *Z*. So that gives me eighty-four to go with the twenty-seven. One hundred eleven—about average for my turn. Right? Oh, and don't forget to add the fifty points I get for using all my letters. That's a total of 161 points added to my 42 point lead. Gee, I'm over two hundred points ahead now."

"Can we get on with the game, please?"

"You mean you want to continue this massacre? I figured you'd want to quit."

"I'm not a quitter," he said firmly. He leaned his head on one hand, studying his tiles. The frown had returned to his face.

Finally it was over and Jane reveled in the final score—493 to 234.

"I guess that makes me twice as good as you." She tossed her head and flashed a haughty smile. John grimaced. He knew her vocabulary exceeded his, although he'd never admit it to her.

Jane got up. "I'll make you a delicious lunch to soothe your bruised ego," she said, planting a placating kiss on his forehead.

In the kitchen, she cut cucumbers and tomatoes to garnish the tuna fish and potato salads. "It looks like the rain has stopped. We should be able to go for our walk after all."

"What, no more Scrabble?"

"Don't you think you've exerted your brain enough for one day? I'd hate to be responsible for causing you permanent damage. By the way, have you decided to what my victory can be attributed?"

"Well, I'm not sure. You may just be a little smarter when it comes to vocabulary." He continued to study the board searching for a way to rig the game.

"You were right the day you told me not having a sister put you at a disadvantage," she said, returning to the dining room. "Women are just smarter than men—it's that simple."

"Oh yeah? Wait until we play Chinese checkers."

They'd been walking for over forty-five minutes, the last ten in a quiet residential area. "Why won't you tell me where we're going?" John pleaded. She threw him a sidelong glance and smiled sweetly, but said nothing. "How about a hint?"

"Nope."

His stream of queries went unanswered. Finally he said, "I've got it. You want to show me a dead animal in the road."

"Yuk, that's disgusting."

John knew he got to her. She had a way of making a face that indicated the extent of her repulsion. Making Jane wrinkle her nose and snarl her lips was great fun.

"You probably won't think it's anything special," she said, "not being the dreamer I am. It's something I've enjoyed looking at for five years now. We're nearly there."

"Nearly there," John repeated, mulling over all the information he had tricked her into revealing. After a short pause, he let go of her hand and confidently patted her bottom. "I bet I know what it is."

"Then tell me."

"It's got to be a house. I bet it's a house you'd like to live in." He smirked, nose uplifted.

Jane stamped her feet. "How did you know?"

"It was easy." John hooked his elbow with hers and began swinging her around.

"What are you doing?" she squealed, as they whirled in a circle right there on the street.

"I'm celebrating your happiness."

"I'm not that happy." Jane knew her laughter only encouraged John to become sillier, but she couldn't help herself. "It's only a house I like to look at."

Finally they turned the corner onto a quiet, tree-lined street. "There it is." Jane pointed to a large, gray house down the street. "Don't you think it's gorgeous?" she said, anxiously hoping he'd agree.

"Wait until we get closer so I can get a good look at it."

It was a two-story Colonial with a three-season porch and two chimneys. As they approached, John was impressed with the well-tended lawn and shrubs. "What do you know? They must be going to have a party," he said, gesturing to the large yellow and white-striped tent behind the porch.

At the front walk, Jane mused, "Wouldn't it be pretty with a white picket fence. I'd plant red climbing roses along it. Roses are so pretty on white fences."

A man came around from the back, examining the grounds as he walked.

"Pretty house," John called to him. "Looks like you're getting ready for something?"

"Thanks. Yeah, my daughter's getting married tomorrow afternoon."

"Jane here has admired your house for years. She brought me by to see it."

The man smiled at Jane. "Would you like to see inside?"

"Oh, we couldn't impose," Jane protested, "with your last minute wedding arrangements and all."

"It's no imposition. My wife and the bride-to-be are out shopping, and besides, the place will never look better. Come on."

With an ecstatic grin, Jane started up the front walk with the man. Extending her hand, she said, "I'm Jane Melrose, and this is John Avery."

"Richard Harrington. Nice to meet you." he said, shaking both of their hands.

Stepping inside, Jane emitted a drawn out, "Ohhh, what a beautiful entrance hall...and the stairway!" The broad, Oriental-carpeted staircase went up to a landing. Walking through the hall, John stepped into the living room on the right. It was big, running the full width of the house. The room had the look of an airy ballroom.

Directly across the room, a set of open doors beckoned to a glassed-in porch. Birch logs gave elegance to the brick fireplace. Noticing the carved detail on the fireplace mantel, John remarked, "Great place for Christmas stockings. How many children do you have?"

"Four. Three girls and a boy. The three older ones are married and have homes of their own. It's our baby who's getting married." Harrington sighed audibly. He led John back into the hall.

Jane lingered in the living room, savoring its graciousness, admiring the built-in floor-to-ceiling bookcase covering half of one wall.

Then the three of them climbed the stairs. "There are four bedrooms and three full baths on the second floor," he said, sounding like a realtor. "Here's the master bedroom. It has its own bathroom and a nice walk-in closet."

John meandered to the window and looked out, while Jane checked the bathroom. "I can't believe how nice this house is," she said, returning to Mr. Harrington. "How long have you lived here?"

"Nearly twenty years. You need a lot of room with four children."

"This house certainly has plenty of that," Jane said, walking into the closet. "Now this I could get used to. This is as big as my whole bedroom." Walking out, she sidled up to John. "What are you looking at?"

"This yard. It must go back nearly two hundred feet, and there's a vegetable garden beyond the tent."

"You and your gardens." She tugged at his arm. "Let's look at the rest of the house."

He resisted, pointing to the far left of the yard. "Back there. You could level that mound and have a great place for a kid's swing set."

"Stop that." She tugged harder. "You know I could never afford a house like this."

They returned to Jane's apartment hot and thirsty. She poured two tall glasses of ice water and brought them into the living room. Sitting beside John on the couch, she caught his eye. "Can we cuddle a little before you go?"

"I'd never refuse the opportunity to cuddle with you."

Jane kicked off her sneakers and moved into his embrace. He was quiet. She looked down, her lips parted and moist. She pressed a kiss, soft and sweet, on his lips, then she slid down and rested her head on his chest.

Running his hands through her hair, he said, "I can't figure you out. Here I admit I'm in love with you, and I'm continually holding back my physical feelings for you. But you? There are times, like right now, when you show your affection in no uncertain terms."

John was right. Jane did struggle with her ambivalent and confused feelings. Finally she said, "I think it's all right for friends to be affectionate. But when one of us finds the right person to marry, we'll have to change the dynamics of our relationship."

It was nearly a minute before John responded, "Are you sure I'm not the right one?"

"Will you stop asking me that?" she snapped. "I don't want to ruin the few minutes we have left today. I'll only hurt your feelings."

"Well then, could you at least put your forehead on mine for a few minutes?"

"Why do you want me to do that again? You acted really strange after the last time."

"Did I? I don't remember. I just want to see if it helps me with my thinking. You know, two heads are better than one."

"That's not what it means," she replied, moving up to put her forehead on his.

"Are you sure you were thinking of the real me when you decided I wasn't Mr. Right?"

"Whenever I think about you, I try to figure out who the *real* you is."

As they lay quietly with their foreheads together, she was nearly dozing with John's caresses to her back. Abruptly he announced, "Time's up."

"Not yet." She grabbed his shoulder to keep him from getting up.

"Not yet," he mimicked, squeezing and gently shaking her as she worked her way down to her serious cuddling position. "Am I acting strangely this time?" he asked, resigned that she only wanted to be friends.

"I don't think so," she murmured, content and sleepy.

"Good," he said, relieved that he hadn't revealed his true feelings...this time.

Chapter 9

The waters of the upper Charles River glittered like diamonds spread out in the hot sun. Tidy rows of aluminum canoes clinked against each other as they rocked gently along the Charles River Canoe Center dock.

John and Jane approached the college girl attendant working the dock. "Ever canoe before?" she asked, handing them paddles.

"Yeah," John said. "When I was a kid at camp. I figure it's the same theory as getting back on a bike."

The attendant smiled. "I suppose you're right."

"Where do you want to sit?" John asked Jane as they approached their canoe.

Her answer came without hesitation. "I'll take the stern."

"I thought you've never canoed before."

"Haven't, but I've seen it done."

He shrugged and carefully stepped into the bow seat. When Jane was safely settled, he pushed off. "Where to? Person in the stern controls where we go."

Shading her eyes, she pointed downriver toward the Marriott Hotel.

"Aye, aye, Skipper." He saluted her with his paddle. "We should paddle on opposite sides to reduce the risk of capsizing."

In no time they were slicing their way downriver. Some of the guests at the Marriott were taking advantage of the hot weekend weather by relaxing on the riverside lawn. "Look sharp," John instructed over his shoulder. "Everyone on shore will be watching, so we have to make them envious."

"Don't worry about me," Jane said, getting into the rhythm of paddle stroking.

They were gliding nicely by the hotel lawn when John shouted, "Rock ahead."

Not seeing anything and knowing how he loved to play jokes on her, she continued the steady rhythm.

"I'm not kidding!" he shouted, with an anxious glance back.

Alarmed by his tone, she craned for a look over his shoulder. There, barely submerged, was a forbidding black mass of rock. Unfortunately, with their momentum and the river's current, they were heading for it dead center.

"Back paddle!" John shouted, desperately back paddling himself. He heard her commotion, followed by a shriek. Then, with the distinct sound of metal slamming into rock, they hit. They instantly became the source of entertainment for the bank-sitting onlookers. John stopped laughing long enough to congratulate her. "You did good, Jane. *Real* good."

The entire hull scraped along the rock as they drifted past. Looking back, he saw her sitting helplessly with her paddle floating away. This brought another burst of laughter from John. "Yup, you did *real* good!"

"Why you...you...." she sputtered loudly, oblivious to the people on shore pointing at them. "You're the one who saw the rock in the first place."

"Me? I did *my* job," he said, still chuckling as he guided the canoe over to the floating paddle. "I warned you about the rock. You wanted the stern. That meant you were responsible for steering us." He fished her paddle out and handed it to her. "Do you want to switch positions?"

"How do you expect us to accomplish that?"

"Well, we could crawl past each other, but that's the easiest way to tip over. So I suggest one of us crawls over the other."

"Are you nuts?"

"It's no big deal. I'll lie down and you crawl over me." With that he inched forward and lay on his back.

"If we tip, I swear...."

She wormed her way over him. "Too bad you're not wearing a dress," he joked as she approached his face. "I bet this looks real kinky from shore."

"You're perverted, John Avery," she said, reaching the safety of the bow seat.

Sitting up in the stern, John chuckled at her look of disgust. "It's all a matter of how you look at life."

When they got underway John changed their direction. "I want to go upriver first. That way we'll have the current with us on the way back when our arms are tired."

They paddled upriver for two miles until they reached the Newton Lower Falls dam, then reversed direction and headed back.

"You can stop paddling," John said. "The current will take us downriver."

Securing her paddle, Jane turned in her seat to face him. "Going canoeing was a really nice idea." She gazed around at their peaceful surroundings. Two gray squirrels, after chasing each other down a tree, rustled among the leaves on the ground searching for hidden treasures. In a birch tree along the bank, a family of finches chirped and darted from branch to branch. A turtle that had been sunning itself on a log plopped into the water, while overhead an oriole perched on a limb warbled a warning of the two intruders.

"My turn to take you someplace nice next week," she said. "Can you get Saturday off? I'll be away at my mother's the following weekend."

"I'm sure Mr. Farris will give me the time off. He's all for this relationship."

As usual she ignored the comment. "We could spend the day in Boston and eat in a fancy restaurant."

"Sounds terrific. I can always use a good meal. So can we consider it a definite date? Just the thought of you being away makes me feel lonely."

"John Avery, you are such a faker. Yes it's definite."

"Even if your dream lover Bob asks you out?"

"Hmmm," she murmured, feigning thought. "I didn't think of

that. Bob *may* have some wild and exciting plans for me."

"See, I told you. I knew you couldn't be trusted as a woman of your word."

"Stop that. You know I'm only giving you a bad time. I promise, no matter what, I'll take you out next Saturday."

They continued downriver in silence. Jane admired his paddling skills. He'd make three strong strokes before ruddering the canoe back on course. "You're good at this," she told him. "You're always in control."

"Hardly." he said, followed by a self-depreciating snicker. "But I *can* control a canoe." Seeing a turtle sunning itself, John steered toward it to see how close they could come before it slipped into the water.

"Until I met you," Jane said, "I thought I was in control of my life."

"So what did I do to mess it up?"

She paused, taking time to organize her thoughts. "I've been thinking about what you said about me last week. Do you think relationships based on sex can survive?"

"Maybe for a couple of years. But I'm sure they'd lose interest in each other before too long."

"That's what I think. That's why I'm worried about my feelings toward you."

John looked perplexed. "I'll probably never understand women."

"I'm sorry. I don't mean to be mysterious. It's just that even though I'm not in love with you, I'm ashamed to say I apparently have strong sexual feelings toward you. And I don't know why."

"I can solve your problem. Fall in love with me. I've heard sex is great when you're in love."

"I'm trying to be serious. I wish you could understand my feelings. You're a great friend, John, but you're not the right man for me."

"How can you be sure? You're nothing like the person I expected to fall in love with, but I have."

Not responding, Jane stuck her hand in the water and idly watched the wake it made. John dug his paddle deep into the water and pulled hard, a motion that created tiny whirlpools. Then, resting the paddle on his lap, he watched as they left the spinning whirlpools behind. Left behind and spinning, he thought. Yeah, he knew those feelings only too well.

Taking her hand from the water, Jane wiped it across her forehead. "Ymmm, the water feels so good."

"Is that so?" John struck the water hard with his paddle. His aim was perfect.

"Eegh!" Jane screeched, as her face and blouse were suddenly soaked. "Why you...!" She jerked forward and leaned to splash him.

"Whoa!" she screamed, even louder, as the canoe nearly tipped over.

John laughed at her frustration.

Fearing she'd end up in the water, Jane fumed and scowled at him. "You'll be sorry, John Avery. I'll get even with you."

"Before we go in I want to put the sprinkler on," Jane said, heading for her back yard. At the outside faucet, she asked John to move the sprinkler to a parched section of lawn. Just as he bent over the sprinkler, she turned the faucet on full blast. With a sudden surge, water shot into his face.

"Gotcha!" Jane jumped up and down at the success of her timing. "I *told* you I'd get even with you."

With a cry of pain, John grabbed his eye and fell, water spraying over him as he rolled on the ground, moaning.

"What's the matter!" Jane rushed to his side. "I didn't mean to hurt you." Kneeling over him, she eased his hand from his face to see what had happened. What she saw was John's determined grin as he grabbed the sprinkler and pointed it at her.

"Why you...," she clamored, as she wrestled the sprinkler free and aimed it at him.

They were both in hysterics as she held the sprinkler to his chest, soaking him. Unable to get the sprinkler from her, John wrapped his arms around her and pulled her tight against him. With the sprinkler sandwiched between them, he rolled on top of her. The water may have been aimed at John, but it was now pouring down on Jane.

"Get off me, you big ox," she yelled, squirming to get free.

"Not until you say you're sorry."

"Never," she declared, continuing her struggle for freedom. Soaking wet, she squished around on the soggy grass.

Their predicament kept them in hysterical laughter. After awhile, John looked around and planned his escape. Rolling off her, he jumped up and ran. In no time Jane was after him. She chased him around the front and backyard, but he eluded her successfully. Finally, in the backyard, he collapsed in an exhausted heap and she fell prone at his side. Lying next to each other with the hot sun beating down, they laughed and told stories of great childhood water fights.

When they were finished with their stories, Jane announced, "I've got to get out of these wet clothes,"

"You're lucky I keep a change of clothes in the car," John said, reaching in his pocket for his keys.

After getting the clothes, he headed for the bathroom. Stopping at her closed bedroom door, he knocked gently.

"I'm changing," she called out.

"Then I'm just in time." He opened the door and stepped in.

"What are you doing?" Jane exclaimed, pulling her partially unbuttoned blouse tight against her body.

"Let's change together. Seeing that we're best of friends it shouldn't be a big deal. It'd be like we were little kids."

Jane quickly secured her blouse. "But we're not little kids."

"Does that make you a prude?"

"No."

"Then think of it as being a way to resolve your dilemma about me," he said, not above using a little reverse psychology. "After seeing me naked, your sexual feelings should be satisfied. The forbidden attraction will no longer exist."

"I suppose you don't get any benefit by seeing me undress? Is this your deranged idea of some sort of conquest?"

John smiled, contemplating her analogy. "I like how you put that. A conquest."

"I think you're putting me on and just trying to get me upset. If you think it's such a good idea, you go first." She was sure John was just trying to fluster her, and calling his bluff calmed her feelings of panic.

But John casually lifted his right leg and began to untie his sneaker. Jane froze, not believing the situation she'd gotten herself into. After both sneakers and socks were off, he wasted no time in pulling his jersey over his head. Jane knew he had hairy arms and legs, but she didn't expect such a hairy chest. She had been right. His body was not gorgeous.

John took a deep breath. "Now comes the good part, but no pictures are allowed." Reaching down to his beltless shorts, he undid the button and pulled the zipper down. Releasing his shorts, they slid down his slender legs.

"Oh my," Jane muttered to herself. She had often thought about those snug-fitting shorts, but never imagined they'd slide down so easily.

Wasting no time, John pulled his underpants down. With a final kick, they went flying against her bureau. Lifting his arms, he turned a circle giving a poor rendition of the hokey pokey.

When he turned around, she discovered he even had a hairy back. But she had to admit, although his buns were hairy, they were cute. His back made her think of a comment she remembered a woman at work once made. "I knew I was in love when the hairs on his back didn't make any difference." Jane was relieved; John's hairy back *did* make a difference to her. Maybe this was the sign she was looking for from God. Robert must be the man she was meant to marry.

"Now it's your turn," John said as he stood naked, ten feet in front of her.

Even though fully clothed, Jane had her arms folded in front of her. "I can't believe I agreed to this," she said, raising her arms.

She pulled the elastic out of her hair and let the tresses fall softly to her shoulders. She slipped her sandals off with ease. But then she froze, face downcast, staring at the floor. She slowly lifted her hands to her blouse and painstakingly unfastened each button, being careful not to accidentally expose herself.

Jane had always felt secure undressing in her bedroom. As a matter of fact, she rarely gave undressing much thought. But today was different. She had never undressed in front of a man before. Taking a deep breath, she slipped her arms out of her blouse and quickly draped it over her chest. Then, dropping it, she reached down and undid the button to her shorts. After unzipping them, she gently swayed her hips to ease them down.

Now vulnerably exposed in her plain white bra and panties, she decided to get it over with as fast as possible. Unhooking her bra she slid it off her shoulders and dropped it on the floor. She lowered her hands to her waist and hooked her thumbs in her panties, pulling them quickly down and off.

During the entire act of undressing, she hadn't dared make eye contact with John. For only a moment she stood before him totally naked. Then, arms soldier straight at her side, she turned a full circle.

John was amazed at how incredible she looked. From the small lamp on her bureau, an intimate pink glow added to her beauty. He'd known she was attractive, but standing there now he couldn't believe how delicate and youthful she was.

With a sigh, she picked up her blouse and draped it in front of her. "I'm glad *that's* over with," she said, finally daring to look at him. "I don't know why I agreed to your idea."

"I rather enjoyed it," John said, with a smirk.

"So I've noticed."

"Do you want to lie down and cuddle for a while?"

"I'm not getting in bed with us naked."

"How about if I put my underpants on? Then I'll stay where I belong. I promise you'll remain a virgin. I'd never do anything you'd regret. I love you too much to ever hurt you. I'll use the same control I've used since I met you."

It was true—up until now he *had* demonstrated that he could be trusted. And she was an adult and could easily control the situation. Besides, after what she had just gone through she really wanted to relax. Feeling John's warm body next to hers had always helped her relax in the past.

"Okay," she said. "We can cuddle for awhile. But only if you put your underpants on. That's if you think you *can* get them on in that condition."

"You'd be surprised," John said.

Jane dashed for the bed, getting in, and quickly covered herself.

John slid in next to her. "Don't make any sudden moves, or I may fall out," he said.

"Just make sure you don't do anything you shouldn't, or I'll push you out."

"I'll behave, I promise." Then, with his hands in the air in front of her, he wiggled his fingers, eyes twinkling.

"Just don't go where you're not allowed," she said, as they became embroiled in a warm embrace.

Lying on his side, John's right arm roamed across her body. At first he only rubbed her back. Then his hand traveled over her hip, down the outside of her thigh. Reaching her knee, he worked his hand between her legs.

In a circular motion he rubbed her lower inner thigh, flexing his hand open and closed, the path gradually moving higher and higher. "What are you planning to do?" Jane asked, clamping her legs tight against his hand.

"Why do you want to know?"

"It's my body. I think I have the right."

"Are you sure you want to find out?"

"Yes, I'm..." suddenly John wiggled his fingers deep into the soft muscle of her inner thigh. "...sure!" she shrieked, as she started writhing in laughter. Backed against the wall, while he unmercifully tickled her, she couldn't get away from his grasp. Twisting in uncontrollable laughter, gasping for breath, she screamed, "Stop it! I can't stand it."

John released her and rolled on his back in his newly acquired space. "You said you wanted to know what I was planning to do."

Her breath back and fire in her eyes, Jane pounced on top of him. She straddled his chest with her knees and sat on his stomach. Making a fist, she put her face and fist in front of his chin, and said, "I don't want you to do that again. Do you understand?"

John pulled her to his lips and kissed her. "I like it when you get angry."

She pulled back to get away from his kisses. "I *mean* it. Do you understand me? I don't appreciate your tickling me."

With Jane's naked chest right before his eyes, he forgot everything. He could no longer ignore her breasts. Totally enthralled, he admired her rather small, yet more than adequate, firm, youthful breasts. From all the commotion, her rusty pink areola had become noticeably swollen. Seeing the extent of her protruding nipples, John said, "Your breasts look like they're really excited to see me."

She looked down at her stimulated nipples. "They got like that because I'm angry at you."

"Is that so?" He reached up and cupped her warm, soft breasts. "If that's the case, you can get angry at me any time you want."

Gently, he squeezed a puckered nipple. Jane's breath hissed

97

through her teeth. Her mind turned to mush and she moaned in delight. Leaning back, she invited him to do as he wished to her unobstructed breasts.

Her yelps of delight became louder and louder with each squeeze and twist, her chest rising and falling in heavy breaths. Leaning forward, he wrapped his arms around her back and pulled her close to him.

His tongue ignited a sudden cry of pleasure. Trailing a wet path, John feasted on her breasts.

"I can't believe this is happening to me," she said, falling prostrate on top of him. Placing her lips hard on his, she drove her tongue deep into his mouth.

Wanting wider access to her body, John leaned against the wall, allowing her to lie flat on her back. She kissed and nipped at his ear. With occasional winces from particular nibbles, John thought back to when she had told him, "You don't have to be scared, I won't bite you." He wondered if she could be believed.

Encouraged by her loud moans, John slowly moved his hand down. Relieved that her landlord had gone to the Cape for the summer, his only worry was Mrs. White's hearing. Moving his hand to Jane's side, he ran it down along her leg. At her knee he worked his hand between her firmly closed legs, easing them apart.

Slowly his hand worked up the soft skin of her thighs until she instinctively closed them tight. Running his hand across her tummy, he worked his way down her right leg. Reaching her knee, he pushed her leg open and again worked his way up her leg until she closed them again.

This maneuver continued. Each time his hand crossed over her tummy a little lower, and Jane was a little slower in closing her legs.

When she not only kept her legs spread, but bent them forward, John knew she was ready. She groaned and nipped at his ear as he slid his hand down from her soft breasts. When she emitted an ear-piercing wail, he knew he had reached her desire.

Jane had been touched there before, by a man she had dated in the past. But it wasn't anything like this. John was unrelenting. Slowly and carefully his fingers built the sensations in her body to a frenzy.

From the intensity of her panting and thrashing, he was sure she couldn't take much more. Then, with a wail that John thought surely caused Mrs. White to jump from her chair, a momentous tremor shot through her body. Soon after that her whole body stiffened. Reaching down, Jane pulled his hand away.

He wrapped his arms tightly around her and whispered, "I love you, Jane."

For the next few minutes, her only response was to hold him tightly and occasionally kiss his face. While she quietly regained her composure, he tenderly stroked her body. To his surprise he felt a moisture forming on her skin. He didn't think it to be sweat, but more of a warm clamminess. He was sharing a very personal part of her that he found most enjoyable.

Sitting up, Jane reached for the top sheet, which had worked its way down. "I don't believe what just happened," she said, lying down with the sheet up to her neck. "What in the world came over me to make me believe that I could lie naked in bed with you and have nothing happen? I lost all control. I would have allowed you to do whatever you wanted. But believe me, John Avery, I'll never do this again with you, or anyone, until I'm married."

He pulled the sheet over their heads to create their own little world. As they talked he noticed her aroma. It was a strong odor that he had never known before, like the perfume from some exotic flower. Deep inside his being, primal impulses were awakening to her pheromones. How he wished it were his bed and pillow she lay on. To lie in his own bed and smell her presence would be absolute heaven. Putting his nose to her neck, he breathed in an aroma he wanted to remember and enjoy for the rest of his life. The sweet essence of Jane.

"You're quite some woman. I hope you enjoyed it."

"How did you learn to do what you just did?"

"I don't know. I was lucky, I guess. I'm just trying to figure out what your body enjoys. Like I told you before, I want to know everything about you."

"After today I don't think there's anything left."

"Oh yes there is," John said, kissing her. "There's a whole lifetime of things I want to learn about you."

"But remember, we're only friends." Jane's mind was no longer like mush.

"Oh, is that so?" he said, sliding on top of her. "You mean you haven't fallen in love with me yet?" Then he placed his forehead on hers.

"No, I'm not in love with you," she said, running her fingers through the soft hairs on his back. "Were you expecting me to change just because you're good in bed?"

"No. I only pray that some day you'll hear God tell you that I'm the one for you." John continued to rest his head on hers.

"He hasn't," she quickly replied. Then, eyes closed, they lay without saying a word.

Interrupting the tranquillity, John suddenly reached for the middle of his back and scratched himself.

"Do I make you itch?" she asked, moving her hand.

"No, some bedbug decided to chew on me."

"I don't have bedbugs!" she exclaimed, pushing him toward the wall.

"Well then, let's hope one of mine didn't decide to move in," John said with a laugh.

"You better not have brought any bugs from your dust-infested apartment."

"Not even a cute little bedbug like me?" he asked, before placing his forehead on hers again.

"Why do you keep doing that?"

"Doing what?"

"Placing your forehead on mine."

John diverted his eyes from Jane's. He lay there silently, then he bit his lower lip. Looking more in himself than at Jane, he searched for courage. "The reason may sound a bit ridiculous. Are you sure you want to know?"

Looking deep in his eyes, she felt a seriousness in him. "I'll risk it."

"Do you remember when I told you about being in the hospital with Steve Farris?"

She nodded.

"Well, I was still in the hospital the morning a nurse told me he had died. My roommate after Steve was an older man who'd had his cancerous larynx removed. Since I had no one to talk to, I spent the rest of that day talking to God. Telling Her how I wished I had died instead of Steve. I was so lonely and everything was going wrong in my life at the time."

As John talked, Jane ran her hand through his chest hairs to soothe his sadness. "I had a dream that night. I remember my throat was bandaged like my roommate's, and I was lying in a hospital bed. I heard a woman's voice say, 'John, wake up. It's not time to die.' And then I heard another woman's voice say, 'Isn't marriage wonderful when we each hear God telling us the same thing?'

"I remember feeling the woman lying down on me and saying, 'Our love is so special you don't need to talk. I can hear what you're thinking.' She put her forehead on mine and we began passing thoughts to each other.

"That is, until the nurse came in with my medication and woke me from my dream." Spellbound, Jane only faintly smiled at John's remark. "My whole life changed that night. I wanted to live, to experience what I had dreamed, hoping and believing I really *did* hear God talk to me that night. I believe to this day the first woman's voice I heard was God's. That's why I refer to God as a She.

"I want to believe that a love between two people can be so special that they can pass thoughts. So when I put my head on yours, I am trying to find out if we have a special love."

"So...*do* we?"

"I guess not," answered John, discouraged that Jane hadn't sensed anything.

Just then the phone rang. "Oh, great," Jane sighed. "Don't you dare say a word while I'm on the phone."

Turning away, she reached to the night table. "Hello." Her face lit up. "Marie! How are you?"

Jane hadn't said he couldn't *touch* her, so he pulled the top sheet down.

Immediately she put her hand over the mouthpiece and turned to him. "What are you doing?" she whispered sternly.

He responded with some nonsensical gestures.

Jane removed her hand from the phone and said to Marie, "Oh, it's nothing." Turning her back on John, she went on with her conversation. "Someone's here for a short visit and he's being a nuisance."

Admiring Jane's naked back and bottom, John began to trace his fingers along her soft skin, making idle designs as she continued talking. "His name's John. No, he's nobody special. Just a friend."

At that point his fingers had made their way to her bottom. Grabbing a handful, he gave her a shake.

Swinging her left hand back, she said in a loud angry voice, "I don't believe you did that!" Then pulling the top sheet off, she wrapped it around her body and walked out of the room, the long phone cord trailing behind her.

Without Jane there to play with, John decided to get dressed.

"Things are going great with Bob," Jane, now in the hall, said to Marie. "Keep your fingers crossed. Unfortunately he's in Paris on business for ten days. Yes, we're going out to dinner and the theater when he comes back. We're seeing *Phantom of the Opera*."

Dressed, John went into the hall and stood next to Jane.

"I have to go," she said into the phone. "So we'll meet for lunch at 12:30 on Wednesday the tenth. The Pillar House is on Quinobequin Road. You'll find it off Route 16, just west of Route 128, on the Newton/Wellesley line."

She listened and said, "Me too, looking forward . . . Say hello to Donna when you see her next week. Tell her I'm praying for her." After Jane hung up the phone, she marched past John to her bedroom without a word and closed the door.

"Who's Donna?" John dared to ask through the closed door.

"A friend from college. She has three little boys and her husband recently died. Diabetes. He was only thirty-one."

"How sad. Must be rough for her and the kids."

Ten minutes later, neatly dressed, Jane came out of her bedroom and walked into the kitchen. John was standing at the patio door holding a glass of orange juice.

"I don't think you see the humor in life the way I do," he said.

"You thought that was funny?" she fumed.

"Of course." His laugh was more irritating than his comment. "Especially when I tried to get your bottom to shake."

Good fortune came John's way that moment as he was literally saved by the bell. The phone rang again.

Exasperated, Jane threw her hands in the air. "Why is this happening?" She looked at him, emphatically pointing a finger. "I want you in the living room. Don't touch me, say anything, or do anything that you think is humorous. Do you understand?" She picked up the kitchen extension. "Hello?"

"Hello, darling."

"Hi, Mother. Is anything the matter?" Jane asked, sitting down at the dining room table.

"Nothing's wrong. I just got home from Aunt Sandy's and Aunt Jean was there. We had to change the date of Aunt Sandy's party to next Saturday."

"Noooo! You told me it was going to be the twenty-ninth."

"That's what we planned. But your cousin Patrick said he and the family couldn't get away that weekend. Since they can make it next weekend, we decided to have it then. Why are you so upset? You told me you were going to keep both weekends open."

"I know," Jane sighed. "But you sounded so sure it'd be on the twenty-ninth I made arrangements to take a friend out to dinner next Saturday."

"Ask her to change it. Besides, your Aunt Sandy's hoping you can come early on Friday and join us for the private dinner I'm preparing for her. It will be nice. Just the three of us."

"It's not that simple, Mother. I promised, no matter what, that I'd spend next Saturday with my friend."

"Then bring her here. The two of you can sleep together in the guest room."

"It's not a she, Mother—it's a he. How can I possibly bring him with me? I can't...."

John smiled. An invitation from her mother—what a nice, unexpected surprise.

"You know about John, the man who works for the nursery."

"A he," repeated her mother. "I didn't know you took men out to dinner. That was never done in my day."

"With John you have to, if you want a decent meal."

"He certainly can't sleep with you in the guest room."

"I know, Mother," she said, looking at John and the smirk on his face. "Look, I have company here now, so I have to go. I'll call you tomorrow. I love you."

Jane dropped the receiver and buried her head in her hands. "I don't believe this day. Do I really deserve all this?"

John, after hanging up the phone, began massaging her shoulders. "God loves you and wants to bless your life."

"You've got to be kidding. God is punishing me, and it's my own fault."

"Lighten up, Jane," he said, sounding a little perturbed. "Let's sit on the couch, and you can tell me what I need to pack. I'll have to wash my shorts so they'll be nice and clean ...."

"Oh, no. You're not going anywhere with me with those shorts."

John gave her a forlorn puppy frown. "I thought you liked them."

"They're indecent."

After a short pause, John ran his fingers through her hair and said, "There's one other minor detail about going to Pittsburgh. Since I'm broke, how am I going to get there?"

Jane's mind was elsewhere. Worrisome thoughts of John's potential for unpredictable and embarrassing behavior were rushing through her head. And how would she be able to explain to everyone that John was only a good friend?

He sat looking at her and her blank expression. "Well?" he finally said a little louder, to get her attention.

Shaking her head of thoughts, she fixed her eyes on him. "I'm sorry, what did you say?"

"I asked you how would I get to Pittsburgh? You must realize that travel to a place that far away is a bit extravagant for my budget."

Eased by the sensation of his fingers combing through her hair, she reached over, wrapped her arms around him, and gave him a kiss. "I guess if we're going to continue being friends I'll occasionally have to keep you."

Tuesday evening Jane stood at her apartment door with dry cleaning slung over an arm. Flipping through the mail, she noticed a letter from John. With nervous excitement she stepped in and tore it open.

On the outside of the note he had printed, TO MY BEST FRIEND. Inside it read, I COULD NEVER THINK OF YOU AS A CONQUEST. LOVE JOHN.

She phoned him immediately. "Hi, I know we've already talked today, but I wanted you to know I received your note. It was really kind."

"I hoped so. I know my odd sense of humor can be misleading. There's more I want you to know, but I'm still having trouble describing my feelings. When I finally feel the words are just right, I'll give it to you."

"I don't need to have in writing how you feel about me. Just being friends is enough."

Ten minutes later the phone call ended, and before they knew it, Friday morning had arrived.

Chapter 10

The whine of the jet's turbines warned passengers to hurry and stow their carry ons in the overhead compartments. John watched from the aisle seat as Jane stretched and pushed to get her bag in. She looked comfortably casual in her loose-fitting, sea-green and seashell print skirt. Static in the air caused it to bunch and cling to her thighs high above her knees. The long sleeves of the unbuttoned sage-colored jacket were folded three inches, revealing the same print as the skirt. The outfit was pulled together with a long, matching, sage sash, tied at her waist in a bow.

She slipped the jacket off, folded it, and carefully placed it overhead. The short-sleeved silk blouse, buttoned to the top of the slightly scooped neckline, was irresistibly feminine. As she stretched to close the compartment, her breasts pressed tightly against the sheer, ivory fabric. The saleswoman was right—the rose embroidery *was* lovely.

Stepping into the aisle, John allowed Jane the window seat. He looked around at all the empty seats. "Not much business today."

"Pittsburgh isn't among the world's great weekend escapes."

"Well, I'd have thought a lot of people would go there to invest in Saturday's Pennsylvania's twenty million dollar jackpot lottery."

"You're not thinking about wasting what little money you have on lottery tickets, are you?

"Come on. We make a lucky pair. We can each pick three numbers and buy one ticket and split the loot."

She gave him an inquisitive glance. "Are you sure you can afford to throw away your money?"

"It's only fifty cents each. Buying one ticket doesn't make me foolish or wasteful with money. Besides, someone has to win the money so it might as well be us." He gave her his weird look.

Jane's serious expression melted into an amused grin. Nestling up to him, she said, "You're so silly when you do that. What makes you think I can trust you not to run off with all the winnings?"

"Trust me? *I'm* the one who should worry. Remember, I'm the one who's in love. You, on the other hand, are still looking for Mr. Perfect."

John paid particular attention to sense any sudden mood change in Jane. Mr. Perfect was sufficient, but who he'd meant was Bob McWilliams. He didn't detect anything out of the ordinary in Jane's slightly nasty dirty look. A look he'd become accustomed to in reaction to his crass remarks. "If it'll make you feel better, I'll write up a formal agreement."

"Sounds fair. Give me some time to think of my numbers. What numbers will you pick?"

"Well, one should be eighteen because you were born on the eighteenth. Then, thirty-three since I've known you thirty-three days. Then forty because I'm forty this year and it's turning out to be a lucky year for me. How about you?"

"I guess I'll start with number three. For the three most important people in my life, my mother, father, and Cathy. Next, I think five because I've always wanted five kids. Finally, twenty-nine. Cathy was born February twenty-ninth. She used to tell me it might be lucky for me, but it wasn't lucky for her. She didn't think it was funny when her friends gave her gifts for a four-year-old on her sixteenth birthday."

"Sound like winners to me. Especially the three and five."

"Why's that?"

John was unsuccessful in holding back his laughter as he told her why. "Well, you have three hairs on your left breast and five on your right."

"Oh you," she said, turning bright red. Clenching her fist, she pounded his leg above his knee. Enunciating each word she told him,

"You are so crude." Then she scrunched up against the window and stuck a magazine studiously to her face.

Encouraged by how irritated she seemed, he chuckled even louder. "What's wrong with hairs on your breast?" he persisted. "I have them all over mine. I think yours are kind of neat. They identify whose breasts I'm looking at."

Turning from the magazine, she informed him sharply, "You can be sure you'll never see *mine* again."

The whine of the engines revving at the end of the runway discouraged further conversation. Once the jet climbed to its cruising altitude the noise receded to a soft drone.

The silence had done little to ease Jane's annoyance at John. Lowering her magazine, she glared at him. "Women aren't supposed to have hair there. What makes you think I do?"

"Because I saw them when you were stretching to put your jacket in the compartment. Accountants like to count things."

"You are a sick man, John Avery."

"Thank you." He grinned proudly at the thought. "Unhook your bra and look for yourself if you don't believe me. There's no one around to see you."

The sneer she gave before the magazine went back to her face clearly indicated what she thought of that suggestion.

"I know more about you than you think. And the more I learn the more I love. That includes your eight little hairs."

As the minutes passed, John knew she hadn't turned any pages. Easing his back rest down, he said, "I feel like taking a short nap, so if you have to use the bathroom, now would be a good time."

She did so, and when she returned to her seat she acted as if nothing had happened.

"Well, was I right?" he asked, smugly.

Ignoring him, she picked up her magazine.

"I guess I'll never know now, anyway. I bet you pulled them out and wiped them off your fingers on your blouse."

Aghast, Jane's mouth dropped. She looked down to where two hairs were stuck on her blouse. "Is there nothing about me you don't notice?" she said, vigorously brushing them off.

John grinned triumphantly. "I hope not."

"Anyway, you were wrong."

"Oh yeah?"

Jane's anger had apparently diminished "Yeah. The three were on my right, and the five were on my left." Wrapping her arms around his neck, she kissed his cheek. "How did you really know?"

"That's easy. I saw them last week and guessed they'd still be there. I was lucky a whole bunch more didn't grow out." John burst into another bout of laughter.

"Oh, you." Removing her hands from his neck, she pounded his leg again.

As Jane stood at her mother's kitchen sink rinsing dishes, John crept up behind her. Wrapping his arms around her waist, he nuzzled his lips to her neck. "Gotcha."

Leaning back, she pressed her body closer to his and tilted her head forward. "I thought we agreed not to be affectionate while we're here."

"I couldn't resist. I needed to tell you how much I love you. And now I can't restrain myself from kissing your lovely neck."

"That's enough," she cautioned. "Mother might come in any minute."

"Well, if you insist." He released her and plopped down on a kitchen chair. "Tell me again who's going to be at this party? I tend to forget names."

"My Aunt Sandy, my mother and me, of course. Aunt Sandy's daughter, Sally, and her husband Larry will be there, but I'm not sure if their daughter Robin will be. They're the ones whose son Douglas killed himself five years ago. And remember, it's very important not to mention Doug's name. I don't want Sally getting upset again."

"Thanks for the vote of confidence." A smile masked his disapproval of such treatment.

"The party will be at Aunt Jean's and Uncle James's. Their son Patrick, his wife Jennifer, and Kevin, their six-year-old son, will be there. Patrick's the bond trader for the Tennessee securities firm."

"You mean the big-shot money maker?"

"Uh huh," she said, finishing the last dish. "The quintessential Yuppie."

❀ ❀ ❀

Jane was uneasy with John at the party, and that uneasiness quickly turned to panic. They hadn't been there half an hour when he disappeared and was nowhere to be found. That was until he casually walked in the front door. Scolding him as if he were a little boy, she demanded, "Where have you been?"

John was nonchalant. "Once your Aunt Jean found out I worked in a nursery, I was destined for a tour of her gardens. She's done a great job with them. Then I had to get a demonstration from Patrick of his new BMW. I think he said it's a 750IL. I'm sure he'd be glad to impress you with a spin around the block."

"No thanks, I'll pass." She grabbed his hand and led him toward the living room. "I want you to meet Sally and Larry."

Navigating through the crowded room, Jane singled out a couple sitting in the corner. "Sally, Larry, I'd like you to meet my friend John."

"How do you do?" John said, his chin rising toward the ceiling to keep eye contact with Larry, who towered over him. He tried not to wince when Larry, the ex-jock, shook his hand. Then looking down at Sally, he thought to himself, *Larry doesn't have to worry about Sally's nose being in his arm pits, his only worry must be whether his belly button's clean.*

"I was surprised to hear that Jane was bringing someone to the party," said Sally.

"You weren't nearly as surprised as Jane was." He threw Jane a grin. "She had promised to take me out tonight. But that was before she heard the day of the party had been changed. So she was stuck dragging me along."

"Still, she must be pretty special, for you to come all the way from Boston."

"We're just good friends. I know Jane will be the first to confirm that." He gave Jane a quick glance. "Won't you?" Turning his attention back to Sally, he added, "Jane tells me you have a child, a daughter named Robin?"

After what John felt was an awkward silence, Larry finally said, "That's correct. She's around here somewhere. She's wearing a Mario Lemieux sixty-six hockey jersey."

"I'll keep an eye out for her," John said, scanning the room, before looking back at Sally. "I was sorry to hear about the death of your son Doug. It must have been difficult for you."

Jane was dumbstruck, then enraged. It was all she could do to control herself.

"It was sad, but we've gotten over it," Larry replied coldly. "If you'll excuse me, I think I'll fix myself a drink."

Trying to read the extent of Larry's anger, Jane watched him walk away. Before she had the chance to change the subject, John said to Sally, "Are you able to talk about it?"

"John!" Jane exclaimed angrily.

"What's there to say?" Sally responded. "He killed himself, and now he's gone."

From the other side of the room Jane's mother called out. "Jane, honey, can you please come and give me a hand preparing the vegetables?"

"Do I have to this minute, Mother?"

"If you expect us to have dinner on time, you do."

Jane turned to Sally. "I'm sorry Sally, you'll have to excuse me." Jane brushed past John without saying a word to him and left the room. Her icy stare had said it all. He had never seen the contortions of her face express such anger.

"Would you like a cup of gazpacho?" John asked, leading Sally to the dining room. "I've tried some, and it's really tasty."

From the dining room, Jane saw John and Sally out by the vegetable garden, talking. Unable to hear them, she studied the intensity of Sally's body language.

She shuddered inwardly, the rage still burning. What in the world made her think it would be safe to bring John to Pennsylvania? She clenched and unclenched her fists. Their departure tomorrow night couldn't come soon enough. At least no one had said anything yet about Sally's crying.

Startled by a sudden tap on her shoulder, Jane twisted around. "How's life at the thundering herd, Cuz?" Lifting his bottle of Coors, Patrick took a swig.

"Why Patrick, things are just fine, thank you."

"Still doing all the grunt work?"

"At Merrill Lynch we call it customer satisfaction."

"Sounds like too much work to me."

"I'm sure it is, Patrick. Would you excuse me? My mother needs me."

Emerging from the kitchen with a platter of salad and a basket of rolls, Jane carefully arranged them on the table.

"That's everything," her mother said, as she inspected the sumptuous spread. Jane's eyes darted to the window. John was nowhere in sight.

The table, set with Jane's grandparents' old silver candlesticks, looked elegant. She dimmed the lights and watched the candles flicker. The smell took her back to her childhood when she and her sister sat around lighted candles and listened to their father tell ghost stories. She smiled. "Mother," she asked, her voice wistful, a little remote, "when you were a little girl did you dream about the man you'd marry?"

"All the time. He was the most handsome of men, just like your father. We'd have tea parties in my room."

"That must be why you and Daddy always had a cup of tea after dinner."

Mrs. Melrose smiled at her daughter and twisted a strand of gray hair as the conversation took her back in time.

"Tell me," Jane insisted, "did you think Daddy would be the man you'd marry? I mean when you first met him?"

Mrs. Melrose kept on playing with her hair, the stare in her eyes now far away. "The very moment I saw him, I knew. I was sitting at my desk on a Monday morning in July. I'd just returned from vacation. He was fresh out of law school. He came up to me to ask a question. That's when I knew." She stopped and studied her daughter. "Why, dear? Why do you ask?"

"I guess I've been thinking about Daddy a lot today...." Just then Larry walked by. "I'd better tell everyone dinner's ready," she said. "Larry, have you seen Sally or John?"

"Last time I saw them they were out on the patio. That friend of yours has been talking to her for over an hour. I bet she'll be a basket case by the time he's through."

Having announced to the guests that dinner was on the table, Jane went out to the patio where Sally and John sat talking. "Dinner's ready," she said. When she saw Sally dab her eyes with a tissue, she feared the worst.

"Already?" Sally said, getting up. "I'm sorry...I didn't mean to keep John from you for so long."

"That's all right," he said, "Jane tells me she gets along fine without me." He wrapped his arms around Sally in a supportive hug. "Remember now, don't be ashamed of your feelings. It's okay to miss Doug. Hopefully, you'll be able to find the kind of support group we talked about."

"Thank you, John." The warmth in Sally's voice seemed to express a genuine sincerity. She released him and turned to Jane. "I'd better go upstairs and freshen up."

When they were alone, John attempted to address Jane's stone face. "I know what you're going to say, but you're wrong."

"Wrong...wrong...." she stammered. "That woman's fragile. God only knows what harm you've done her."

"Harm? I don't think so, Jane. Didn't you see the pain in her eyes? Can't you see she's suffering?"

"I specifically—make that *emphatically*—asked you *not* to mention her son. This family has seen her fall apart too often and I didn't want *you* to open old wounds."

"Why are you so blind to reality? One person starts crying when their son is mentioned, the other goes and grabs a drink, and you don't think anything should be done?"

"Was it too much for you to do as I asked and not prove to be an embarrassment to me?" Jane said. She turned and headed for the house.

"Do you understand me?" John called out. "I'm not the one with the problem. You're the one all bent out of shape,"

Jane spun around. "What I understand is that I really wish you'd start walking home right now, so I'd never have to see you again."

She shook her head and walked away.

"Jane," he said loudly, as she reached the door. She stopped, but didn't turn. "We should have a way to resolve our arguments, because no matter how irritated I get, I still love you."

Jane turned and declared vehemently, "Don't you understand, *I don't want your love.*"

❀ ❀ ❀

By nine-thirty that evening most of the guests had left. Jane, her mother, aunts, and some cousins were in the kitchen cleaning up. The gaiety of the girl talk often spilled out to the living room where the men were. Except for John, all of them were clutching beers while they listened, or pretended to listen, to Patrick. "I tell you I've got it all planned. I have over a hundred and fifty thousand invested now. In five years I'll have a million—unless, of course, Jennifer and I continue our current spending. But why not? I'll be making from a half to three quarters of a million a year."

"I'm proud of you, son," James, his father said. "You've got it all."

Suddenly there was a burst of feminine laughter. "What's going on in there?" James bellowed.

"Nothing, just girl talk," came the hysterical reply.

As Patrick again launched into a soliloquy about his investments, his son Kevin, wearing Luke Skywalker PJ's and hugging a teddy bear, padded in. "Daddy, the *Star Wars* video is over."

"Upstairs, young man," ordered his father. "I told you when the video was over you had to go to sleep."

"But I want a drink of water."

"Then go in the kitchen and ask your mother," Patrick said, not bothering to hide his irritation at the distraction.

When Kevin had left, Patrick picked up his discourse, rambling on about his job buying and selling in the bond market.

Exiting the kitchen, Jennifer carried her son in her arms. "Say goodnight to the men, Kevin."

"Goodnight," he said, waving his teddy bear as he passed.

Patrick again returned to his captive audience. "With my experience and education I can...."

Now it was John who interrupted. "Hey, Kevin, may the force be with you."

Kevin waved his imaginary light saber as his mother climbed the stairs. "And with you," he called back. John smiled. Kevin giggled. Patrick scowled.

115

Mrs. Melrose must have known something was bothering her daughter. During the party and the drive home, Jane had barely spoken to John. "I'm exhausted," Mrs. Melrose said as she entered the house. "I think I'll be off to bed. See you two in the morning."

"Good night, Mother. I'll be up in a little while."

"Good night, Mrs. Melrose," John added.

Jane followed John into the living room and chose a chair opposite the couch. John had hoped she would sit next to him so he could lighten her mood by cuddling.

"So what did you want to say to me?" she questioned, in an icy tone.

"I thought we could talk about what's upsetting you."

"Oh, I forgot, *I'm* the one with the problem. And you're all knowing, unable to do any wrong."

"Jane, that's not what I meant," John replied, frustrated and hurt. "Can't you see I'm trying to salvage our friendship? Why can't we *talk* about what happened tonight?"

"If you want to talk, go ahead and talk."

"Okay, but hear me out. I know you specifically asked me not to mention Doug to Sally and Larry. And even though I didn't agree with how your family was handling Sally, I didn't *intend* to say anything. But no matter what you believe, I did see extreme pain in her eyes.

"There's something you have to know about me. There are certain things I have to do, even if you disagree with them. Ignoring Sally's pain, was one of those things I couldn't do. It's like my work with the Samaritans—all I did was offer her the chance to talk. You know full well she hasn't healed from Doug's death. She desperately needs someone to listen to her, to acknowledge her feelings. I did my best not to cause a scene. That's why I suggested we go outside. I'm sorry if I ruined the party for you."

"You didn't ruin the party, but you did get me really upset. You don't know my family like I do. The thought of Sally making a scene, because of something you said, terrified me. Even though she seemed fine afterwards, I don't think you were right to discuss Doug with her."

Sensing forgiveness, John desperately wanted to relax and hold her. "Do you want to sit next to me and cuddle for awhile?"

"No." Her voice was firm. She stood up as if to leave. "With the events of tonight and last weekend it wouldn't be right."

"Well then," he said, as Jane headed out of the room. "I'll see you in the morning. I'm going to sit here for awhile."

When Jane reached the stairs, she turned to John. "Did you ever play lacrosse in college?"

"What's that got to do with anything?"

"Did you?"

"No. Something like that was too dangerous for me."

"That's what I thought," Jane said, then climbed up the stairs.

In the ensuing silence with Jane in her mother's bedroom for the night, John sat trying to understand his lonely situation. He glanced at the chair where Jane had sat and muttered, "To thine own self be true."

Resigned to his fate he stood, and with a reflective snicker, he said, "So you can mess up the rest of your life."

Jane was still in her mother's room packing when John came out of the guest bedroom carrying his bag. On his way downstairs, he saw Mrs. Melrose fixing her hair in front of the hall mirror. She was eyeing him in the reflection as he set his bag down. "It was nice meeting you, Mrs. Melrose. You and your sisters made me feel right at home. I especially enjoyed learning about Jane's childhood."

"And I enjoyed meeting you, John. I didn't know what to expect when Jane said she was inviting you. Give me a big hug and please call me Connie. I hate the sound of Mrs. Melrose. Makes me feel a hundred years old."

Upstairs as she finished packing, Jane had begun to feel relief. The dreaded weekend with the unpredictable John was about to end. At least her mother seemed to genuinely like him.

When she started down the stairs and saw John pressing his forehead to her mother's, she froze. Now what was he trying to accomplish? He couldn't really believe that telepathy stuff is real.

"Why, you rascal." Her mother began to laugh. "You'll have to get Jane to invite you again."

Seeing Jane on the steps, John sensed a mother-daughter moment was at hand. "I'll be out by the car," he said, gathering up their bags.

Jane hugged her mother. "It was a really great party. I understand your decision to move back to be near your sisters, but I miss having you nearby."

"It was a delightful weekend, wasn't it? All us girls together, yakking away. Just like old times."

"Yes, Mother, it sure was."

"And it was wonderful to see Sally in such good spirits. John seemed to have a really good effect on her."

"He's a very understanding person."

"I can see that. I'm so glad you brought him."

Jane moved uncomfortably, wanting to go, clearly not wanting to talk about John. How could she? She couldn't even figure out her own feelings toward him. At the door, she turned to her mother. "Mother, what were you and John talking about when he put his forehead on yours?"

"Nothing. Why?"

"You laughed. Called him a rascal."

"Oh that. We didn't say anything. I only happened to be thinking about the two of you."

"Tell me, Mother. Please."

"Consider it my little secret, darling," she said, rubbing her daughter's cheek. "I will say that I think John's very special. He has a friendly, childlike sincerity about him. You may say he's just a friend, but I saw the way he looks at you. I also noticed your icy glares last night and today. I hope you two work things out."

"I'm sure you do, Mother. I just wish you didn't have to tell him every embarrassing thing that's ever happened to me. It was tough enough to be with him as it was."

"Oh, I thought he was so cute when I showed him your baby pictures. Especially when he saw the one of you naked in the tub when you were four months old. He sounded so innocent when he said, 'Oh, is that what she looks like.' Not that I believed him for a minute."

"Mother! How can you say such a thing?"

"Come on, darling, you're a grown woman living on your own. Besides, there's little doubt he's in love with you."

Jane dropped her head. "I know. I really wish he wasn't." Feeling guilty and ashamed, she faced her mother and pleaded her case. "I'm really not in love with him, Mother. He's wonderful...sometimes, but he's not the man of my dreams. He's older. He's in debt. He has medical problems. What if we got married, had children, and he got sick again? He could die. What would I do then?"

"I don't know, dear," her mother said. "You'll have to let God worry about that. I'm sure He will give you the answer to the questions that are obviously bothering you."

On the plane back to Boston, John informed Jane, "We didn't win the lottery."

"I told you it'd be a waste of money."

"Nobody won it, so I bought another ticket. You owe me fifty cents."

"You're really making this an expensive weekend." She opened her pocketbook and rummaged around. Pulling out a handful of change, she said, "So are you glad to be going home?"

"Not as glad as you are, I bet."

She handed him two quarters. "You're right. I guess I was a little apprehensive and overreacted at times. I'm sorry."

"I did my part and played the just friends role." He hesitated and looked out the window at the setting sun. From the heavens above, golden shafts of sunlight beamed down. "Even though I really wanted to tell people how much I love you."

"John. I...I...."

"Shush," he told her, patting her leg. "I know. I understand. Really."

She kissed him on the cheek. "You really are the best friend a girl could have."

After the stewardesses served drinks, John took a pen and paper from his carry-on and began to write. Deep in a book, Jane glanced at him as he reached for a tissue. Feigning concentration on the book, she saw him wipe his eyes. A lump formed in her throat. She wanted to reach out, but feared she'd distract him. He wrote on. She watched peripherally, with careful cursory glances. He wrote furiously sometimes, sometimes with more thought. Pausing, he read what he had written. Then he energetically lined out words, replacing them with new ones.

When he allowed her eye contact, she asked, "Can I read what you wrote?"

"It's just a poem."

"Please?"

"It's sad. A bummer like my life. That's what I write about. Writing about my pain helps me."

"Friends should share their sadness."

"Like I said it's a bummer," he said, handing her the paper. Even though John knew the poem wouldn't change anything, he carefully watched her read it.

HEAVENLY BODIES

A lonely star travels through time.
A lost satellite swings into orbit.
Renewed life unfolds from the sun's tender touch.

Solar flares nip the celestial body.
Warm salty moisture permeates the surface.
A sweet musky cloud rises.

Resisting gravitation a night flight into space.
From the final transmission a super nova becomes
     a black hole:
"But I didn't love you."

After a minute, Jane's gaze and the hand holding the paper dropped to her lap. Such a momentous reaction caused John to snicker at his uselessness. When she looked over at him with what seemed to be a studious but disappointed expression, the ache inside only worsened.

"It's about us," she said, "isn't it?"

"Yeah," he murmured, turning toward the window. At thirty thousand feet, the golden shafts were still above them. He watched them fade away.

"I'm sorry I'm not in love with you, John. But that doesn't mean we can't go on being as we are."

John sat there quietly soaking in the meaning of her statement—the dreaded reality of their relationship. Finally he said, "As important as that is to me, you'll never know how much it hurts to hear you say that's all we'll be. I had hoped, by expressing my feelings toward you, you'd have heard God tell you what I believe She's been telling me."

He bit his lip to hold back his tears. Avoiding her eyes, he looked down at his lap wondering what he'd say next. "There's no hope," he said. "I don't get any better than this. You've seen my best and it wasn't good enough.

"But...." John put his hand to Jane's lips to keep her from speaking. He needed to finish telling her what was burning inside him.

"It's a lot easier to leave someone than it is to fall in love with them. I know you well enough to know you're too good a person not to have the right man come along and discover what you've been trying to hide all these years. The beauty one can easily see on the outside is nothing compared to the real beauty you have inside.

"When you give your heart to your dream lover—who knows, it's probably Bob—you'll no longer need me in your life. Even if it's not Bob, I'm sure someday you'll wake up and see me as an obstacle. You have such ambivalent feelings toward me, you'll probably decide what you need is freedom to concentrate on your search." He stopped to gather more courage. "I'll always love you, Jane, but as painful as it'll be for me, I'll give you that freedom. I'll have no choice but to let you drift away, believing only you know what's best for your heart."

She lifted his hand to her lips and kissed it tenderly. "Don't say such things. I'll always want you as my friend."

He knew it was hopeless. But he had always lived with honesty. "I believed I heard God tell me the day we met that you were the one. I also believe you when you say God hasn't told you I'm the one for you. Which can only mean She intends for you to be with someone else. I'm sure a marriage can only work when God tells both people exactly the same thing. My love for you is one of many things God does that I just don't understand. However I have to live with my faith. I know that my love for God has to be greater than my love for you."

Emotionally exhausted, he turned to the window and ended the conversation. With one hand clutching the poem, the other in Jane's, he sat quietly, wanting so much more. To hear her say, "I love you, John," would have truly been a gift from heaven. The plane droned on over the mountains of New York State as full darkness enveloped them. *Why God? Why wasn't I good enough?* From the corner of his eye, a tear trickled down.

Chapter 11

A mass of jubilant humanity poured from Fenway Park onto Yawkey Way. The Red Sox 5-0 shutout over the Cleveland Indians seemed to justify to some fans a bit of late Saturday afternoon rowdyism. Insulated from all the pushing and shoving, Jane gazed from the limo.

She looked stunning in her long, peach colored crepe dress. The fan-pleated platter collar with the romantic rosette must have been made with her in mind. Reclining on the lush leather seat, her dress fell open at the side slit, exposing an abundance of leg.

"You're so amazing," she said to Bob. "When you told me to get dressed up, I thought you were only kidding about seeing a Red Sox game."

His smile bordered on conceit. But why not? He was the most self-assured person she'd ever met, and she was thoroughly charmed by his manner. Who wouldn't be, knowing all it took was a quick phone call to a Red Sox official and he had his 600-Club tickets—sky boxes behind home plate. He acted as if he had planned everything, even the fortuitous introduction to Jean Yawkey, the majority owner of the Red Sox.

"I felt like a foreign dignitary," she said. "I never dreamed I'd be served lunch while watching the action on the field."

"I'm glad you had a good time, sweetie." Reaching for her hand, he folded her fingers in his and kissed the back of her hand.

Jane responded with an enraptured smile. After the fiasco with John in Pittsburgh last weekend, it wouldn't have taken much to please her. But this was more than she could have asked for—she was being treated like royalty by the man of her dreams. Sliding closer to Bob, she leaned her head on his shoulder.

Bob slid an arm around her and pulled her tight to his chest. Lowering his head, he pressed his lips firmly on hers. Bob and Jane were on their way to the Harvard Club, where City Youths was sponsoring a wine-tasting fund-raising party.

"Can I offer you a quick drink?" Bob asked, reaching for a glass.

"No thanks. I'm not much of a drinker. Sampling wines will be more than enough for me tonight."

Bob fixed himself a Chivas Regal on the rocks, with a splash.

"How long have you been involved with City Youths?" she asked.

"Over three years now. I'm proud to be associated with them. Their activity centers keep a lot of kids off the streets."

"That's really admirable. My father used to spend a lot of time with disadvantaged youths. What activities do you and the kids get involved with?"

"Unfortunately I haven't had time for the kids. I've been involved with the organization's fund-raising events. For instance, last January they had a slave auction and I brought in the highest bid of $1,700. I offered to spend a ski weekend with someone. Two women got caught up in a bidding war over me."

"I hope she got her money's worth."

"I'd say she did. Not only did she prove to be an excellent skier, she even owned her own ski chalet. You can't beat that. We managed to have a few good weekends together."

Jane could only imagine that they did more than just ski. "Where is she now?"

"Oh, I've seen her around town. But we kind of lost interest in each other."

Stuck in the usual post-game gridlock, Jane looked out at the people passing them by. "I've never gone to or from a Red Sox game by limo before. I've always traveled with the common folk and took the T."

"You're anything but common, sweetie," he said, leaning over for another kiss. His lips were wet with the taste of Scotch. "A limo is the only way to travel to a ball game or concert. When you live in the city, it's like a second car."

Jane surreptitiously wiped her lips with the back of her hand when Bob looked out the window.

"Wouldn't you like to escape the city congestion by having a pretty house in the suburbs?" she asked.

"And give up my condo on the wharf? Hell no. I grew up in a large house with the big yard and hated it. Yard work is such a waste of time. When I have a problem now, I call maintenance. You'll fall in love with it once you see it. And you can always change your mind and enjoy the experience tonight." Bob ran a hand along her leg.

Jane pressed her legs together and reached for his hand. "Another time."

He kissed her cheek and mused, "Settling down with an investment consultant will fit in really well with my legal travels. You have a job that allows a lot of freedom."

Jane tilted her head, quizzical.

"Whenever I have to go some place nice, like Europe for business, you can take time off and join me."

The limo stopped in front of a building on Commonwealth Avenue. Jane looked out at the familiar five-story brickstone which housed the Harvard Club. "We're here."

"Let 'em wait." He engulfed Jane in his arms and planted his lips once again on hers. When the chauffeur opened the door, she broke free of their tangled embrace and stepped out.

Bob took her arm. "You look spectacular, sweetie. Let's go dazzle them."

"You're a great cook, sweetie," Bob said, getting up from the dining-room table. "You stay seated and look over the brochures while I clear the table and open the champagne."

Figuring Bob had—after their wine-tasting date two nights ago—understood and accepted her desire not to rush into things sexually, Jane had invited him to her apartment for dinner. For eight days now she had not allowed herself to see John, hoping to purge herself of the intrusive desire to be comfortably nestled in his arms. But not willing to go completely cold turkey, she had allowed a few phone calls. She rationalized that there was no reason why she couldn't keep her friendship with John while she fell in love with Bob. After all, Bob was her Adonis. And, once she'd found out he was raised a Catholic—although now a nonpracticing one—she was convinced he was the one for her.

Now she was lost in thought, dreaming of enchanted evenings walking along the Cannes shoreline, admiring the expensive yachts, when Bob returned with glasses and a bottle of Dom Perignon. In dramatic splendor, he worked the cork out with a loud pop. Handing her a bubbling glassful, he said, "To what shall we drink?"

"How about to the joining of great minds," she offered.

"I like that." He gave her a cunning smile. "And may it lead to the joining of great bodies." With a clink of crystal, he took a sip.

Slightly taken aback, Jane barely had time for a sip when the doorbell rang. "Who could that be?" she muttered, putting down her glass.

Peering through the peep hole, she opened the door right away. "John! What are you doing here? You know I have company tonight."

"I'm sorry, but this can't wait." He huffed in heavy breaths. Then he turned a full circle. "Am I any different from the last time you saw me?"

"Stop acting ridiculous."

Disappointed that she didn't sense his excitement, he reached in his back pocket. "Okay, how about this?" Eyes beaming, he pulled out a small date book and showed it to her. "Does this make you think of anything?"

Jane shook her head and shrugged her shoulders. "That you've finally decided to go out with other women and you just had to show me?"

"No." John's arms flopped down in frustration. "Don't you remember me telling you why I never planned anything?"

Glass in hand, Bob walked over to Jane's side. Glancing quickly at him, John said, "I'm sorry to interrupt, but this will only take a minute." He looked back at Jane, biting his lip. It was all he could do from blurting out the information. "Well, let's see how you take it."

"Take what? I'm in no mood for your games."

126

John spread his arms out wide and announced, "You and I are now officially millionaires. Our numbers won last week's Pennsylvania lottery."

Jane gaped.

John was grinning broadly, his head nodding exuberantly, up and down with his body.

"You must be kidding," she said. "I...I don't believe you." She headed for the couch and sat down.

In the apartment, John reached into his pocket and pulled out a piece of newspaper. "I'm not kidding. It's listed in today's paper. We're not as rich as you may think, though. Four other tickets had the same winning number. Which leaves us with approximately four million, two hundred thousand dollars. Which means you and I will each receive just under one hundred six thousand dollars a year for twenty years before taxes."

Bob went over to the table to retrieve Jane's glass. "Sounds like a toast is in order here," he said, refilling his own. "Let me pour you a drink, John."

"I prefer juice," John said flatly, heading for the kitchen. After coming back with a glass of cranberry juice, the three of them stood and Bob offered a toast: "To new wealth."

John put down his glass and noticed the French Riviera brochures, then he glanced at the expensive bottle of champagne. With a look at Jane and Bob, his heart froze. Bob had the grin of a triumphant conqueror.

Bob looked straight at him and draped his arm around Jane. "Jane and I have been talking about a trip to the Riviera."

"I wouldn't go so far as to say we were planning anything yet," Jane corrected.

John was defeated. Cold sweat beaded his forehead. What a fool he was, barging in on them, and in tattered clothes no less. There was Bob McWilliams, the tall, blond, movie star handsome, successful lawyer, wearing a suit of Italian silk. Worst of all was that Jane seemed to enjoy having Bob's arm wrapped possessively around her.

And Jane. He had never seen her look so alluring. The clingy black dress wasn't tight, but it still suggested the feminine symmetry of her curves.

"I should go now," he said abruptly. "It was rude to barge in like this."

"No!" Jane broke away from Bob to reach for John's arm. "We have to plan how we'll get our checks," she said, leading him into the living room. He sat down opposite the couch where Bob and Jane were sitting. In no time the new millionaires made their plans.

"So, Jane," Bob said, placing his hand on her knee, "what exciting cravings will you satisfy with your new wealth? One thing's for sure— Boston's jet-setting crowd will welcome with open arms someone as lovely and intelligent as you."

John squirmed in his chair, staring at Bob's aggressive hand as it kneaded Jane's smooth skin above her knee.

"I'm not like that. I'll probably help my mother. And I know of a nice house. Maybe the owners be willing to sell it to me." Bob started to run his hand along Jane's leg from her knee to the hem of her dress. "And I can't forget about saving for a rainy day and donating some to charity.

"I'd like to do something to help women who choose not to have an abortion, but are willing to give up their babies for adoption," Jane said, taking Bob's hand in hers and discreetly sliding them onto the couch. "It's a sad commentary of our society where women suffer more shame if they give their babies up for adoption rather than having abortions. Even if someone believes a woman should have the right to choose, there has to be a better choice than terminating the life of an innocent, unborn child. I wouldn't know where to begin, but it's something I've thought about for a long time."

"I didn't know I was involved with such a socially-conscious rabble-rouser." Turning to John, Bob said, "And you, John, what are your plans?"

"That's easy. I'm in debt, so paying most of it off will wipe out this year's check. In the future I expect I'll give some of it to my nieces and nephews for their college education. I'm used to living without things, so I figure each year I'll give half of it away to charities."

Bob sat back on the sofa and took a long sip of champagne as John went on.

"I'm involved with the Samaritans, so I'll give some to them. Then I'd like to do something for kids with cancer. I've seen stories on TV about camps for kids with cancer. When I was a kid, I went to an overnight camp and I still have fond memories of my summers there. I'm sure for a boy or girl suffering from the nightmare of cancer a week or two away at camp would mean a lot. Not to mention the respite it'd give their parents whose lives have been consumed in worry about their childrens' illness."

"Sounds admirable," Bob replied, "but I'm sure once you actually *have* money for awhile you'll find ways, like the rest of us, to spend it on yourself."

Jane's mind wandered as she heard them speak. She was imagining John eating an ice-cream cone—a Brigham's black-raspberry ice-cream cone.

Chapter 12

The dog days of summer had settled in by August ninth when Jane left work early to spend a leisurely lunch with her friend Marie. The Pillar House, named for its facade with four stately pillars, provided an ideal ambiance for easy conversation. Sliding out of her Mercury Sable, the noisy traffic from the adjacent Route 128 seemed unfitting for such an elegant restaurant. But over forty years ago, the state highway department plowed through many fine neighborhoods to construct an eight lane, Boston beltway.

Jane was dressed in a breezy white blouse with a long, side-buttoned skirt. The green of her skirt matched the four rows of scallop embroidery down the front of the blouse. A welcoming maroon canopy shielded her from the blazing sun as, with a bounce in her step, she climbed the outdoor carpeted stairway.

As she stepped into the foyer, everything about the Pillar House suggested the splendor of a time gone by, from the sparkling crystal chandelier, the flowing bouquet of flowers, and the thick Persian rug. To the side a stairway wound its way to an upstairs bar. Gentility filled the air—soft music, murmurs of conversation, the clink of china.

Jane's glance met a woman's looking up from a menu. There was no doubt in their instant expressions of recognition. Marie was wearing a knee-length, rose-print suit. The fitted jacket, accented with a fancy shawl collar, implied a most stylish woman.

"It's so good to see you," Marie said, as they greeted each other with loving hugs.

"Far *too* long," Jane said, giving Marie an affectionate squeeze. "I should make myself spend more time with the people I love."

Marie pulled away and looked her friend over. "Get a look at you, honey. You get prettier every time I see you."

"Cut it out. I'm the same old me." Jane took Marie by the arm. "I hope you're hungry. The food here is absolutely delicious."

Settled at their table, drinks ordered, Jane glanced out the window to where gardeners were tending flower beds. Thoughts of John flashed through her mind. Looking back at Marie, their joy shined in their smiles. Jane had always thought Marie to be one of the prettiest women she had ever known. She was graced with a radiant smile and a magazine ad, flawless complexion. Her eyes, big and brown, were so deep a person could swim in them.

"How's Stanley doing?"

"Lots better, praise the Lord. Can you believe it's been two years since the car injury? He has good mobility in his left arm, but nothing like he had before the accident. He still struggles with some words."

"I'm glad he's recovering so well. I shudder every time I think of that awful accident. That first week, not knowing if he'd live or die. I prayed so hard for him."

"We all prayed a lot back then. Thousands of prayers from fans all over the country helped pull him through. And our prayers are still being answered. Stanley's just been appointed Illinois Assistant Commissioner of Human Relations."

"Oh, that's wonderful! It may be a far cry from being the Bears' all-pro wide receiver, but what he does for the handicapped is so important."

"One drunk driver sure changed our lives. But you know," Marie said, becoming reflective, "our love is stronger than ever because of what we had to endure."

A formally attired waiter approached their table with two glasses of Chardonnay. After the waiter served their drinks, Jane raised her glass and proposed a toast. "To good friends."

Marie, glass in hand, added, "Who'd ever believe it? But here we are twelve years later, all the wiser for having known each other."

"Yes, we certainly were the odd couple in college—the shy white girl from the suburbs and the street-wise black girl from Chicago."

With a clink of crystal, they each took a sip.

"How's little Lacy doing?" Jane asked.

"She's an absolute doll. I only wish my job didn't require me to travel so often. It's especially difficult when I'm out of town over night. Children grow up too quickly these days. Can you believe she'll be going into second grade this fall? She played T-ball this spring, and of course Stanley was her team's coach. If he has his way, there'll be women professional baseball players by the time she's out of college. She loves her summer day camp and is already a better swimmer than I am."

"And Hilliard? Is he still the cutest baby that ever lived?" Jane asked.

"You mean Mr. Big Boy. He's the moose of the two-year-olds. A future lineman, I'm sure. Not the lean wide receiver like his father."

"Do you have any pictures?"

"Now you sit back, honey, and make yourself comfortable. I brought a whole mess of 'em." Marie pulled out a bulging envelope from her designer bag.

With a running commentary from Marie, Jane attentively admired each picture, emitting sighs, oohs, and aahs. "You don't know how I envy you," Jane said, handing them back. "We had the same dreams back in college. You have it all now, a gorgeous husband and two beautiful children."

Marie reached over and took Jane's hand, giving it a squeeze. "Don't you worry, honey. I know your time will come. Besides, you told me over the phone you *have* met the man of your dreams. Tell me all about this Bob McWilliams of yours."

"He's definitely what I've dreamed about. He's great looking, very intelligent, and successful. Everywhere he goes people notice him." Jane paused and her gaze became distant. After a few moments, she focused on Marie and said, "John's nothing like Bob. John turns into a wallflower when we're in a group of people."

"John? Who's John?"

"I've mentioned him to you. He's nobody special, just a friend I met two months ago. We see each other about once a week. We mostly talk on the phone. He's really weird, but I've gotten used to him. We go for walks and talk a lot. It's strange, but it feels like we've known each other all our lives."

"Does Bob know about him?"

"Of course. He's even met him. Bob was over for dinner the night John came by and told me we had won the Pennsylvania lottery. It was a bit awkward having John see me with Bob. John looked like a bird with a broken wing."

"We? I didn't realize you had won the lottery with someone else."

"How else do you think I'd win? I'd never buy a ticket on my own. John and I were flying to my mother's when we picked the numbers."

"Hold on, honey," cut in Marie, "I don't think you're telling me everything about this John what's-his-name. You took him to meet your mother?"

"His name's John Avery, and believe me I'm telling you everything. It's not what you think. I didn't take him to meet my mother. He's only a good friend. The reason he went to my mother's was that I'd promised him I'd spend that Saturday with him. Then I found out that Aunt Sandy's party was changed to that weekend. I had no other choice but to invite him. You know how I am about keeping promises."

"No choice, huh?" Marie scrutinized her ex-roommate with a sly grin. "So if you go for walks and talk with John, what do you and Bob do for excitement?"

"Well," Jane paused, realizing she had started off what she had to say the way John often did, "one Saturday he picked me up in a chauffeured limo and took me to a Red Sox game. Everything Bob does is lavish. He knows someone with sky-view box seats. The view from those seats and the amenities were fabulous.

"John's idea of impressing me was for us to have a high-speed drag race."

"Sounds exciting. Who won?"

"Marie, I don't believe you. We could have been killed. I've never been so scared in my life."

Jane tried to ignore Marie's expectant stare. A look a mother would make while patiently waiting for her child to divulge the truth. Giving in, Jane sat up tall, held her chin high, and said, "We did."

Marie made no comment, instead she just gazed at her friend. It was a look Jane recognized—a look Marie always adopted before coming up with the answer to a difficult question. Then Marie's face gradually brightened to a big smile and she started to laugh.

"What's wrong?" Jane said, wiping at her chin. "Do I have something on me?"

"I don't believe it. I would never have guessed."

Jane's face paled. "Tell me. You know I don't like it when you do this to me."

Marie leaned forward and in excited happiness she said, "You're in love!"

Jane took a relieved breath. "You've got to be kidding," she said with a short laugh. "I hardly know Bob."

"Forget Bob. You're in love with John. You can't stop talking about him."

Instantly Jane tensed. "No, I'm not." The force of Jane's denial threw Marie back in her chair. "Don't even say such a thing. We're only friends. He's nothing like the man of my dreams."

"Okay. I'm sorry I said it. It was only a thought."

For the next minute there was silence. Jane stared out the window biting her lower lip. Then she felt the comfort of Marie's hand on hers.

"Jane, honey, let me tell you a story about my love for Stanley."

Lost in a whirl of thoughts concerning her feelings for John, Jane simply looked at Marie.

"For months after Stanley's accident, I worried that my love wouldn't be strong enough to withstand the misfortune life had brought us. I had fallen in love with a famous football star. You saw how he was in the hospital. It seemed his whole body was shattered—ribs, left arm, jaw, and a fractured skull. The doctors said the punctured lung should have killed him."

Jane's heart ached as she remembered what Stanley and Marie had gone through.

"Before the accident, he had accepted an invitation to speak at a national conference on employee benefits in industry. He had given his talk on the benefits of hiring the handicapped many times, but now he had to present it as a handicapped person himself. He had four months to recuperate and prepare for it. His physical and speech rehabilitation was going painfully slow. The day of the presentation eventually came, and I will always remember that night and his speech."

Thoughts of John were lost for the moment; Jane leaned forward in total concentration.

"As he walked to the podium, I felt sick. I didn't have faith that he was ready. I thought for sure he'd embarrass himself. I didn't believe my love for him would survive his imperfections. When he started speaking, his speech faltered and he began stammering. Then he just froze. It was like my worst nightmare.

"But then he composed himself and with considerable effort continued. I must say Stanley's spirit never shined brighter. The audience was rapt. Tears streamed down my checks as I realized how very much I loved him. I discovered too, my love wasn't based on appearance, but on respect for the man I knew he was inside."

Jane picked up her napkin and wiped her eyes.

"He ended the speech by saying that since his accident, it had been his employer, the State of Illinois, that gave him the opportunity to go home to his wife, daughter, and new son, a proud man. As he headed back to his seat, the audience gave him a thunderous, standing ovation."

"I'm so happy for both of you."

"Jane, honey, what I'm trying to tell you is that there's more to love than appearances. Respect for the person and how he treats you is what *really* matters."

"That's just the point. When I first met John I had no respect for him. I thought he was goofy—intellectually lacking. His greatest joy seemed to be making a fool of himself and embarrassing me."

"But there's something else, isn't there?"

Jane wasn't sure of what Marie meant.

"Tell me," Marie said, "who do you look forward to seeing the most, Bob or John?"

Jane didn't have to think about it. She already knew the answer. Ashamed with guilt, she looked at her dearest friend and confessed. "I like being with John. He's a nice person. He's sincere. He's funny. It sounds so silly, but he makes me happy."

"But you don't respect him?" Marie said, cutting in.

"I don't know what I feel," Jane said, throwing her napkin on the table. "He did something at my Aunt Sandy's birthday party that really upset me. You may recall my cousin Sally whose seventeen-year-old son, Doug, committed suicide five years ago. Sally's never recovered from that loss and her subsequent depression. For over a year, family members tried to be supportive, to help her through it, but nothing worked. By the second year, we felt she'd had enough time to get over her depression and it was time to get on with her life. And for the last two years, it's been an unspoken agreement among family members not to talk about Doug when Sally's around.

"I told John all about the situation. But what do you suppose he did when I introduced him to Sally and her husband Larry? *He mentioned Doug.*"

"You've got to expect such things from a man," Marie said, whimsically. "They're always doing or saying the wrong thing."

"Maybe, but needless to say, I was furious. But it seemed Sally needed to talk and John was there to listen. They talked for over an hour. Later Sally seemed better and she laughed while cleaning up. She even told a mildly off-colored joke about a yellow toad and a pink elephant. We all roared when she told the punch line.

"I refused to give John credit for her change. But Sally called me yesterday to thank me for bringing John, and for the chance to talk to him. She had just returned from her first meeting with a survivors support group John had suggested. She told me Larry had agreed to go with her to the next meeting. She now knows she'll never be completely healed from her pain, but she believes she's found the support to help her move on with her life."

"So what's your problem? Why be so stubborn? John sounds pretty special to me. How did you two meet in the first place? The last I knew, you were making it difficult for a man to catch you."

Jane laughed; her eyes sparkled now. "That's exactly what happened. One morning I was walking peacefully by myself, when I stepped in a crack and twisted my ankle. He came out of nowhere and caught me."

"Such gallantry!"

"Believe me," Jane said, pointing her spoon at Marie. "There was nothing romantic about his behavior. Not like the day you met Stanley. You were walking on air. For days you swooned about this hot shot, freshman football player. Saying how you had met your dream man."

"I suffered that year. I thought he'd never see me as an eligible woman."

"Oh, but your magic finally worked and you two had a fairy tale courtship."

Flushed, Marie drank some wine. "Falling in love was such an aphrodisiac. But you already know about my courtship, I want to hear about yours. What attracted you to John?"

"It's not a courtship, I'm telling you."

"There must have been something about him for you to have allowed him into your life."

Jane paused and reflected on that day. It wasn't long before a grin flushed her cheeks. "Have you ever experienced the sensuousness of black-raspberry ice cream?"

"Black-raspberry ice cream?" repeated Marie, accentuating each word. "Now why does that suddenly sound so naughty?"

Jane's pink mask betrayed her innocence. "We were in a grocery store and he chose some black-raspberry ice cream for me and proceeded to tell me what it'd be like eating it while looking at me."

"Honey, you've found *my* kind of man. What'd your love machine say?"

"Marie, you're not making this easy for me." Jane chuckled nervously. "He said some stuff that belonged in a trashy romance novel. But that was nothing compared to actually watching him eat the ice cream."

Marie's eyes widened. "Ooooh, do tell me more—every juicy detail."

Jane took a long sip of wine. "I had invited him into my apartment for an ice-cream cone to thank him for carrying my grocery bags. He sat on a chair facing me—licking his cone. His smile drove me crazy, as I watched his tongue and imagined him devouring my body."

"*You*? Impure thoughts? You wicked woman."

"I may be a virgin, but believe me I have a very good imagination."

"So what happened?"

Jane looked around the dining room and leaned forward. "Disaster. With my last spoonful, when I thought he wasn't looking, I stuck my tongue into my ice cream to experience the sensation myself. 'Nice tongue' he says, causing me to swallow the wrong way. I nearly died choking."

"This is a Jane I never knew existed. I must meet this John of yours. And you can be sure I'll bring the black-raspberry ice cream along to watch you two in action."

"Marie!" It was like their old school days were back. Telling shameful tales with funny grins on their faces. "You wouldn't."

"I guess if you're still a virgin, it means you haven't gone to bed with your man yet?"

"Marie!"

"People who date have been known to do that you know. Besides, I sense a real change in you. You've loosened up."

During their meal, Jane mulled over whether or not she dared tell her friend about how she and John had been in bed together. She thought back to how Marie had trusted and confided in her and knew she had to tell her. So during dessert, she bit the bullet and told all. Giving special elaboration on how John had given her a whole new and wonderful meaning to the Pointer Sisters' song, "Slow Hand."

As time passed, the two women talked about other things. Then, before they knew it, it was 4:30. In the parking lot they paused by Marie's car. "When will you be seeing John again?"

"Tomorrow night. He's taking me out to dinner."

"I don't care what you say, honey. I think you know you're in love, but are too afraid to admit it."

"Please don't say that. I can't be. I can't let myself fall in love with him."

"Why not? I think you've finally found Mr. Right."

Jane stood silently, trying to figure out her feelings. "If John is the one God intends for me to marry, Marie, why hasn't He let me know yet?"

"What do you expect, girl? Do you expect the Lord to write it in big letters across the sky?"

"I don't know what I expect, but I'm sure I'd know it."

Chapter 13

Sitting at her desk, Jane glanced once more at her watch. Minutes were passing like hours. At four o'clock she decided to leave work to get ready for her six o'clock dinner date with John.

Dressed by 5:30, she lay on the couch, sedated by the warm summer breeze and the serenade of birds. Since John's ridiculous performance, the feeders had hosted a variety of birds. She could now identify the distinct calls and songs, from the lamenting "coo-coo" of the mourning dove to the lively "purty-purty" of the cardinal.

As she started to doze, the doorbell jolted her. It was not yet six. John was never early and she wondered who it could be. But when she looked through the peep hole, there he was. "You're early," she said, opening the door.

"I hope not too early?" he said. "I've heard that catching a woman in the middle of her transformation can be very risky."

"No, you're safe, I've been ready for awhile. Besides, why would there be a need to make a special transformation?"

"Some people do it for love." He gave her his weird look.

"But some people aren't in love," she said, looking out at the yard.

He wasn't going to let that comment—or Bob—discourage him. Especially tonight. He had finally found the exact words. Tonight was the night. He knew there wasn't a cloud in the sky, and the new moon would be shining.

"I see your mourning dove is still out there. He's becoming fat from all your food. And what do you know, he now has a mate to coo at."

"Yes, he does," Jane said, sounding like the proud parent. "She's been around since we got back from Pittsburgh. They look pretty content out there, wouldn't you say?"

"Speaking of content, have you adjusted to being a millionaire? You haven't decided to quit your job yet, have you? Giving up those business meetings with Bob may prove too difficult."

The sarcasm hung in the air—thermal underwear wouldn't have kept John from feeling the chill of Jane's lingering expression. He gave her his silly look, and her glare finally melted.

"It's uncomfortable," she said, "the way people look at me now, wondering how I've changed. Being constantly asked for money is what bugs me the most. How about you?"

"I feel great. I'm finally released from the chains that have dragged me down for years. I spent the day writing checks. I still owe my parents some money, but I feel great. Are you ready to celebrate with a most memorable dinner?"

"All I have to do is go to the bathroom and fix my hair, and I'll be ready."

John parked in front of Casey's, a tiny, bright yellow with a black trim, historic Worcester-style diner in Natick, built in 1922.

"This is it?" Jane said, stepping in. There wasn't much to it; ten counter seats and a take-out window.

Sitting at the counter, John asked Jane, "I hope you like onions, relish, and mustard?"

"Sure do!" she said, eyeing the menu behind the grill.

Jimmy, the short order cook, closed the screened take-out window and walked over to John. "It's good to see you, John. What'll it be tonight?"

"We'll each have two dogs all around."

In less than a minute, Jimmy slid paper plates with hot dogs in front of them. "May I have some ketchup?" asked Jane.

Doing a double-take, John acted like he was nearly knocked to the

142

floor.

"What's wrong? I've always enjoyed my hot dogs with ketchup."

"Nothing," he replied. John watched her take a bite and smiled to himself. He could imagine her as a kid—a scrawny little girl with beautiful wide eyes and knobby knees, sitting with her family enjoying a big, fat hot dog, dripping with ketchup and all the trimmings.

By the continuous flow of regulars from near and far, it didn't take long to realize Casey's reputation. After dinner, Jane wanted to go to the Natick Mall to buy a raincoat. At Filene's, she searched for a beige London Fog. She was deep into judgment when John approached her with a large yellow sou'wester hat.

"Here. Try this."

"I'm not going to try that on. I'll look ridiculous."

"Of course you won't. You're so pretty you can wear anything." She eyed him dubiously. "The trick is to look confident. Come on, give it a try."

She grumbled, but put the hat on and looked in the mirror; her frown was instantaneous. "Even Christie Brinkley wouldn't look confident with this on her head."

"You look great. I'm going to buy it for you. What a threesome we would've made on puddle days."

"Dream on. That'd be the day I'd jump in a puddle."

Walking through the mall, packages in hand, John convinced Jane that they deserved a dish of black-raspberry ice cream at Brigham's. She didn't argue, even though they'd already shared slices of Boston cream pie and banana cream pie at Casey's.

John had seemed standoffish during the evening, and his mood worried Jane. Approaching her apartment door, swinging her hand in his, she said, "I want you to know, nothing happened the other night between Bob and me."

"Why should that concern me?"

"It shouldn't, but I saw how you looked when Bob rubbed my leg. And I'm afraid you're going to say goodnight to me here at the door. You must have put some kind of spell on me, because I've really missed cuddling with you."

"Is that supposed to make me feel better? Knowing you can resist my love, but not cuddling with me?" he said as she opened the door.

"None of that now. We agreed not to pressure each other with our feelings." Jane closed the door and led him to the couch. "I've thought about this all day."

"I'm not sure I dare lie down with you, especially after the way you ate your ice cream. I thought you were going to attack me and start a family right there in Brigham's."

"I did not!" Her vehement denial was followed with a whack to his shoulder. "How could you say such a thing? If anyone acted improper, it's you. You eat ice cream as if you're devouring me."

"So that's what you're fantasizing about when you get that dreamy, dazed look."

There was another swift whack to his shoulder. "I do not."

John only laughed. "Let me call the store manager and ask if we can see their security video tape. Then I can prove how you looked." He walked over to the phone.

"You wouldn't dare." Jane came up behind him, staying close to his side.

"Sure I would." He picked up the phone. "After all, I'm the one who's disappointed you didn't attack me."

Jane grabbed the phone from him, put it back, and led him to the couch. "I'm sure some friendly kisses will ease your disappointment." With that they collapsed on the couch. Jane pressed her open lips against his, forcing her tongue between his soft, warm lips. His passion ignited, he plunged his tongue deep into her craving mouth.

Coming up for air, he told her, "I think I'd better go. If I stay any longer, you'll have to pack me in a tub of ice. My willpower isn't very strong tonight. So for your safety, you'd better take a rain check on the cuddling."

Leaving the warmth of her goodnight hug, John walked out the door. Disappointed, Jane stayed back, just inside the threshold. Standing by his car, he glanced up at the clear night sky. "The stars are really pretty tonight. I'll call you tomorrow afternoon."

Dispirited, Jane closed the door and went to her bedroom. Switching the light on, she noticed a sheet of paper on her pillow. Puzzled by what it was, she picked it up and saw that it was a poem signed by John. Bewildered by how it got there she sat on her bed and began reading.

MY PILLOW

God, will you grant a wish for me?
I know exactly what it needs it to be.
You have already blessed me with so much.
But what I want takes your loving touch.
A pillow for the mind is all I ask.
To create this pillow will be a delicate task.
A special pillow for the woman I love.
Send it to her on the wings of a dove.
I want to be the person she sees in her mind.
This woman I love I never thought I'd find.
Such a pillow will not take much space.
But what it will do, once it's in place,
Is soften the fall.
Her falling for me, I want most of all.
Like a child trusts her parents when learning to float.
Please let her feel secure with my I LOVE YOU note.
The pillow will cover her mind like new-fallen snow.
No matter when or where she falls in love I want her to know.

Dearest Jane, it's not for me to make judgments of who you are.
Use my love for your continued growth to shine like the brightest star.

Make the pillow as pure and soft as cotton.
So the feeling from our love will never be forgotten.
She'll learn about my sensitivities in the bed we sleep.
All memories of my love, I want her to keep.
Make the pillow like a fluffy white cloud.
I want her so happy she'll sing out loud.
This pillow will make our love have no end.
I'm so happy that she's my closest friend.
Am I wrong God, to ask for this pillow in my prayer?
You know I love her and want our lives to share.
She's so beautiful in the moonlight.
Please God, may I give her the pillow tonight?

145

Jane's eyes were blurred with tears when she finished. His love was as comforting as the finest goosedown pillow. Why couldn't she love him back? Getting up, she went out to the patio to ask God once more to resolve her internal struggle.

Even with a light sweater, she shivered in the cool night air. Looking up at the sky, she was amazed at how clear and dark the sky was. The stars were especially bright with only a sliver of the new moon on the horizon. Pulling her lawn chair to the center of her yard, she wrapped her arms close to her body and began identifying the different constellations.

Two shooting stars zipped across the night sky and distracted her meditative mood. She recalled that it was the second week of August, and the Perseid meteor shower was providing its annual fiery spectacle. Earth was traveling past the trail of dust and debris left behind the comet Swift Tuttle.

After seeing over twenty shooting stars, clouds overtook the night sky, so Jane went to bed. She read and reread the poem, praying for God's answer. At last sleep came, and the poem fell to the floor.

Jane awoke to the sound of rain beating steadily on the windowpanes. The forecast was for continued heavy rain until the afternoon when a cool, dry air front would pass through. With the sou'wester so handy, she decided to wear it to work. As she walked to the office building entrance, she ran into Wayne. He had managed to reach the door just before her and held it open.

"Good morning," she said, with greater cheerfulness than the weather.

"Love that hat, Jane. At first I didn't recognize you. All I could see was bright yellow on your head. I wondered who'd be brave enough to wear such a hat and was shocked when I realized it was you. You've always been so conventional, but I guess becoming a millionaire is starting to change you, after all."

"Thanks for the compliment, Wayne," Jane said, approaching her desk, "but you guessed wrong." At her desk, she flipped through yesterday's phone messages. Being at work didn't change her state of mind. Thoughts of John kept her from concentrating on her research, so after lunch she took the rest of the day off to clear her mind. It was still raining quite hard, but since it was comfortably warm she decided to go to Nahant Beach.

People were either reading or having a late lunch in the few cars in the parking lot. She buttoned her new raincoat and adjusted her sou'wester. Bending over, she took off her shoes and tossed them into the car.

Walking toward a path to the beach, a big grin formed under the yellow brim of her sou'wester. "What the heck," she said and started running. She lifted the hems of her coat and dress and without stopping, jumped into the middle of a puddle, landing with a large splash.

Cool, sandy water dripped down her legs. She laughed like a delighted child. Oblivious to onlookers, she made a couple more jumps. The rain still pelted down as she strolled along the nearly deserted beach at the water's edge. In the distance, some kids played in the water, and an old man with an umbrella was walking his dog. Sea gulls either glided overhead in the wet air currents or scurried along the water's ebb ahead of her.

With raindrops dripping off her sou'wester, she headed for the softer sand beyond the high-tide mark, and prayed to God to let her know what to do. She kicked the soft, damp sand, thinking of something her mother had told her on the phone: "Make sure what you're hearing is God and not just your confused rationalizations."

Her shadow appeared on the sand, and she looked up at a wall of clear, blue sky. The cooler, drier air from Canada was bulldozing the steamy storm eastward over the ocean. It was rare to see such a distinct squall line. She sat down to watch the changing weather pattern. Soon the curtain of rain had drifted out over the ocean.

With the warmth of the sun beating on her back, she dug her toes into the cool dampness of the sand. Putting her hands together, she closed her eyes and began praying. "God, will you please let me know what my life would be like if what I feel for John is truly love."

Then she opened her eyes and continued to restlessly dig her toes into the sand, until an unusually loud screech from a sea gull flying overhead caused her to look up. The moment she lifted her head, she forgot about the sea gull. Her eyes stopped at a sight so startlingly beautiful and dramatic, she couldn't believe it was real. A rainbow had filled the sky. Rising out of the ocean, its arc stretched across the dark stormy sky before curving back down into the ocean.

It was so clear and close she felt like she could have easily reached out and touched it. Never before had she seen colors so brilliant and wide. She watched in wonder as a second rainbow, smaller, not quite so vivid, appeared under the larger arc. She was sure there had to be a pot of gold at the end of it. Then she realized what was happening. God was telling her that the pot of gold at the end of this rainbow was John.

For the next few minutes she watched the rainbows, thinking of all the previous signs she had ignored—how John had mysteriously come from nowhere to catch her, to the shooting stars she'd seen last night. She could hardly control her excitement and happiness, wishing he was there to share this moment with her. How would she ever be able to describe the beauty of these rainbows and how she now knew her true feelings? When the last of the rainbows had faded away, she knew what she had to do.

Entering Farris' Nursery, Jane went up to the woman at the counter. "Do you know where John Avery is?"

"Yes, he's in the orchid greenhouse. Do you want me to call him?"

"No, that's all right. If you could direct me, I'd like to surprise him."

"Are you Jane?" The woman gave her a warm smile.

"Yes, I am," she said, slightly embarrassed.

"I thought so. He often mentions you." Then she pointed behind Jane and gave her directions.

Jane walked silently on the soft dirt floor between rows of orchids. The greenhouse was hot and humid, thick with the odor of moist dirt and mulch and the sweet fragrance of orchid blossoms. John was standing working on something. She paused behind him. "How are all your children this wonderful afternoon?"

He turned, a delighted smile filled his face. "As usual they're requiring a lot of attention." He looked her over from head to toe. "To what do I owe this unexpected visit? I called your office and your secretary told me you were playing hooky this afternoon."

"I wouldn't quite call it playing hooky. I'd rather think of it as doing some successful soul searching. Have you got a minute? I don't want to interrupt."

"For you, I have all day."

She wrapped her arms around him. "Do you remember the day we met, and you asked me why I had been crying and I told you I wouldn't tell you? I want to tell you now.

"As you know, I'd recently turned thirty. The morning we met, I had woken up from a bad dream, crying hysterically, not knowing what I should do. I was feeling so depressed thinking how all my dreams about love and marriage would never come true. It wasn't until I was in church later that morning, praying for God's help, that I started to feel better. I asked God to help me find the man He intended for me. I was on my way to the store from church when you caught me.

"This afternoon I'm not sure I found my soul, but I do know I found my pot of gold at the end of the rainbow. It's you, John. Your pillow has been so soft and comfortable I haven't realized I've had it since the day we met. You are the pot of gold at the end of my rainbow. I love you, John Avery. I love you very much."

Lost for words, John hugged her tightly in their first loving embrace. "Oh Jane, I love you *so* much. I can't believe the way I feel. Do you feel my heart? I think it's doing loopty-loops."

He kissed her, then said, "I want to hold you so hard against me....I want to always remember what it's like having you in my arms, knowing you love me."

"Can you forgive me for not realizing sooner that what I felt for you was actually love?"

"How could I ever be upset with you? Besides, we've known each other less than two months. It takes time to understand feelings. Now we'll have to figure out what our love for each other actually means."

"I know one thing it'll mean," Jane said. "I'm going to stay awake tonight thanking God and thinking about you."

"I've been thanking God every day since we first met. Who else but you would put up with a person like me?"

John looked around the greenhouse. "You know, for years I've been in absolute awe of the delicate beauty of these orchids. Now that you're here next to them, I can see they don't compare to the precious beauty *you* possess. How will I ever be able to tell you what I feel for you, Jane? It will take me more than a lifetime."

Chapter 14

October and the maple grove beside Sacred Heart Church blazed with color. It was a typical New England church, white, with a majestic spire and, today, a backdrop of red, yellow, and burnished-orange leaves and a crisp, blue sky. It represented a postcard setting at its pastoral best.

When John, with Jane at his side, pulled into the parking lot for the nine o'clock Mass, they sat for a minute to take in the beauty of the scene.

"You're certainly enthusiastic this morning," Jane said, after John hopped out of the car and opened her door.

"Must be because you look particularly beautiful today." He reached in the backseat for his suit jacket and a small box. The box looked like the type a nursery used for small flower arrangements. But if it was a corsage, she thought, surely he would have pinned it on her at her apartment.

At the church steps, a brisk gust swirled the few fallen leaves around them, and Jane shivered in her new, three-piece ensemble. The pleated, navy-blue, knee-length skirt flattered her legs. The floral-print, silk blouse, and the navy-blue blazer personified the conservative Jane Melrose.

"What do you have in the box?" she finally asked, as they entered the church.

151

Instead of an answer she got his weird look. Like an alarm going off, her sensors for potential embarrassment went on full alert. He was enthusiastic and secretive. He must be planning something.

After they'd prayed, they sat back, and John nonchalantly reached for the box. He opened it carefully and pulled out a scarlet rose corsage with white babies' breath.

Seeing the flower, Jane's body temperature skyrocketed. "Put that back!" she said in muffled anger, glaring. She couldn't imagine why he had waited until the Mass was about to start to give it to her. "I'm not going to let you make a scene by pinning that on me now."

His hand covered the ends of the white satin ribbon as he reached over to pin the corsage on. "I'm not making a scene. I want you to wear it, so sit still while I pin it on."

Reckoning he'd only attract more attention if she continued fussing, she sat still and acted as if nothing was happening while he pinned the rose. Yet sitting there, she sensed everyone in the church was watching them.

After securing the corsage, John kissed her cheek. "I hope this means as much to you as it does to me." He settled back in the pew as the sacristy bells rang, announcing the priest's entrance and the beginning of Mass.

Even after the opening prayer Jane kept her eyes on the lector. Feeling a thousand eyes on her, she didn't dare look down at the corsage. But inevitably her hand was drawn to it. She caressed the soft, cool petals and fingered the satin bow, noticing an unusual roughness along the middle of each ribbon. Unable to hold her curiosity back any longer, she pulled one end and glanced down. There, embroidered in scarlet thread, she read the words, I LOVE YOU VERY MUCH JANE. She looked over at John, who must have been watching from the corner of his eye. He greeted her with his silly look.

Smiling back, she grasped the other end and glanced down. Her body froze. The sudden, rapid pounding of her heart caused her blood to rush. Immediately lifting her head, she looked straight ahead at the large, stained-glass window. Jesus smiled down at her. She didn't know what to do, but she certainly didn't want to just sit still.

Perhaps she had misread the words, but she didn't have the courage to take another look. To her relief, everyone stood while Father Kiley read the gospel. She knew she couldn't look at John; there was no telling what he might do. Heart still throbbing relentlessly, she took a deep breath and closed her eyes. "Please God," she said in a low voice, then quickly looked down at the ribbon and reread the words. *Yes,* they were exactly as she had read them the first time. She wanted desperately to jump up and down, but remained composed as the priest continued with the gospel. *Why,* she wondered. *Why had John waited for this moment?*

Eventually she looked at him, her heart racing in happiness. This time he didn't greet her with his weird look. Instead he gave her his kind and loving smile as he reached for her hand. She knew he meant it. It *was* real. She looked down again at the wonderful question: WILL YOU MARRY ME, JANE? JOHN AVERY.

Jane entered an ethereal, blissful contentment. She squeezed John's hand. Now she would add her own sense of the dramatic. She waited. John fidgeted and kept looking at her. The Mass continued. Finally, at the sign of peace, she uncharacteristically threw her arms around him. "Yes. Peace be with you, John Avery." She kissed his cheeks and lips. "I love you so much. Yes, I will marry you. Yes, yes, yes," she murmured, as all eyes and smiles looked on.

Jane went to North Carolina with John to get acquainted with his parents. She saw firsthand his loving family background and the values his parents had instilled in him. It was only fitting she should learn about John's childhood, and some of the antics described by Mrs. Avery made even the unflappable John wince in embarrassment.

Mrs. Avery had pointed to her gray hairs and said she could explain how each one got there. For instance, there was the time the three boys waged the ultimate plastic toy, cowboy-and-Indian war in the basement. They had lit kerosene-soaked cotton balls for the flaming arrows. Luckily the house didn't burn down like the fort did. Then there was the chemistry set and the various fireworks production experiments.

Jane also met John's friend, Tim. Here she felt she really learned the essence of John Avery. For a long weekend she was privy to their boyhood reminiscences covering everything from puddle jumping to dating.

❀ ❀ ❀

In early March, Jane managed to buy her dream house, and the renovations were completed before their mid-May wedding deadline. Now, three days before their wedding, the love-starred couple sat on the couch in Father Kiley's study waiting for him to come and go over the final details.

As soon as he entered the room, Jane noticed that his normally amiable greeting was serious and businesslike.

"Jane," he said, "I received an unanticipated request from the cardinal this morning which will impact your wedding. He wants all the area priests to attend a special diocesan meeting this Saturday."

Her stomach tightened in one big knot. "Does this mean we can't get married on Saturday?"

Father Kiley smiled. "Of course you can get married Saturday, Jane. It's just that I won't be able to officiate."

"No!" Jane wailed. Suddenly erect, her eyes were wide open in shocked disbelief. "It's not fair. I want *you*, Father Kiley. I've always wanted you to perform my marriage ceremony."

"I know how you feel, Jane, and I appreciate it, but duty calls. Now, don't worry, I've found a wonderful priest to take my place."

Maybe it was her unreasonable wish for perfection, or too much last-minute stress, but Jane broke down, sobbing hysterically. John wrapped his arms around her and rocked her back and forth. "It's okay, darling. Everything will work out just fine." He kissed her tear-soaked cheek.

"Jane," Father Kiley pleaded as she wiped her eyes with a tissue, "last week I was at a reception for a Father George O'Boyle. He's in Boston for a scriptural scholar's convention. With the help of the Chancery Office, I asked Father George if he'd officiate your wedding. He said he'd be honored to."

Jane looked at his earnest face, but so far she was unimpressed.

"He was born and raised in the Burren section of Ireland. When he was twelve he moved with his family to Jerusalem. He studied at the Patriarchal Al Seminar in Beit Jala, outside of Bethlehem and was ordained in 1970—that's the same year I was. Isn't that a coincidence?"

The good father seemed to be selling now, but Jane remained

impassive. She shifted in her seat, her eyes still glistening and red.

Father Kiley continued Father George O'Boyle's resume. "The last fifteen years he's been studying scripture at the Gregorian University in Rome. And, Jane," he said, pausing until she made eye contact, which she was reluctant to do, "he's the most inspirational man I've known to wear the garment." The last words were clear, even, punctuated.

"But I only want you, Father," pleaded Jane. John squeezed her hand. She looked at Father Kiley, thinking about her own father, who also wouldn't be there, and her tears flowed again. After a short silence she said, "I'm sorry, Father. I'm no teenage bride. I should know better than to act this way."

Jane dug in her pocketbook for another tissue and blew her nose. With her emotions under control, Father Kiley picked up his pre-wedding checklist to make sure he had everything required to make their marriage legal. After fifteen minutes, they had gone over all the final details and Father Kiley asked them how their I'M MAD. ARE YOU MAD? envelope was working out. Jane was quick to inform her priest that they've had to use it twice already, each time was due to John's unreasonable attitude about their wedding plans. Father Kiley said he was optimistic that their novel approach in settling disputes would serve them well throughout their marriage. He went on to discuss the sanctity of marriage and the church's concern that couples understand that marriage was a sacrament entailing a life-long commitment.

During this spiel, Jane began thinking about Father George and wanted to know more about him, so she said, "You said Father George O'Boyle grew up in the Burren?"

"Yes, until he was twelve."

"Two years ago Mother and I visited relatives in the Burren region in County Clare. We stayed at a small village in Kilforna. Years before I had read a quote by General Ludlow who, in 1651, led Cromwellian forces through Clare and described the Burren as 'a country where there is not water enough to drown a man, wood enough to hang one, or earth enough to bury him.'

"Throughout the area there are fissures in the limestone rock formations and over thousands of years, soil has filed those fissures and plants have taken root. The extraordinary flora is so diverse you can find plants there unique to the arctic region as well as the Mediterranean. After seeing for myself its breathtaking beauty and diverse landscape, a quote like that could only come from an Englishman."

"Watch it." John said, giving her a hostile glare before he chuckled. "Those are my ancestors you're talking about."

They left Father Kiley on an upbeat note. He told them he'd try to have Father George at their 6:30 rehearsal on Friday.

On Saturday John slept later than usual. Impeccably dressed in his tux, he arrived at the church around 10:17, where he was greeted by Tim and the ushers.

"Well, old buddy," Tim said, patting him on the shoulder, "it's not too late to back out."

"Are you kidding? I may *pass* out, but I'd never *back* out of marrying Jane."

Standing there with his childhood friend, John began to feel an uneasiness in his stomach. They entered the sacristy to wait for Father George. When he arrived, they went over the wedding procedures.

John's butterflies were now swarming.

Then the word was given. It was time to start the ceremony. The uneasiness in John's stomach was joined by a vibrant pounding of his heart. As he stood at the end of the aisle, he observed the waiting guests. Then, with a blast, the organist started Handel's "Water Music Suite." John's heart nearly popped right out of his chest.

He watched the bridesmaids come down the aisle followed by Marie, the Matron of Honor. He wondered how Jane was holding up. Swallowing hard, he looked over at his mother, who had a tissue to her eyes. He gave her a little wave. He turned his attention to Mrs. Melrose, who blew him a kiss; John responded with his most nonchalant thumbs up. Jane's mother smiled at him, then strained to look up the aisle for her daughter, and he followed suit.

There she was. His beautiful Jane, his true love, at the back of the church, on the arm of her Uncle James. To ease his tension, he gave her a discreet wave and smiled when she responded in kind.

Suddenly there was the resounding call of trumpet and organ.

Everyone stood and turned toward the back of the church. Then, as Clarke's grandiose "Prince of Denmark March" filled the church, Jane began her walk down the aisle.

Overcome with emotion, tears filled John's eyes. Throughout his life he had become familiar with tears, predominantly those of sadness. But today was different. Today he only knew tears of pure happiness.

When Jane was halfway down the aisle, a blessed vision came to John. His tears, with the red light from the side stained-glass windows, produced a soft, rosy glow which seemed to radiate from Jane. There was no doubt about it, a vision of an angel was walking toward him. He knew without any doubt he was about to marry the angel sent to him by God.

The service went smoothly, with everyone saying their lines properly. At the end of the ceremony, Father George, in his lingering Irish brogue, declared, "Go, may the blessing of the Almighty God come upon you. In the name of my Father, and of the Son, and of the Holy Spirit, go in peace to love and serve the Lord. You may kiss the bride."

Jane remained motionless, staring at the priest.

In a low voice, John repeated, "You may kiss me."

Jane sought Father George's eyes. He smiled and said, "Yes, it's true." After a brief hesitation he added, "You are really married."

John couldn't wait any longer. He leaned over, lifted her veil, and kissed her lips. The spell was broken. Jane responded to the ceremonial kiss, and the guests cheerfully applauded the ritual.

The reception was held on the lawn of the Concord Academy under warm skies. Later the party moved indoors, and it wasn't until eight o'clock that Jane threw her bouquet and John tossed the garter. Jane had a childhood dream of leaving her reception in her wedding gown, so there was no need to change. Their plans were to spend the night in their new home and tomorrow fly to Aruba.

"I must say," Jane said, as they approached their front walk, "you did an excellent job putting the picket fence in."

"Well, thank you, my love. I wanted to make sure the fence had a firm foundation. Like our marriage, I want it to last forever."

"Look how long the stems have grown on the roses I've planted."

"It's going to be just the way you imagined it." John pulled her into a tight embrace, and they kissed each other passionately.

157

"Are you ready?"

"I'm so happy. Only with you could this day be so special." She put her arm around his neck. "Yes, I'm ready."

With a swish of her wedding gown, he gathered her up into his arms. She wrapped her own tightly around him as he proceeded up the front walk to their new home. Jane stopped her kisses only long enough to say, "I can't believe this is really happening. This day has been so much better than any of my dreams."

Inside the house, John carried her past the living room and up the beautiful Oriental-carpeted stairs. In their bedroom, John carefully placed her on the queen-size bed. Feeling sensuously secure, Jane pulled him down on top of her, whereupon they rolled around in one long, amorous kiss.

Later, still nestled together, Jane lay on top of him, her forehead resting on his. Suddenly, letting go of him, she sat up straight. "I didn't feel anything," she exclaimed in frustration.

"Couldn't you have at least faked it?" John said. "I gave you the best I knew how, and this is what I get. I think you've permanently broken my heart. I don't know how this marriage will ever survive."

"Stop *that*. That's not what I meant. I didn't feel any of your thoughts being transmitted to me."

"Oh that." He pretended to let out a sigh of relief. "Well, I guess it must mean I'm not the one you were meant to marry. You should never underestimate the lengths to which a male will go to get a woman in bed." With a hearty laugh he added, "When you think about it, men are the scum of the earth."

"Oh you." She clenched her fist and pounded his chest in frustration. "For all these months I wanted to believe you."

John pulled her close and kissed her. "Do you believe?"

"I want to." Her voice was wishful, faint.

"Well then, put your forehead against mine, close your eyes, and concentrate real hard."

Doing as he suggested, they lay peacefully together. After a minute or so Jane asked, "Do you *really* think I'm beautiful? Do I excite you?"

John continued to lie there saying nothing.

After a few more moments Jane spoke again. "You're not just saying that because it's my wedding day?" She lifted her head, bouncing on her husband in excitement. "I did it! I could feel your thoughts.

We really *can* pass thoughts to each other."

John smiled. It was too dark for Jane to see the tears in his eyes. "I know. It's just the way I dreamed it would be."

"It is. It *really* is." Jane smothered him with kisses. "Let's do it some more."

For the next few hours—in between their loving entanglements— they lay together passing thoughts to one another. Some time during the early morning hours Jane lifted her head from his chest. "Did you notice anything strange about how Father George said the Mass?"?"

John shook his head and uttered a weak, "No."

"How could you have missed it? You notice everything."

"Only things about you. I'll admit I did begin to worry when you didn't kiss me. It was so weird how you froze. I envisioned you having second thoughts while you were standing there staring at Father George."

"That's when I realized it. I thought I had noticed something unusual before. But the last time he said, 'In the name of my Father, and of the Son, and of the Holy Spirit,' that's when I knew."

"What's so unusual about that?"

"It's not *my* Father, it's *the* Father."

"It's probably just his style."

"It wasn't. I know it wasn't. It was Jesus. Just the way I always dreamed it would be. Jesus was at our wedding!" Tears of happiness filled her eyes.

"Well, I'm definitely not going to argue with you over something as important as that. The idea that Jesus presided over our wedding certainly makes it that much more special."

"Do you know what else made yesterday and last night special?" Jane snuggled close. "In nine months we're going to have a baby."

"Jane, we're married now. You don't necessarily get pregnant the first time you make love, like they taught you in parochial school."

"I know that," Jane said, ignoring his attitude. "But I can feel it happening inside me. You'll see, Mr. Smarty."

He turned on his side, studying her face. He was in a dreamy kind of contemplative-philosophical mood. "Do you think you would have married me if I weren't Catholic?"

"Why do you ask that? You are, so I did." Then she paused and thought about a more definitive answer. "My religion is so important to me, I don't think I could have. How about you? Would you have married me?"

"I believe it's more important to pay attention to what God tells you, regardless of your religion. There's only one God, no matter what religion you belong to—be it Protestant, Jewish, Muslim, Catholic, or whatever. So even if you weren't a Catholic, I would have married you. I didn't hear God tell me, 'Marry her, she's Catholic', and I certainly didn't know you were Catholic when I reached out and caught you."

They were near sleep when Jane asked one last question. "John, if you had an event in your life to experience again, what would it be?"

He ran his fingers through her hair. "The day I met you. I'll never forget the time we had and the way I felt with you."

Her smile was lost in the darkness. "It *was* a special day, wasn't it? For me it would be our wedding day. Especially last night and now in these early morning hours. Wearing my wedding gown, having you carry me into our home, being here in our home....It's what dreams are all about. Or, as you would say, a little girl and her dreams of marriage."

"Hey, guess what, I found the answer," John yelled, as he lay fully dressed on the bed, reading. It was mid-December, and they were enjoying a relaxing morning before he went to work.

From her bubble bath, Jane called back, "Found what?"

"The reason you blush." He walked into the bathroom and stood beside the tub, book in hand. "Here, on page fourteen of Dr. Xenakis's book on funny feelings. It says you blush when the body experiences unrequited lust."

"That's not true," Jane said, reaching for the book.

While Jane examined the book, John admired her in the soapy water. Most of the bubbles had disappeared, revealing her almost-seven-month pregnant body. "Boy, you're certainly big."

"I am not." Jane rubbed her swollen tummy. "The doctor says my tummy's in really great shape."

"I wasn't referring to your tummy. I was looking at your breasts."

"Oh, you." Jane flicked a handful of water at him. She grabbed the shower curtain, the one from her old apartment with the snow

160

scene, and yanked it closed. "I thought you were impressed with big-busted women."

"That was only a boyhood fantasy. After meeting you, I no longer desired a woman in a size 36C bra. Little did I know...." John's laughter was cut short by the phone ringing.

A few minutes later Jane strolled from the bathroom and wrapped her arms around him. "Who called?" she asked, looking out at the raging snowstorm.

"The nursery. They suggested I stay home because of the storm."

"I like *that* suggestion."

John looked at the snow swirling outside the window. "Do you realize with last year's snow drought, this is the first major snowstorm we've had since I've known you?"

"I was thinking the same thing when I was in the tub."

"Oh yeah?"

"Yeah, and do you know what else? I dreamed about the fun we'd have making snow angels together."

"Well, if you're up to it, we could go out and make them today?"

"Um...." she purred. "Today would be a wonderful opportunity to go out and play. But you have to promise not to get upset when you see how much better my angel will look, compared to yours."

"That'll be the day. You'll probably get on your back and discover you can't move. You'll be like a beached whale, floundering helplessly in the snow."

"John Avery!" She jabbed him in the ribs to stop his laughter. "I'll show you. Even pregnant I'm in better shape than you'll ever be."

"Ha. Bigger isn't better."

"I don't believe you."

Receiving a more noticeable jab, John stopped laughing. He begged for a truce and hugged her with one arm, rubbing his ribs with the other. Giving her a kiss he asked, "Do you think there are any pregnant angels?"

She nuzzled his shoulder, looked out the window, then at him. "This one certainly is."

Chapter 15

"Look who's finally awake, Neal. It's your mommy," John said, strolling into the bedroom wearing pajamas and slippers. He had their four-month-old son comfortably nestled into his neck. Seeing them, Jane kicked off the sheet, stretched her arms to the bedposts, arched her back, and sighed luxuriously. Her spaghetti-strap, violet chiffon nightgown clearly revealed the return of her figure, except for her breasts, which swelled against the sheer fabric.

"Tell Mommy I came in and rescued you from boredom, hunger, and a dirty diaper."

Like a kid guiding a model airplane, John navigated the baby through the air and zeroed in on Jane for a landing. "And now that you're clean and smell so nice, tell Mommy that you're ready for breakfast."

Making a soft landing on his mother's stomach, Neal lifted his head and gave her a Gerber's-baby-food grin.

"What a wonderful smile to start my day," she declared.

Neal was an absolute delight to his parents. Lifting him, Jane rubbed his creamy, velvet skin across her face as he chortled from the loving attention.

"I can't believe what a happy baby you are," said Jane. "I'm so lucky. Are you ready for breakfast?"

Propping two pillows against the headboard, she sat up to nurse him. Once he settled down, she looked over at John who was lying next to her, fiddling with Neal's baseball. "I'm glad you're not working today," she said. "I do look forward to our family days."

John's heart was bursting in joy as he admired her. Her nose and lips nuzzled Neal's peach fuzz hair. The sweet kisses and tender rubbing of his back was the essence of maternal love and contentment.

"There are times I miss the excitement and challenges I had at Merrill Lynch, but I don't regret my decision to be a full-time mother," she said.

"Well, Ralph Daniels certainly did."

"He only acted that way because I made him so much money. I'm sure he wouldn't have given us such a nice wooden swing set if he was really upset."

"Look how Neal grips the ball." The baby's chubby little left hand was curled over part of the ball John held between Jane's breasts. "He's going to be a famous lefty for the Red Sox. A feared defender of the turf in front of the 'green monster,' the way Williams and Yaz were."

"What's with you and baseball? Before Neal was born you hardly ever mentioned the Red Sox. Now it's baseball, baseball, baseball."

"Well Neal's my clone, so that means he'll follow *my* dream—playing for the Red Sox."

"How can you possibly believe Neal is your clone? Look how gorgeous he is."

"You're saying I'm not?" John said, pumping himself up.

Jane laughed at his futile display. "You're cute. Neal's gorgeous."

"Does he or does he not have my cute buns and brown hair?"

Jane refused to concede. "His hair's brown, but it's a lot thicker than yours." Her voice then became somber and subdued. "He has my heart."

"Well, that's the only thing." John knew what she meant because Neal had an unexplained irregular heartbeat, like his mother. "But I consider that a blessing, because no one has a nicer heart than my wife."

John quickly launched into some affectionate horseplay, nuzzling her ear with his lips and tongue.

"Stop that," she squealed when he blew in her ear. "You know that drives me crazy." She looked down at the contented baby. "You're not mean to your mommy like your daddy is. Even your daddy's Mommy says you're nicer than your daddy."

John chuckled. "You know, Neal, I think us guys have some serious female educating to do."

"Is that so?"

The child was oblivious to his parent's affectionate bickering as he went on suckling. Jane sighed and caressed the back of Neal's head. "I love mornings like this. Just the three of us."

No sooner had she spoken than there was the patter of little feet from down the hall.

"Well, not for long."

Brown hair flowing, a small bundle of energy careened through the doorway, squealing in delight.

"Could that be our Mary?" Jane asked, as the little girl hurled herself onto the bed next to her father. It was their two-and-a-half-year-old daughter, born exactly nine months and a day after their wedding. For the next hour the four played together on the roomy, queen-size bed.

After breakfast, Jane prepared Neal for his regular doctor's appointment. Mary stood and watched as her mother changed him. It was a hot July day, so he only needed to wear a T-shirt and diaper.

"What's the doctor going to do to Neal?" Mary asked.

"Same as he does to you, princess. He'll weigh and measure him. And you've grown a lot, haven't you?" Jane said, gently poking her finger into Neal's stomach, causing his fat, milky-white cheeks to puff out even further in a wide grin. "The doctor will listen to his heart," she went on. "Maybe the doctor will let you hear *your* heart again, wouldn't that be fun?"

"Will the thing be cold on my tummy?"

"We can ask the doctor to warm the stethoscope first. Go tell Daddy we're ready now. And don't forget your sun hat. You'll need it for the park this afternoon."

After the nurse took Neal's measurements, she led them into a cramped examining room and said, "Dr. Merrill will be right in."

Mary climbed up on her father's lap with her favorite book, *Play*

Ball, Amelia Bedelia, by Peggy Parish. Though she knew the story by heart, she never tired of it. She carefully studied each picture as her father read to her. She knew when to turn the pages, a job she had claimed as *hers*, letting everyone know in no uncertain terms.

Pointing to Amelia's dress-up trunk, Mary looked up at her father. "I have a dress-up box like Amelia Bedelia."

"That's right, you do."

"Do you know what I want to be for Halloween?"

"Let me guess." He rubbed his chin in feigned puzzlement. "I think you're going to be a...a...bunny rabbit, like I used to be."

"Noooooo...." Mary giggled at her father's silliness. "I'm going to be a princess. Know why?"

"Uhhh, noooooo."

"Because you and Mommy call me princess."

The examining room door opened and Dr. Merrill came in. "I see we have the whole family here today."

"Yes," said Jane. "Today's a family day. We're going to McDonald's for lunch, then we're going to the park. Neal's never been to the park."

"I'm going to show him how to feed the ducks," Mary piped.

"What a nice big sister," said Dr. Merrill, smiling down at Mary. The child beamed at the compliment.

Scanning Neal's chart, Dr. Merrill quickly reviewed the nurse's figures. "Ninety-eight percentile in weight and height. Pretty good there, Neal."

He placed his hand on the baby's stomach, skillful fingers gently pressing in along his ribs. This brought a big grin to Neal's face, along with little chortles of laughter.

"You're certainly ticklish today, Neal," Dr. Merrill said, putting his stethoscope to his ears. "Now, let's hear how your heart and lungs are doing."

A shiver shot across Neal's body as the metal instrument touched his chest.

Jane intently studied the doctor's every expression as he moved the stethoscope across her son's chest and back.

Straightening, Dr. Merrill gazed down at the baby, then turned to Jane. "I would feel more comfortable if we took some more tests at the hospital. His heart beat sounds more irregular than his last visit."

John's body went cold; Jane put her hand to her mouth.

166

"I don't think there's anything to be alarmed about," the doctor assured them. "I want to do it only as a precaution. Get him dressed while I go and schedule an appointment. I'll try for 1:30 so Mary can have her McDonald's lunch."

"Thank you, Doctor," Jane said, reaching for Neal's T-shirt. The hidden fear she'd had since Neal's birth raced through her mind. She had always had an irregular heartbeat, but the doctors had assured her it was very common, and not to worry about it. Why was Neal's so different?

When Dr. Merrill stepped out, Jane said, with a strained pale look on her face, "John, what do you think's the matter?"

"There's nothing to worry about," he said, trying to reassure her. "Neal just wants to be like you with his irregular heart."

Mary tugged on her mother's slacks. "But Mommy, the doctor didn't let me hear *my* heartbeat."

"I'm sorry, princess. Today isn't a good day to ask him. We'll ask next time we come."

To Neal nothing was different. He cooed to his mother's touches, and his playfulness quickly diminished Jane's concern. She let go of him and he rocked unsteadily in his newly learned sitting position. "Look at our big boy," Jane said, "sitting up all by himself."

Neal chortled with glee. It was a pleasant, memorable moment. One that's all too soon forgotten. Suddenly Neal's eyes rolled back, and he slumped backwards on the table.

Jane panicked. "What happened?" she shouted, scooping him up. "What's the matter with my baby?"

John ran from the room and yelled for the doctor. Two nurses immediately came running.

"Help him! He's turning blue!" Jane howled. One of the nurses took the baby and laid him on the table. Mary, lost in the commotion, looked up at all the legs rushing around and cried out in fright. Amid the chaos Dr. Merrill rushed in. Quickly examining Neal, he shouted, "Call an ambulance! Immediately! Get me a monitor!"

Jane hovered behind the doctor, trembling. Turning to the Averys, he said, "I'm sorry but you're going to have to leave the room."

John picked Mary up and went outside with Jane. Jane, her heart racing, craned her neck to see Neal.

Almost immediately a nurse came out. "The doctor will ride in the ambulance with Neal," she told them. "Why don't you leave now for the hospital so you can meet them there?"

As they ran to the car they heard the mournful whine of the approaching ambulance's siren. It pulled in while John was strapping Mary into her car seat.

"I'll be right back," Jane shouted, running toward the ambulance. Scared out of her mind, she watched in muted silence as Neal was rushed out, the doctor performing CPR while he carried him. The moment the door was slammed shut the ambulance sped off, its siren screeching.

Back in the car, Jane wailed hysterically. "Oh God, don't let Neal die. Please...." She kept repeating the word "please" until it became a mantra.

Her mother's hysterics made Mary cry in fright. As they raced to the hospital, John managed to calm his daughter down, but Jane was beyond his help.

Reaching the hospital, Jane was out of the car before John had braked to a full stop. By the time he got Mary out of the car and caught up with his wife, Jane was pleading with the emergency room nurse for information. Totally helpless, she clutched John, bawling, "They won't tell me anything. Why won't they let me see my baby?"

The couple clung to each other in fear.

"I'm going to need some information," the emergency room nurse said.

John released Jane. "I'll take care of it," he said. "Why don't you and Mary sit in the waiting room."

The waiting room was standard hospital—decorated in calming pastels and a television playing in one corner for distraction. It did little to calm Jane as she sat there with Mary on her lap. Mary twisted her neck and looked up at her mother. "Mommy, what's wrong with Neal?"

"He had trouble breathing, princess."

"Is he okay, Mommy?"

"I don't know," she said, clutching her daughter. "I hope so."

Mary soon became fidgety and scanned the room, her eyes coming to rest on a ten-year-old boy with a bloody bandage on his foot.

It seemed to fascinate her.

When the paperwork was completed, John came back and sat down beside his wife.

"What's taking so long?" Jane asked impatiently. Her foot tapped on the floor from the tension filling her body. "Why hasn't someone come out to tell us what's happening?"

John held her hand. "I'm sure Neal's doing all right. If there was anything seriously wrong with him, they would have told us by now."

Jane saw a nurse standing at the registration desk.

"I can't take this waiting any longer, this not knowing," Jane announced. She got up and went to the nurse. After a short conversation, the nurse headed down the corridor toward the treatment room where they had taken Neal.

Jane returned to her husband and Mary. "The nurse is going to find out what's happening," she said.

The door to the treatment room opened and Dr. Merrill emerged.

"It's about time," Jane said, rushing to the doctor, followed by John with Mary.

"How is he, Doctor?" John asked.

Placing a hand on Jane's shoulder, Dr. Merrill said somberly, "I'm so sorry. We tried everything, but little Neal's heart simply gave out."

"NOOOOOO!" Jane wailed, grabbing her head before her body went limp.

Stricken with disbelief, John saw his wife collapsing and instinctively reached out to catch her.

Lost in the commotion, Mary was left in the middle of the stark, unfriendly hallway. Nobody heard her plaintive cry, "Mommy, Mommy! What's wrong with my mommy?"

Four months later the lead-gray, cold November skies reflected the mood in the Avery house, the chill seemed to pervade every room. Mary, alone in the living room, turned off the television. *Sesame Street* over, there was little more to interest her. She climbed the stairs to her mother's room, something she had already done three times that morning. The room was still dark at ten o'clock. Mary could see her

169

mother lying in bed amid a pile of crumpled tissues. "Mommy, will you play with me?"

With a sullen face, Jane looked up and admonished the child. "No. I already told you, not now. Mommy doesn't feel well. Where's your daddy?"

"He's downstairs writing on things." Rejected by her mother, Mary turned away, but instead of leaving, she plopped down by the door. The minutes wasted away as Jane lay, wiping her eyes, unaware of her daughter's presence.

The child stared at the dusty-rose carpet, idly running her hand across its smooth pile. "You wish I died, and not Neal, don'tcha?"

Jane was startled, shocked. She sat straight up and looked over at her daughter. "No, Mary. That's not true. Why would you say such a thing?"

"You never play with me anymore. You used to always play and laugh with Neal."

Jane got out of bed and went over to lift Mary up. She gave her a big hug and said, "Oh, Mary dear, I'm sorry. I don't mean to ignore you. I would feel the same no matter who had died."

She sat back down on the bed and put the little girl next to her. "I loved both you and Neal the same. It just takes a long time to feel better after someone dies. I'll be feeling better soon, you'll see. Then we'll play and laugh again, just the way we used to. Right now, though, I'm sure your daddy will play with you."

Mary had heard it all before. She slid off the bed and left the room.

Later John came into the bedroom carrying some papers. He walked to a window and raised the shade. "You've got to get up and get yourself busy with something, Jane. You can't keep lying here, allowing your depression to fester like this."

"I know. I wish I could get busy. Oh John, I don't know what's the matter with me. I don't feel like doing *anything*. I've become useless even to my own daughter. I can't get it out of my mind that I should have done something sooner for Neal. Why didn't I realize something like that could have happened?"

John lay down on the bed beside her. "It's not your fault," he said, stroking her hair. "It's nobody's fault. It's easy to second guess what we should have done. But we *must* believe in God's will. For some reason

She wanted Neal to be with Her. You can't change it, I can't change it, so let it be, Jane. Try to concentrate on the things you *can* change."

She buried her face in his chest. "Oh John, how did you do it? You cried for days after Neal died, yet you were able to carry on. Why haven't I been able to cope, to get the pain out of my system?"

John looked down at the papers he was holding and rolled them up restlessly. "Long ago I learned the best method for me to deal with pain was to write about it. My poetry has been my vehicle of expression. Once I've written about the pain, I'm able to deal with it." He kissed her cheek. "I haven't needed to write about Neal's death, because I had already written about it. Over fifteen years ago. For a long time after Amy left me, I was seriously depressed. One day I was thinking about how lonely and depressed I felt. I was sure my depression was only temporary, that if the right woman came along, it would go away. I was right, because you came into my life and gave it meaning.

"But at the time I thought about the people who suffered permanent losses, like a loved one. How would they start laughing again? With those thoughts running through my head, I wrote a poem. I couldn't possibly have known back then that part of it would really happen."

He held up the papers in his hand. "I have a copy here. While I take Mary to the mall and to the library, please, read it. Afterwards, think about doing something *positive*. Get involved in something— something our son would be proud of. I'm sure he's terribly sad seeing you in such pain. He wants to give you back your laughter. Please...take it, Jane, share your laughter again with Mary and me. We need it back almost as much as you."

He got up and kissed her forehead. "No matter what, in sickness and in health, I'll always be here, loving you with all my heart. We're a family and, as hard it may be, God wants us to face up to our problems and work on them together. She's waiting to give you the strength to carry on and live your life without Neal. Read the fortieth psalm—it's so clear there, you'll feel it happening."

After her husband and daughter left, Jane unrolled the papers and read the contents.

WHERE DID THE LAUGHTER GO?

I can remember meeting her and saying, "With her, I'll do it right."

We would talk and laugh at the crazy things we'd say.

I felt so secure with her as we shared our vulnerable thoughts and became such intimate friends.

I hoped I was doing it right as my laughter was turning to love.

My heart sang with joy when I heard her voice the night she unexpectedly called.

But how my heart and life collapsed when she said we should stop seeing each other.

The pain was not new, but this time the laughter was gone.

Did she forget to give me back my laughter when she said good-bye?

Where did the laughter go?

I remember seeing the little boy laughing with his brother and sister as their parents packed for the flight.

As the baby of the family he required a special love.

His laughter and joy seemed fueled by the love and attention that flowed from his parents.

He purposely stayed close to his parents when he needed that extra dose of love and affection.

With a hug and kiss he said, "I don't need a present, I only need you."

But when a tearful aunt told them what had happened he became so confused.

Now he plays quietly without the sound of laughter.

Did his parents need his laughter to help soften their crash?

Where did the laughter go?

I remember the father laughed as he watched his daughter joke with her brother.

His pride for her seemed to climax the day she wore her cap and gown.

How he loved her bright smile highlighted by her mother's eyes.

She had matured with a look that clearly said, "It's my time to live."

As she drove off with her friend he realized that daddy's little girl
was now a woman.
But after a knock on the door, a policeman said his daughter
was never coming home again.
Now he spends more time lost at work where there's no need to
laugh.
Did she need to take his laughter to comfort her in the car that
night?
Where did the laughter go?

I remember the mother laughing and playing with her baby
before putting him to bed.
For nearly a year and a half he had filled her life with constant
joy and laughter.
She was lucky to have a baby so late in life.
Since she was a child, she had hoped and prayed to be a mother
to such a child.
How she loved waking in the morning to see him smiling in the
crib.
But how her body was gripped with a sickening horror when she
saw her child lying so blue and still.
Now she hardly leaves the house 'cause she can't face a world
with joy or laughter.
Did he need her laughter to take with him when he took that
last breath?
Where did the laughter go?

Every night when I lie down and pray.
I ask for strength and courage to make it through the day.
Why God, did you allow the laughter to go away?
I have laughed again, but it's not as it should be.
It feels so hollow, like there's nothing inside of me.
Will true laughter grow in me again someday?
Or are fading memories of my love the price I have to pay?

But what of the mother, father, and little boy?
Are they still living a life without joy?
What can they do to take away their pain?

How can they find their laughter when their tears still fall like
   rain?
Tonight, I'll say a prayer around eleven.
Please God, send their laughter back from heaven.

Tears streaming, Jane buried her face in her pillow, her anguish
swelling to a howling cry. Pain poured from her and, in the end, she
permitted herself to think about Neal being safe in heaven.
Remembering what John had said about the fortieth psalm, she rolled
over on the bed and picked up the Bible.

PSALM 40
Gratitude and Prayer for Help

I have waited, waited for the Lord, and he stooped towards me
   and he heard my cry.
He drew me out of the pit of destruction, out of the mud of the
   swamp;
He set my feet upon a crag; he made firm my steps.
And he put a new song into my mouth, a hymn to our God.
Many shall look in awe and trust in the Lord.
Happy the man who makes the Lord his trust; . . .
. . . may all who seek you exult and be glad in you,
and may those who love your salvation say ever,
"The Lord be glorified."
Though I am afflicted and poor, yet the Lord
thinks of me.
You are my help and my deliverer;
O my God hold not back!

She read it three times. Each time sensing the weight of her sorrow lessening lighter. She remembered how John had advised her
cousin Sally to find a discussion group to help in her grief over Doug's
death. Perhaps she, too, could find a bereavement support group.
   She put the Bible back and picked up the phone. Calling the hospital, she learned there were grief-counseling meetings every other
Tuesday.
   She knew she would be at the next one.

She started thinking about what she could do in Neal's memory to bring happiness to others. While her mind busily considered different ideas, she got out of bed and during her shower she made her decision. She was sure Neal would be proud of his mother, and now she was determined to carry it through.

After sharing three slices of pizza and milk, John and Mary wandered around the mall, observing the activities. They approached a kiosk selling personalized newspaper headlines. The last twenty years of the *Boston Globe* or *BostonHerald*. Curious, John examined some samples. "Any headline I want?" he asked the young woman.

"That's right. We print the headline and two sentences detailing it, then end up with 'Cont. Page 2'."

"That sounds neat. I think I'll try it. But I have to figure out what I want to say." He sat on a bench with Mary. She squirmed and looked around while he thought and wrote. Ten minutes later he handed the woman a slip of paper. "Can you make it the *Boston Herald*, dated August 8, 1989?"

She read the slip and her face flushed. "Is this...true?"

"Partially. It applies to only two of the numbers."

The young woman laughed. "I guess that makes sense." She typed the information into her computer. A short time later Mary watched spellbound as the newspaper came out of the printer.

As John paid the woman he said, "You should try it. Get two friends together and play your numbers."

She chuckled as she gave him his change. "I just may do that."

"Only make sure one of you doesn't have more than forty-two if you do it in Massachusetts."

The woman laughed. "I certainly hope that won't be a problem."

They had returned home and discovered Jane was out. Mary had fallen asleep riding in the car, but didn't want to go to her room to finish her nap. Instead she got out her Amelia Bedelia book and sat on her father's lap. After reading it to her father from memory, it was time for *Mr. Rogers*.

Before long Jane returned home. "You two look comfy," she said in good cheer, as she entered the living room. "Can I join you?"

She sat down on the couch close to them and Mary slid off John's lap and climbed onto Jane's.

Feeling left out, John moved next to his wife. "You're looking a lot perkier. The fresh air must have done you good."

"That's not all. I've done some really positive things for myself. You know how I've always wanted to do something for women who've chosen not to have an abortion, but to give their babies up for adoption? I thought about what you said this morning and I decided it's time to actually *do* it. I went to a realtor and told her what I had in mind—and guess what? I think I've found a house where pregnant single women can live safely before giving up their babies.

"It has ten rooms, five of which are bedrooms. I figured if two women shared a bedroom, we could have eight women living there, along with a live-in housemother. Plus, there's enough land around it to build on a four-room addition. That would mean between twenty to thirty babies could be saved each year. Think about how happy those families would be to finally have the baby they've dreamed about but were unable to have themselves."

John couldn't remember when he had seen his wife so excited. She was bubbling over with enthusiasm.

"With the money I receive each year from the lottery, I can more than afford what it'll cost. I've even thought of a name for it: ADOPTIONS FOR LIFE."

While Mary was occupied with Mr. Rogers, Jane and John talked about what could be done to make her dream come to fruition.

When the children's television program was over, Mary got off her mother's lap and went over to the window and looked out at the back yard. Thick clouds had darkened the late afternoon sky and large, lonely snowflakes were slowly drifting to the ground.

"Mommy, Mommy!" Mary cried, running from the window. "It's starting to snow. I saw great *big* snowflakes falling!"

"Is that right?" Jane said, getting up with John and going to the window. "You're right, Mary, it *is* snowing. Do you know what we can do tomorrow if there's enough snow? We can go out and make some angels in the snow."

"Can we, Mommy? I've never made angels in the snow before."
She looked up at her mother with the happiest and brightest smile
she'd had in months.

"Of course we can," Jane said lovingly, beaming as she looked up
at John. "Let's go up to my bedroom window to see where we should
make them." With that the three of them ran up the stairs.

"Where should we make them, Mommy?" Mary asked, looking
out at the increasing number of snowflakes floating down from the
sky.

"Do you see over there?" Jane asked, pointing down to the left at
the lawn. "That's where your daddy and I make ours, so you need to
have your own special place."

"How about near the swings?"

"That would be a wonderful place."

John pulled his wife back from the window and drew her into his
arms, embracing her deeply and warmly, welcoming back the happiness he had so dearly missed.

Jane was delighted that Mary wanted to go to bed early that night.
Even though the child could hardly control her excitement about
playing in the snow tomorrow, Mary was exhausted from not having
had a full nap. On his way upstairs to tuck Mary in, Jane whispered
into John's ear. "I want to go to bed early also and not because I'm
tired."

"Mmmm, I like the sound of that," he said. "But before we do
that, I have something to give you."

"Ooohhh...." she purred, brushing up against him, rubbing her
breasts across his chest. "I wonder what it could possibly be...."

"None of that now," he said, easing her away. "Let me get Mary
tucked in first."

Jane turned away and flopped down on the couch. She was sure
John would ruin things and get Mary laughing out of control, like he
always did when he put her to bed. Then surely Mary would come
alive again, and not want to stay in bed. But happily she was wrong.
After her fits of laughter, Mary settled down and a few minutes later
John came downstairs carrying a rolled up paper tied with string.

"I found this at the library today while going through some old microfilmed newspapers," John said, handing her the paper.

Jane carefully slipped the string off and unrolled it. At first, all she recognized were the words *Boston Herald*. Then the headline caught her eyes: WOMAN WINS LOTTERY BY THE HAIRS ON HER BREASTS." Below the headline she read, "You've all heard about someone winning something by the skin of their teeth. This woman won over two million dollars by the hairs on her breasts. Cont. Page 2."

Jane's body temperature rose as she read the story. When she saw the date—August 8, 1989—her blood boiled. Rage in her eyes she glared at John. "How would they know something like this! It's not true! ! *You*! You're the one who thought of that crazy idea."

She was ready to take a swing at him. "Did you tell somebody at the paper your crazy theory?"

"Me? Why would I do something like that?" John laughed innocently.

She knew that laugh—it indicated guilt. "Because you have a sick sense of humor and you'd do anything to embarrass me. You enjoy seeing me turn red. Tell me the truth. Did you tell this sick story to someone?"

"I certainly did. A woman." John put his arm around Jane's shoulder and pulled her closer. "Don't worry, my love, she works in the mall kiosk where they create personalized newspaper headlines. I *had* to tell her in order to get this printed."

Relief cooled Jane's face, as she realized it was only a joke and not something for the whole world to see. "So when did you have this made?" she asked.

"Today—when Mary and I went out. I thought you needed a good laugh."

"Laugh. Do you see me laughing? I suppose Mary now knows this and she'll tell all her friends."

"She only knows it if she really knows how to read like she pretends, and going by *Amelia Bedelia*, you may be in big trouble," John said.

Jane, now laughing in spite of herself, said in faked anger, "It's not funny."

"It is funny. That's the whole point. Laughter is very good for healing the body and mind. And from the way you're starting to laugh again, I'd say that you're starting to heal at last.

"If it makes you feel any better, the woman got a real kick out of it. She's thinking about doing it herself with two of her friends. I told her to go for it, but I warned her that it wouldn't work here in Massachusetts if she had more than forty-two hairs."

"You didn't?"

"Sure. Everyone needs some humor."

Jane again tried to fake anger in spite of laughing. "How can you go on letting me suffer in embarrassment believing all your stories?"

"You look so beautiful in your multi-shades of blush. I must be attracted to it." He gave her his weird look.

"You know, someday I'm going to get the better of you. And you make sure you laugh," Jane said, with a twinkle in her eye. Once more rubbing her body against his, she kissed his cheek where his dimple had been. "I think we're ready to go upstairs now."

While she went into the bathroom to prepare for bed, John carefully took the bedspread off. When Jane emerged, he stood by his side of the bed for a better view. With a customary yank, she pulled back the sheet and blanket. Instantly, tiny hearts, about two inches in diameter, spilled out and around the bed. Jane looked at a smiling, glistening-eyed John.

The hearts had writing on them, and Jane picked one up. I LOVE YOU BECAUSE OF YOUR SILKY HAIR, it read. John's face radiated his unending love for her. With a broad smile she reached down for another, then another.. I LOVE YOU BECAUSE YOU'RE TICKLISH IN THE RIGHT SPOTS, I LOVE YOU FOR YOUR PASSIONATE KISSES.

When she read I LOVE YOU BECAUSE YOU LET ME MAKE BETTER ANGELS IN THE SNOW, she shook the paper heart at him and said in a stern voice, "Now this isn't true. I make better angels and don't you forget it." Picking up more hearts, she asked, "How many are there?"

"Two hundred and twenty-nine, one for each week I've known you."

She went to her closet and brought back an empty shoe box and proceeded to carefully gather up all the hearts. Holding on to one in particular, she put the box on her night table and slipped into bed.

"What do you have in your hand?" John asked.

She snuggled up to him and read, "I LOVE YOU BECAUSE YOU MAKE BEAUTIFUL CHILDREN."

With an adoring look, she told him, "I'd like to try again. I think Neal would like it if Mary had another brother or a sister."

PART TWO

Chapter 16

The years passed following Neal's death. For the Averys—Jane, John, and their two daughters—they were years of blessed normalcy. .

Late one April afternoon, John, in the living room, took advantage of some quiet time alone. Jane was at ADOPTION FOR LIFE's Newton home, and the kids still hadn't arrived home from school. Finished with his warm-up stretching, he began his Jane Fonda video aerobic workout. Before long, from the front door he heard, "I'm home."

"I'm in here," he answered, as he continued to hop and clap. Mary, now a lanky sixteen-year-old, came in. "How was school today, princess?"

"Awesome." Sitting down on the couch she watched her father do his jumping jacks. "Did Mommy say you were getting flabby again?"

"Noooooo," huffed John. "Besides, I don't have flab, I have love handles. I keep them so your mother will have something soft and warm to wrap her arms around when we're in bed."

"Dream on, Daddy....Guess what? We got our history test back. I got a ninety-seven."

"That's great," he puffed.

"I felt that way, too, until I found out Joy White got a ninety-eight."

"It's about time you gave her a break, isn't it?"

Thud. The whole house reverberated from the front door slamming. John's eyes went to the hallway where he saw his twelve-year-old daughter, Patty, breeze in.

"*All right*, Daddy!"

"If it isn't Patty T. What'cha been up to?"

"I stayed after school to play an intramural baseball game. The boys needed a good pitcher." She dropped her knapsack and plopped down next to her sister. "You know, you're not kicking your legs high enough to do any good."

"I've been doing this for years now, and not once has Jane Fonda criticized me. Tell me about the game."

"We played six innings. My team won six to four. I hit two home runs and struck out seven batters."

"Did your nemesis Warren Dezotell play?" Taking the workout tape's advice, John paused for a water break.

"He pitched for the other team. He struck out more batters than me, but he didn't get me. My first homer was a shot over the left fielder. The other should have been a single, but it got by the center fielder. Hey, don't drink the water so fast. You'll get sick."

With the break over, John went back to his exercising.

"Did you hit anybody this time?" Mary asked, a bit sarcastically. Mary wasn't interested in sports the way her sister was. But she often went with her parents to watch Patty's little league games and knew about Patty's famed brush back pitch.

Patty laughed. "Yeah, I still got a problem with the old brush back. I hit Warren his second time up. I guess I got carried away after he hit a home run off me his first time at bat." She centered her attention on her father. "Daddy, you should suck in your stomach and straighten your legs when you do those sit-ups."

"You two can leave if all you're going to do is laugh and criticize me."

"Why don't you watch Mommy? She does it the right way."

"Believe me, when you're both at school and we do this I spend a lot of time watching her. So Patty T, how's science going?"

"Not so good. I think I'm getting a B minus this quarter."

"A B minus? Just because Mary gets all A's like your mother did, I don't want you to be like me and get the grades I did."

"Like you? This will be my first B minus, Daddy. I've seen your old report cards and I'd never have as lousy grades as you. Besides, how could I be like you? I don't even look like you the way Mary does. Luckily, I look like Mommy."

"Well, school was harder when I was a kid."

"Did you hear that, Mary? Let's teach Daddy a lesson not to tell lies." Patty pounced from the couch onto her father's side, rolling him on his stomach. "Grab his legs so he can't get away," she yelled, as she tickled her father's ribs.

"Careful of my left arm," John cautioned, between bursts of laughter. "It hasn't fully healed yet." As usual, he put up only enough of a struggle to make them work hard to achieve their goals.

"Do you take back what you said and admit we work harder than you did?"

"Yes, I admit it." He laughed as Patty determinedly wiggled her fingers deep in his arm pit.

"That's better," Patty said, releasing him.

"For such a scrawny girl you're pretty tough. Thank goodness I only have two incorrigible teenagers to deal with." He poked his fingers into Patty's stomach to add greater emphasis to his next comment. "Thanks to you and the problems you created with your difficult delivery."

"Eeigh," Patty squealed, squirming to get away.

"Okay, let's get serious here," John said, getting to his feet. "I got a call from Marie this morning. She, Stanley, and Hilliard are coming in two weeks to spend the weekend. Boston College has offered Hilliard a football scholarship."

"Does that mean I have to sleep in Mary's room?" Patty moaned. The question was academic; she knew the answer.

"It's only for two nights. Besides, I thought you looked forward to their visits."

"It's not the Ruckers Patty looks forward to the most," Mary said. "It's the black-raspberry ice cream they always bring."

"Ah, there's nothing like Brigham's black-raspberry ice cream," John quipped, with a sly grin. "I'm going to start making dinner. What do you two have for homework?"

"I have to write an essay and study for a Latin test," Mary offered.

"I have a joint science project due in a few days. Mommy said it's okay for Lizzie to come over after dinner so we can work on it."

"That's fine. If you think Lizzie would like to partake of my famous beef soup she's welcome to join us." Culinary art wasn't John's specialty, although, through years of hit and miss attempts he had concocted an extraordinary beef soup recipe.

"I'll call her," Patty said. "When's dinner?"

"Depends on when your mother gets home from Newton. Should be around six." Going to the kitchen, he began cutting up vegetables.

Twenty minutes later the phone rang, and Patty made a mad dash to answer it. Afterwards she bounded into the kitchen. "Lizzie's willing to take a chance on your soup."

Eyeing the big pot on the stove, she lifted the lid and sniffed the aroma of the vegetables and elbow noodles simmering in the tomato sauce and beef broth. "Is it ready?"

"Not yet." Lifting the cutting board over the pot, he dumped the mushrooms in.

"Is there any bacon?" she asked, dipping a spoon in for a taste.

"Do you want it with bacon?"

"Yeah," she said, dipping the spoon in again. "It's really good that way."

"Then I'll do it, special for you." Lifting his wooden spoon, he chased her away from the stove.

"Can you drive Lizzie home at 9:30?"

"No problem. I'll take her on my way to the Samaritans. I'm doing an overnight shift."

"Don't you ever get tired of being a Samaritan? It sounds so boring. Waiting up all night for someone to call and say they're going to kill themselves. Yuk."

"I don't have to stay awake all night. I can lie down on the couch till someone calls. Besides, it's rare for a caller to be in the actual act of suicide. I do it because there's a need to help. You can't sit back and do nothing, believing someone else will be doing it."

He reflected on one case in particular. "I still remember a young woman who called during my first overnight shift." Unlike her older sister, Patty was still at the age where she idolized her father. She sat down willingly and listened as he gave her a full account.

"She was crying hysterically, begging for someone to commit her to a mental hospital. She had recently separated from her husband

and could no longer cope with her life and the pending divorce. For months she'd no one to talk to about her feelings. No one bothered to take the time to ask her how she was doing.

"I knew I hadn't solved her problems that night, but over an hour later, when she had finished talking, she was more in control of her emotions, believing she had a glimmer of hope. I never knew what happened to her, but to this day I believe I made a difference in that woman's life. Volunteering as a Samaritan isn't glamorous work, but it has its rewards."

Patty stretched up on her toes and kissed her father's cheek. "I'm proud of you, Daddy. Someday, in my own way, I hope I can make a difference like you."

"I hope you do. I certainly don't want you to go through life believing there are already enough people helping the less fortunate, because there's not. Each one of us has to make an effort to help others and to follow through on that commitment. But first you have to go and do your homework."

"Okay." She headed for the hallway, stopped, and turned to her father. "By the way, I agree with Mommy. You do have great buns." Laughing, she ran out of the kitchen.

"You better believe I do," he yelled back to her, as she scampered up the stairs. Chuckling to himself, he went to the refrigerator to find the bacon.

"I smell something good," Jane said, walking into the kitchen.

"It's Daddy's famous beef soup."

"Mmmmm, yummy. But what I really need right now is one of Daddy's famous hugs."

Wrapping his arms around Jane, he noticed her eyes were puffy with a hint of red. "What's wrong, honey? Didn't things go well in Newton?"

"Yes, everything went fine," she answered. Having to talk about it nearly brought a new wave of tears. "I don't know what happened. I was driving home and I started thinking about the way things have turned out. I don't even know if I was crying happy or sad tears.

"Susan has definitely decided to keep her baby. She and the baby's father plan to get married after he graduates from high school in June. Susan was really happy to know we'd let her stay at the home until she delivers the baby next month."

"Well, Susan sounds like another success story to me. You should be proud of yourself. Through your direction and efforts, ADOPTIONS FOR LIFE, with its three homes, has grown to national renown. And with nineteen women currently waiting for the births of their babies, I think it's terrific that you've convinced them to focus on their futures by insisting they continue going to school or working."

"You're so sweet," Jane said, kissing him on the cheek. "But there's something else I was thinking about. It's Neal. Do you think it was God's will to take his life so I would save many others?" With her finger, she wiped at a tear trickling down her cheek. "Like maybe this is my hymn to our God?"

Chapter 17

Sunshine poured through the open kitchen window as Jane prepared breakfast. Outside the birds chirped and squabbled as they jockeyed for position around the feeders, a constant reminder to *John's* mourning dove from years ago. The spring air, fresh, clean, and soft, intoxicated her. Even the hardiest New Englanders appreciated May after yet another mean Yankee winter. Except for John's absence, it was a perfect morning.

The stairs of the old house shook under Mary's thundering footsteps. She sprinted into the kitchen, heading for the cabinet to get her Cheerios. "Morning, Mommy. Where's Daddy?"

"He's not feeling well. He coughed most of the night and feels like he has a fever. You know your daddy when he thinks he's coming down with something."

"Yeah. Good old daddy and his bed-rest doctrine."

A proud grin came over Jane's face as she sipped her coffee and studied Mary, who was definitely more animated than usual this morning. "Big day today. Are you excited? You're not worried, are you?"

"I may have blown my finals. You know how I am about exams."

Jane smiled. Her oldest daughter was a bit of an over achiever. Like all parents, Jane saw some of herself in Mary and in the seeing, liked some things better than others.

That afternoon Mary pulled on the front door. Locked. Digging a key out of her school bag, she let herself in.

"Hey," she shouted, "anybody home to congratulate me?"

Only silence greeted her, so she sprinted up the stairs and gingerly entered her parents' bedroom. The light was dim but she could see her father in bed. He turned toward her as she entered exuberantly. "I did it. I'm the class valedictorian. I beat out Joy White. Isn't that awesome?"

John struggled a bit to sit up and held out his arms. "I'm so proud of you, princess." He hugged her. "I love you very much, not for this one achievement. It's terrific, of course, but my love for you is forever—for *all* reasons."

Mary threw him a puzzled kid-to-parent look. Then she said, "Where's Mommy? I can't wait to tell her."

"She's in Newton. She's taking care of some administrative stuff with a new girl who's moving in. I don't have the energy to slave over dinner, so that will have to be women's work tonight."

"Oh, Daddy, I know you. You love it when you can get us women to wait on you. But *I* can't spoil you tonight, I'm going to Maximus with Paul. An awesome new rock group, the Body Parts, are playing there."

His grunt at the name didn't dim the girl's excitement. She rattled on. "I heard the keyboard player is incredibly cute. I hope Mommy gets home before I have to leave. I want to be the one to tell her I'm the class valedictorian."

"Can you back up a minute, Mary? You're going with your boyfriend to see an incredibly cute guy in a rock band? Is this your idea of being a liberated female?"

"Oh Daddy, it's not like that." Her tone was patronizing. "You wouldn't understand."

"Well, that makes me feel better. Now I can lie here and worry about my own problems rather than trying to figure out how illogical you sounded."

"I'm sorry, Daddy. I didn't even ask how you're feeling." She put her hand to his forehead. The maternal gesture reminded him so much of Jane.

"I had a killer of a headache a while ago, but the Tylenol is beginning to work. I'll live. I've got to, so I can enjoy your exciting days ahead."

When Mary got home from the concert, she dashed up the stairs to her parents' bedroom. Her mother was sitting in bed reading; her father lay with his back to her in his sleeping position. "Mommy, I had the greatest time tonight. The Body Parts are totally *awesome*. Everyone was yelling and screaming."

"Sounds like lots of fun," John moaned, his sarcasm unnoticed. "Was the keyboard guy cute?"

Ignoring his directness, Mary said, "Mommy, you wouldn't believe it. I pushed through the crowd and got right up front. The keyboard player is so *gorgeous*. His name is Ted Santini, and the group's from South Bend, Indiana." As an aside she added, "Daddy, I'll have you know he's a very good keyboard player and singer."

"How did Paul enjoy your acting like a rock groupie, drooling over this Ted Santini?"

Petulant now, she told her father, "Paul had a great time and thought Ted was fantastic, too. Mommy you won't believe what happened—I noticed him looking at me! At *me*!" Mary screeched, then sighed as if she were going to faint.

"What'd you expect?" John piped up with a laugh. "You said you were right in front of him."

"Daddy!" Mary flumped her hands down to her sides.

"She's right, John," defended Jane. "Why don't you go to sleep and let Mary talk to me."

"I'll behave, but I do want to hear about this night."

Jane threw her daughter a conspiratorial look and gave John some love taps on his bottom. "The old stick in the mud has been silenced."

The excited Mary continued. "So whenever he looked at me I smiled at him. And guess what?" Jane waited, paying full attention. "He smiled back. *I thought I'd die!* I would never have thought someone with hair down to his shoulders and a stud in his ear would make my heart pound the way it does. You wouldn't believe what happened during their last song. I thought I was going to die for sure. The song was about falling in love and when-

191

ever they sang the word 'you,' he pointed to me. At *me*, Mommy. Can you believe it?"

"Paul must have loved that," John chimed in, until Jane gave him a reminder—a swift slap to his bottom, given with an extra dose of love.

"I can't wait to tell everyone in school tomorrow."

Jane smiled. "It's getting late, darling. You should be off to bed."

"Ha," John teased. "She probably won't sleep again till next week. By the way. Isn't South Bend where Notre Dame is?"

"Yes.... So?" questioned Mary.

"That's what I thought. Just wanted to know where to send your college tuition payments. That's all."

Once again, somewhat peevish, Mary said, "Just because I've been accepted doesn't mean I'm going there. Notre Dame was never high on my list. You know I'm debating between Wellesley and Stanford. Besides, I would *never* choose a college just to be near some guy. I'm much too smart for that. After all, it's not a rational thing to do when it comes to a good education and my future."

For the first time, John turned and looked at his daughter. He had his familiar expression of unconditional love. "Love isn't rational." With that, he lay back down facing the crucifix on the wall.

"Good night, Mommy." Mary leaned over and pecked her mother's cheek. Then, sliding off the bed, she went over and kissed her father. "Hope you feel better, Daddy."

"Good night, princess. I promise, I'll get better as quickly as I can."

As she turned to leave, he reached for her hand. Pulling her toward him, he whispered in her ear. "I didn't fall asleep the night I met your mother. Just remember though, always listen carefully to what it is God's telling your heart."

Mary smiled down at him. "Thank you, Daddy. I love you, too."

"Is Daddy any better this morning?" Patty dumped her school books on the kitchen counter, paying no attention to her mother's haggard appearance.

"No, he isn't." Jane sighed heavily. "I'm going to call Dr. Lewis this morning. Your father says it's probably the flu, but it's been three days now, and he's getting weaker."

"That's too bad. Tomorrow's our Saturday to serve breakfast and lunch at the food kitchen," Patty said, between mouthfuls of cereal. "I'll have to get someone else to help."

Mary peeked in on her father and ventured a soft, "Daddy? Are you awake? How ya feeling?"

"Morning, princess. Not so good, I'm afraid. Your mother's going to take me to the doctor today. Don't worry, I'll be back in shape by the time your big day comes in two weeks."

As Mary descended the stairs, the hacking cough from the bedroom sent goose bumps down her neck.

Dr. Lewis released his stethoscope and sunk his hands deep in his pockets. "You can put your shirt back on." Apprehensive, hand in hand, John and Jane waited for him to speak.

"You've got pneumonia. Normally I wouldn't be concerned, but with your history of kidney problems I think you should spend a few days in the hospital. We need to conduct some tests, find out exactly what we're dealing with."

A weak and pale John moved slowly as he went to his bedroom to pack. He sat on the edge of his bed, hands on knees, while Jane gathered his things. She tried to hide her worry, but seeing him, she broke down in tears.

"Don't worry, Jane," he consoled, "it's only pneumonia. I don't have any swelling in my ankles, so there's nothing wrong with my kidneys." John knew the swelling would be the last symptom to show up. The others could only be detected with the medical tests he'd probably be given in the hospital. He didn't want to let Jane know the sudden terror he had felt when he learned he had pneumonia. If he couldn't control his own fear, he would never be able to convince his wife not to worry.

On the drive to the hospital, they agreed that after dinner Jane would bring the girls in for a visit. No stranger to hospitals, John settled into his room and the routine. It wasn't long before a nurse came in and drew seven vials of blood. He looked away, making gratuitous wise cracks, as she worked.

That evening, while Jane and the girls were visiting John, Dr. Lewis stepped in and asked Jane to join him in the corridor. The girls exchanged looks, but John kept up a brave front.

Out in the hall, Dr. Lewis, with a directness that came from years of practice, informed Jane of her husband's condition. "John has septicemia. It's a bacterial infection in the bloodstream. We've administered antibiotics and he'll soon be hooked up to a peritoneal dialysis machine to insure proper kidney function."

Jane paled. "He's going to be all right, isn't he?"

"I...don't know. We should know better by morning. It depends on how he responds to the antibiotics."

"Doctor, I'd better stay with him tonight. Can he be moved to a private room? He needs to know I'm at his side."

Dr. Lewis took her hand and squeezed it. "I'll check with the nurse."

John was moved to a private room. On one side of the bed was the CCPD cycler. Three bags of solution hung from an IV rack. From one of the bags, a catheter led to under the blanket where it had been surgically placed in John's abdominal cavity.

A nurse hovered over him, taking and recording his vital signs. To John's right was a large stuffed chair where Jane knew she'd spend the night, close to his side.

There was no change in John's 101.6 temperature. When the nurse had left, Jane moved the chair closer to John and reached over, gently putting her hand in his.

"We should have made reservations with a double bed," he joked. "Tomorrow night you can have the bed and I'll take the chair."

After awhile, his eyes closed. Not asleep, he told her, "I may not be talking or looking at you, but you don't know how much it means to me to have you here."

"You're wrong, dear. I've known from the first night we ever talked

194

on the phone what it means. And after all the years of sharing our love, I could never let you be alone at a time like this." Not answering, he clasped her hand and drifted off to sleep.

Jane also managed to sleep, her arm stretched out, holding on to her husband. Every two hours, when a nurse came in to check on him, Jane woke up. Her tired smile seemed to melt a bit of the nurse's professional stoicism. Once the nurse left, she'd drift off to sleep again, knowing all vitals were stable.

By the time the doctor came to see John the next morning, Jane was a nervous wreck. John's temperature had risen to 102.3. But even worse was his listlessness. He still did whatever the nurses asked, but with only a minimum amount of energy. She hoped it was the medication that was making him more lethargic.

Dr. Lewis put his stethoscope in his ears and listened to John's lungs. Then he took Jane aside. "There's no change in his breathing, and this morning's blood tests indicate he hasn't responded yet to the antibiotics."

"How long does it take before they have an effect?"

"He should have shown signs of improvement by now. The antibiotics are very strong and effective for this type of infection. I'll look in on him this afternoon."

John perked up when Mary and Patty came in for a visit that evening. Summoning up his stamina, he assured them that although it was taking more time than he thought, he was trying real hard to get better. Patty told him how well things went at the food kitchen. Her friend Lizzie had helped her. Since John was so tired, they didn't stay long. As they left, each girl solemnly kissed his cheek. Mary felt his forehead and reminded him about her graduation.

Jane awoke near dawn, sweaty and frightened as if from a nightmare, with no sensation of having slept. Outside the sky looked brighter; a church spire, against a pinkish glow, rose above the lower buildings. She looked over at John to assure herself he was sleeping. She wished she could open the window and smell the glorious spring air and hear the chirping birds. But the strict hospital rules couldn't be violated, so she had to be content with the sterile, antiseptic odors which permeated the atmosphere.

When Dr. Lewis arrived that morning, John was drifting in and out of sleep. He looked over the chart and the results of the latest tests, then said quietly to Jane, "The infection has gained strength."

Jane felt full-fledged despair. "Isn't there anything else you can do for him?"

"All we can do is rely on the antibiotics and keep him on dialysis. Saying a prayer won't hurt."

Jane dropped her face to her hands. The doctor touched her shoulder and left.

On Monday morning, John couldn't eat and had to be fed intravenously. Dr. Lewis remained hopeful during his morning rounds, assuring Jane everything possible was being done. He told her there was still a good chance John would respond to the medication.

That evening Jane kept talking to the non-responsive John. "Remember our trips to the beach after Patty learned to walk? She was fearless. Always heading right for the water. Even after a wave knocked her over, she'd just get...."

"How's our patient doing, Mrs. Avery?" It was Felicita, the Rubensesque, Hispanic, night nurse. Over the weekend, she'd become the most caring of nurses to both John and Jane.

Jane shook her head, on the verge of tears. Felicita had such a maternal, caring manner about her, Jane felt she wasn't all alone in this nightmare. She looked at the concern on the dark, cherubic face, the worried expression prompting Jane to reassure the attentive and car-

196

ing nurse. "I'm praying, Felicita. God will see us through this."

Felicita understood. The brave front, the denial. The dependence on God. She had seen them many times before.

"He occasionally opens his eyes and moves his fingers. But sometimes, Felicita, the only way I know he's alive is by looking at the monitor."

Felicita put her arm over Jane's shoulder and hugged her. Jane wanted to lose herself in the humanity of the gesture.

"He likes it when I talk to him. I can tell by watching the monitor. When he hears my voice, he doesn't have any of his wild fluctuations."

Felicita knew the workings of the heart were extraordinary. If anything could save John now, it would be God and Jane's love. "I'll be nearby," she said. "Call if you need me."

Startled by the presence of someone else in the room, Jane shook herself awake. "Oh, it's you...what time is it?" Jane's eyes instantly focused on John, who was apparently asleep.

Felicita was taking his pulse. "It's a little past six in the morning."

"No, I couldn't have slept for two hours."

Felicita turned to Jane. "I'm afraid he's slipped into a coma. I'll get the doctor and come back."

Jane buried her face in her hands. "Nooo! I didn't mean to fall asleep. Please forgive me, John."

Felicita walked over and rubbed Jane's shoulder. "Don't talk foolish, dear. You're doing more than anyone could expect. In fact, you're one of the bravest women I've seen."

"I'd better call my daughters." Jane reached for her pocketbook and fumbled through it, muttering, "I should have prepared them for this."

"I'll be back," Felicita said, walking out of the room.

Alone, Jane turned to John and sunk her head on his chest. "Why God?" she moaned. "Why aren't you here when we need you? It's too much for me to do all alone."

She stroked her husband's forehead. "I need you darling...I need you so much...."

The girls had to restrain themselves from crashing into their mother as they rushed headlong into their father's room. "How's Daddy?" Mary's voice quivered. Patty stared as if frozen with fear.

Jane looked up.

"Oh Mother, what happened to you?"

Jane was a wreck. Matted hair stuck to her tear-soaked cheeks. Dark, raccoon-like circles sunk deep in her eye sockets. Her red eyes were rimmed with even brighter red eye lids.

"It's very bad, dears," Jane said, reaching for her daughters. "He's in a coma...he may...he may die any time now."

"No! You're wrong!" Mary stepped away from her mother.

"Daddy's going to die?" Patty said, rushing to her father's bedside, tears beginning to stream. "Don't die, Daddy. Please don't leave us. Daddy, don't die."

Mary looked at her father and defiantly told her mother, "He's only sleeping. He's going to wake up and he's going to get better."

"I wish it was true," Jane said, approaching Mary. "But the doctor says there's no hope."

"They're wrong!" Mary, struck out and hit her mother's shoulder. "He can't die. He has to see me graduate. He's *got* to get better."

"Daddy, wake up. Please Daddy. It's Patty. Can't you hear me?"

Jane, her body numb, reached out for Mary. "I know how you feel."

"No, you don't know how I feel," Mary cried out hysterically, pounding her mother's shoulders with her fists. "He promised me. He told me he'd get better. He's always kept his promises...always...."

Dropping her arms, Mary shook in uncontrollable sobs. "He promised me, Mommy."

Jane pulled her close. "I know, Mary. I know."

"But Mommy," Mary sobbed weakly. "He promised me."

"Why won't you wake up for me, Daddy?" Patty pleaded, gently shaking her father's shoulder. She kissed his cheek. "It's me, your Patty T."

Reaching for Patty, Jane eased her into her arms where the three of them hugged in a circle of grief.

"Oh, Mommy, it's so unfair. He's going to miss everything," cried Patty. "I haven't even had my first date yet."

"He doesn't *want* to leave us." Her soothing tone seemed to reach the grief-stricken girls. "As hard as it is, we have to believe in God's wisdom. The doctors don't know how much longer he's going to live.

So we must say good-bye to him while we have the chance. Do you understand?"

Mary and Patty looked down at their mother, tears dripping down their cheeks, and nodded.

"Mary, you should be first. What I want you to do is to put your forehead on your father's and think about everything you want to say to him."

Mary gave her mother a puzzled look. "Why do you want me to do that?"

"He'll know what you're saying, remember...? Like when you were a child."

Mary went to her father's bedside and looked down at him, then back at her mother.

"Go ahead, it's okay," Jane encouraged.

Slowly she leaned over and awkwardly put her forehead on her father's. At first she didn't know what to do, but then she reached for his hand and closed her eyes. For five minutes she stayed fixed to her father, her warm tears dropping to his face.

"I love you, Daddy." Lifting her head, Mary kissed her father good-bye.

Then in much the same way, Patty bade farewell to her father.

Felicita had come into the room. "I want to lie with him," Jane told her. The nurse, somberly fighting her own emotions, nodded.

Slipping off her shoes, Jane climbed on the bed, careful not to disturb any of the tubes and wires. With her forehead on his, Jane stroked his face and head. "I know you love me," she said to the silence. "I know you don't want to leave us. I understand, John. I really do. Of course it was worth it. Every minute of it. My life was empty before you."

The girls were in too much trauma to comprehend anything unusual in their mother's behavior. That was until she cried out in a loud voice, "No!...I'm not ready for you to go."

Calming herself, she became subdued. "Of course I don't want you to be in pain."

The room was still. Mary stood, watching. Then she shifted her eyes to the EKG monitor, seeing how erratic her father's pulse was.

Jane put her forehead back on John's and said in a soft, consoling voice, "I will always love you, too."

Softer yet she said, "Good-bye, John Avery."

Hearing that, Mary looked over at the monitor and saw the EKG line go flat. "Oh no," she gasped, releasing Patty to put her hands to her face.

Seeing Mary's stare of fright, Patty looked at the monitor. "DADDY!"

Patty ran to the other side of the bed and wrapped her arms around her father. "Daddy," she whimpered over and over with her head on his shoulder. "Come back! *Please* come back!"

Mary, frozen in disbelief, stood there looking down at her father, mother and Patty. This is all a bad dream, she told herself. Daddy promised me he'd get better for my graduation. But it wasn't a dream. She reached out weakly to her mother's shoulder and gently rocked her crying mother.

The organ at the Sacred Heart Church sounded especially poignant that Saturday morning. John Avery's funeral Mass was about to begin. Bach's "Chorale Preludes" greeted everyone who had ever liked, loved, and still loved John. Waves of otherworldly music penetrated each person's private prayers and thoughts.

A deep silence came over the church—John's body had arrived. Father Kiley walked from the sacristy. Bowing before the altar, he turned, walked up the aisle and greeted the casket, blessed it, sprinkled it with holy water, then covered it with a white pall. He led the procession of pallbearers with the casket, followed by Jane, Mary, and Patty, toward the sanctuary.

Inside the sanctuary, Father Kiley addressed the congregation. "You all have been handed a sheet of paper with two hymns printed on it. We will begin this Mass with the hymn 'We Are Climbing Jacob's Ladder' and end the Mass with 'God Be With You Till We Meet Again'. But before we begin—John had asked me to present this to his wife Jane as a sign of his eternal love for her." Opening a small box, he lifted out a red rose corsage.

"The day of his request he told me Jane had lived in high honor. Since I've known Jane even longer than he, I had to agree. But I didn't give much thought to his words until after his death, when Jane told me *John* had lived in high honor. So I'd like to add, not only is this rose a sign of John's eternal love for Jane, it's also a symbol that they had a most honorable marriage."

Father Kiley crossed the sanctuary and approached Jane in the first pew. "I'd pin this on, but I'm all thumbs," he said in a low voice.

"I'll do it, Father," offered Mary, as Jane fought back tears.

Once Father Kiley made his way back to the sanctuary and stood at the presidential chair, the organist introduced the hymn. As the congregation stood, Jane pressed her hand to her heart.

We are climbing Jacob's ladder,

Looking down at the rose, she ran her fingers across its cool, delicate petals.

We are climbing Jacob's ladder,

As the hymn became a distant serenade resonating in the far reaches of her heart, Jane thought about John, and how he had often expressed himself with flowers.

We are climbing Jacob's ladder,
Soldiers of the cross.

She remembered his proposal to her in that church, with a red-rose corsage. How hard it had been to control the happiness she'd felt.

Every round goes higher, higher,

How could she ever have doubted that she loved him?

Every round goes higher, higher,

Why had it taken a beautiful rainbow for her to realize God's intent?

Every round goes higher, higher,
Soldiers of the cross.

She remembered her excitement to see him, to tell him about the rainbow and its revelation. Of her love for him....

Brother, do you love my Jesus?

She remembered the beautiful orchids in the greenhouse. He'd told her the delicate orchids didn't compare to her beauty.

Brother, do you love my Jesus?

Then there was the vacation lunch that John had prepared for her on the beach in St. Martin.

Brother, do you love my Jesus?
Soldiers of the cross.

He had surprised her by pulling out an orchid and positioning it over her left ear.

If you love him, why not serve him?

He had loved to see flower blossoms in her hair.

If you love him, why not serve him?

In their yard on warm spring afternoons, he'd pick off individual lilac blossoms and sprinkle them in her hair as they walked.

If you love him, why not serve him?
Soldiers of the cross.

Every spring he'd start seeds in their basement... Suddenly Jane realized the music had stopped and her ethereal meanderings were sadly cut short.

Father Kiley stepped to the podium for the eulogy. "I had a chance to talk to John before he died. He didn't believe his death would be an end to his life—rather it would just be a stage of his life. A time of passing from the life we know here on earth to the eternal life we all can have with God and his Son, Jesus Christ. John, of course, was right. That is why we are here, to rejoice in the life John shared with us all and his life that still lives on here with us.

"When I look out at Jane I am reminded of how John's love helped her grow to become a stronger and more dynamic woman. That part of Jane will certainly live on. As for his daughters, Mary and Patty, they will carry with them throughout *their* lives so much more of their father than a few inherited traits. His love will continue to guide them. And when they have children of their own, John will surely live on in their lives. So, as you can see, we are here to celebrate in the continuation of John's life.

"Even before he had children, John was a man who believed that laughter was vital to happiness. For instance, he experienced such joy at camp as a youth, and later in life he gave time and money to support Camp Sunrise, a place for children who suffer from cancer. What he gave them will never be forgotten. Hundreds of youngsters still carry smiles and happy memories of camp with them today. Yes, John's life continues in us all.

"For over twenty years he gave a great deal of his spare time to the Samaritans, a suicide hot line. He tried to encourage the hundreds, if not thousands, of callers to choose life.

"He supported his wife in her efforts to promote life through ADOPTIONS FOR LIFE, a home for pregnant women choosing to give their babies up for adoption. There are many hundreds of happy families who are living fulfilled lives because of Jane and John's continued efforts.

"John's joy and love of life was constant. As a young adult he overcame several bouts of a life-threatening kidney disease. He was keenly aware that each day was a precious gift from God for all of us." A broad smile spread across Father Kiley's face.

"When I think back on some of his antics I can't help but question Jane's sanity. Who can forget the time about ten years ago when Sacred Heart's Parish Council was in need of an Easter bunny to make an appearance at our April Fool's Fun Fair? Who volunteered? One guess. Where he got that white rabbit body suit and those floppy ears, I'll never know.

"But a grand appearance he made, carrying a Santa's bag full of candy over his shoulder, a large carrot in one hand and a bucket of pink carnations in the other. Instantly he became a pied piper as he walked around the parish hall followed by the children. They had to wait patiently while he handed out carnations to every woman there.

"I was sworn to secrecy so it must have been four years before people were convinced it had been John in that outfit. Just like Clark Kent was never around when Superman was, it seemed John was never around when our Easter bunny showed up."

A smile came over Mary's face as she thought about that first year. Even she hadn't realized it was her father at the Fun Fair. Early that Easter morning her mother had entered her bedroom and woke her, saying, "The Easter bunny's downstairs." She followed her mother to Patty's room where they woke Patty. The three of them quietly went and sat on the landing of the stairs where they had watched as the Easter bunny scurried around downstairs with his Santa's bag of candy. Without looking up at the children, the Easter bunny went about hiding candy, saying loud enough for them to hear, "This is a nice low spot for Patty to find, and Mary will have to look up high if she expects to find this one."

Mary realized right away that it was her father in the outfit. But the three-year-old Patty thought it really was the Easter bunny. That was until she watched him go from the living room to the dining room, hearing him talking about his hiding spots. Suddenly Patty excitedly squealed loud enough to be heard throughout the house, "That's not the Easter bunny, that's Daddy."

When the Easter bunny announced in the dining room, "All the candy's hidden, it's time to wake the children," Jane told the girls to hurry and get in bed and pretend they were asleep. After John sneaked in to wake them, they saw him disappear into their parents' bedroom. Then their mother came out announcing, "I think the Easter bunny was here; let's go look and see if he left us anything." The three of them ran down the stairs to search for the candy while John got out of his costume.

Much to Jane's surprise, a special Easter basket for her was hidden on her kitchen chair. They had decided to have pancakes for breakfast that morning before getting ready for Easter Mass. When Jane asked John to get the pancake mix from the cabinet, he was surprised to discover his own hidden Easter basket.

Mentioning the Easter outfit brought tears to Patty's eyes. Her mother, years ago, had decided it'd be nice if they'd take turns planning and hiding their father's Easter basket. Next year was to be Patty's turn again, and she had already started planning the special basket she'd fix and hide for her father. She now realized that she wouldn't be doing it next year or ever again. She'd never known an Easter morning when she hadn't sat with her sister and mother on the landing and watched the Easter bunny go about hiding candy.

A smile came to Jane's face when she heard Father Kiley mention the Easter bunny outfit. That was the year she called John at work a few days after Easter. "John, you have to come home immediately," she'd said, hysterically, "I left the front door open and a wild rabbit came into the house. I'm too frightened to get near it and I'm scared it'll damage the furniture."

John rushed home. "Where are you?" he yelled from the front door.

"In here," she answered from the living room.

Prepared to save his damsel in distress, he carefully walked to the living room, ready to do battle with the wild animal. John never expected to find Jane lounging seductively on the sofa in a Mrs. Bunny Rabbit outfit.

Ending the Mass, Father Kiley stood with the congregation and led them in the concluding antiphon.

"May the angels lead you into paradise;
may the martyrs come to welcome you
and take you to the holy city,
the new and eternal Jerusalem."

The organ began "God Be With You Till We Meet Again," and the people began singing. Jane thought back to the night she was in bed in with John and he told her why the hymn was so special to him.

"God be with you till we meet again;
By her counsels guide, uphold you,
With her sheep securely fold you:
God be with you till we meet again."

Back when John was at camp, the Sunday evening ecumenical service always concluded with that hymn. Leaving the security of the lodge and other campers, John walked alone in the darkness of the Maine woods, with that hymn running through his mind. Only his flashlight beam and his faith in God led him back to his cabin. John had told Jane that night that it was only with God's guidance he was able to find her that warm June morning.

"God be with you till we meet again;
'Neath her wings protecting hide you,
Daily manna still provide you:
God be with you till we meet again."

As the second verse resounded, Father Kiley stood before the altar, bowed, and led the procession down the aisle toward the entrance. The final committal ceremony would be held at St. Joseph's Cemetery. When he came to Jane and her children, he stopped to speak to them. To Patty he said, "Your father has left you a wonderful example." To Jane: "John carries your love with him. His soul is at peace." Reaching over, he took Mary's hand. "I know you wanted so much for your father to be at your graduation, but you must believe God has a reason for everything. Believing that, your father will be with you forever."

"God be with you till we meet again;
When life's perils thick, confound you,
Put her arms unfailing round you:
God be with you till we meet again."

Wracked with pain, trying to understand God's will, the Averys stood together and gave what comfort they could to one another. They saw the world and the people through a veil of tears.

"God be with you till we meet again;
Keep love's banner floating o'er you,
Smite death's threatening wave before you:
God be with you till we meet again.
Amen."

"Good-bye Daddy."

Chapter 18

Jane Avery had set her alarm clock for 5:30 AM in order to get Patty to Lizzie's house before seven. Patty had been invited to go with Lizzie and her family to Martha's Vineyard for the long Columbus Day weekend. But Jane had wakened much earlier than 5:30. Something had disturbed her sleep—a haunting dream demanding interpretation, but only leaving her more confused. It was so vivid, so real.

After showering and dressing, Jane fixed Patty and herself a quick breakfast. On the drive to Lizzie's, Jane repeated instructions to her fifteen-year-old. "Remember your manners, and be helpful."

"Mom, please," the youngster pleaded. "I know how to behave."

Whenever Jane performed her parenting responsibilities she felt John's presence, reminding the girls of their behavior, their attitude, their roles in life.

They arrived at Lizzie's ahead of schedule. As Patty helped Lizzie and her father load the family car, Jane went in to say hello to Beth, Lizzie's mother. "I'm so jealous," Jane said to Beth as she entered the kitchen. "The weather forecast says it's going to be an absolutely perfect weekend, and the island is so delightful this time of year. Most of the tourists will be gone. It'll be like having the island to yourself."

Beth smiled. "That's why Michael chose this weekend. It will be like a second honeymoon for us, but with kids this time."

"I should get away myself. With Patty with you, the house will be so empty. It's hard to believe that Mary's started her sophomore year of college."

"Is she still enjoying Notre Dame?"

"She absolutely loves it, and is so happy there."

"That's wonderful. Can I offer you a quick cup of coffee?"

"No thanks. After the night I had, I just want to go home and crawl back into bed."

"What happened?"

"I had the weirdest dream. I was on a plane, sitting by a window reading a book when I heard a duck quacking. Looking out the window, I saw a cloud shaped like a duck. Then I saw John walking on the cloud toward me. I insisted to the stewardess that the plane turn back because my husband was out there. Next thing I knew I was floating around on that cloud, and I distinctly heard John's voice saying, 'I'm home. Is anyone here?' I woke myself up yelling for him."

"You're right, that *was* weird. Sounds like it's straight out of Stephen King. Do you dream of John often?"

"Not in that way. I didn't even eat anything strange for dinner that I can blame it on. It's been haunting me all morning."

With their packing completed, Lizzie and Patty bounded into the kitchen.

"I better be going now. I don't want you to miss your boat." Jane walked over to Patty and wrapped her arms around her. "Let me warn you about Patty. Don't let her see any hungry children or homeless people unless you want to spend the weekend setting up a soup kitchen. Patty has become determined to save the world from hunger."

With a parting kiss and hug, Jane once again began reminding her daughter how to behave.

"I know, Mother. I'll do everything you said; now good-bye." Patty turned her mother toward the door and gave her an encouraging push.

❖ ❖ ❖

By 7:30 Jane had lowered the shades, slipped off her shoes, and crawled into bed. With her head on John's pillow, she fell promptly to sleep. Soon she became agitated and flailed wildly, her legs pumping as if she were trying to walk. At first she moaned unintelligibly, but then cried out clearly, "Please come!" With her hand reaching for John's side of the bed she moaned, "I can't find you."

Peace returned, and she slept soundly; only soft breathing penetrating the hushed room.

Then suddenly her whole body jerked up. "John!" she wailed. She awoke, damp with perspiration, and scared. The clock read 8:25. Dazed, she looked around the room, convinced John was in the house. She jumped out of bed, ran to the landing, and looked down at the front door. But there was no one. She descended the stairs and checked the door. Locked. She ran from room to room. Only when she came up from the basement, was she convinced she was alone.

Upstairs in her bedroom she opened a shade and looked out. Her eyes focused on the spot where she and John used to make their snow angels. Then her attention wandered to the children's swing set, now motionless. To the left were the lilac bushes John had planted the year they were married. Today they formed a thick wall along the side of the property.

In front of the lilacs was one of John's gardens, now in profuse autumn colors. There were bright yellow and gold marigolds along with the various colored mums she had planted back in August. Sadly she thought, a frost would soon kill everything.

In the distance a lone, fluffy cloud drifted lazily in the bright, blue sky. She thought about her dream of the duck-shaped cloud. As she looked at the cloud, she saw it take the shape of what she imagined to be a duck's tail. After awhile, the wind dissipated the tail, only to have it take the shape of webbed feet. Engrossed in the cloud's metamorphosis, she watched as it continued to drift toward her. Now a long, narrow part of the cloud started to separate from the main body. For an instant she saw a perfect duck's head, complete with a blue sky hole for the eye. "That's it," she shouted. "He's coming."

Dashing to her dresser mirror, she pulled off the old knit jersey and jeans and rummaged through her drawer. Tossing bras and panties on the bed, she began sorting through them, wondering which he'd enjoy most. From the closet she chose a verdant, tropical wraparound skirt. She remembered how he constantly tried to unwrap it to see what was underneath. After rifling through another drawer, she chose a sheer, floral, stretch camisole top, a bit too revealing she thought, but this was a special occasion. Braless, she blushed as her erect nipples protruded against the tight material. A pair of green satin tap pants under the skirt would be the finishing touch.

Back at the mirror, she undid the elastic, freeing her ash-blond hair, now streaked with silver. She vigorously brushed it back to life, avoiding hair spray, knowing how John liked the silky, natural feel. She accented her eyes with a touch of makeup. A dab of lily-of-the-valley perfume applied to her pulse points and she was ready.

At the stairs, she looked down. He wasn't there. Disheartened, she slowly descended. She checked the living room. Empty. Then to the front door, still locked. She released the catch, opened the door, and stepped outside. An inspection up and down the street revealed nothing. It was deserted. She went back inside, closing the door behind her. Sadly, she searched the downstairs all to no avail.

She settled in the living room with a book to wait for him. But she couldn't concentrate as reality began to set in and tears filled her eyes. What a foolish woman she was. The dead don't visit the living. With defeated hopes and dreams, she went upstairs to cry in the sanctity of her bedroom.

At the window, she didn't see any special spots, only clear blue sky. No cloud shaped like a duck. No John walking toward her, waving. Her head throbbed from all her tears. Crawling back on her bed, she collapsed. With her face buried into John's pillow, she cried, "Oh God, I'm *so* lonely."

Whether it was God's answer or not, she began to come out of the emotional turmoil, and a kind of calmness took over. Hours passed as she relived her memories with John and their times together. A blessed, mellow feeling filled her with contentment.

Then it happened—a strange noise. Ears perked, she lifted her head. The clock read 1:03. From downstairs she heard a loud, familiar voice. "I'm home. Is anyone here?"

Jane leapt from the bed and ran to the landing. There he was, just inside the front door. "Is that really you?" she cried.

"Well, by the look on your face I'd say that plain Jane has a gas pain."

"Ahhhhh. It is!"

She raced down the stairs and flew into his arms with such force that, if he had been only a ghostly vision, she would have damaged the front door. In between a swarm of kisses, she squealed with delight, "I knew you were coming today. The dream was so real."

John returned her kisses. Seeing her red, puffy eyes, he pulled back. "I know crying eyes when I see them."

"Don't worry about my eyes. They're happy tears now."

He picked her up and gallantly carried her up the stairs to the bedroom. He set her on the bed where she stretched out enticingly. "This is *my* bed now. You have to ask permission if you want to get on it."

John looked despairingly at her. She loved his lost puppy dog look. "May I join you on your bed, Jane Avery?"

There was no hesitation. "Yes. Yes. A thousand times yes."

John lowered himself on the bed and crawled toward her like a stalking cat. When he found the spot from which to maneuver, he reached out and delicately caressed her face. Her warm green eyes beamed, radiating her unending love. "You're so pretty," he said. "I've missed you so much."

Jane couldn't believe he was really in her arms. "What's heaven like?" she asked.

He traced his fingers across her lips, leaned over, and pressed his own to hers, soft, moist, and loving. "I'm sorry. I can't tell you. Please, for the short time I'm here let's pretend nothing has happened to me."

He ran the back of his fingers across her smooth skin. Stopping occasionally, he kissed a favorite spot.

Unable to hold back any longer, Jane's body trembled with a burst of tears. "But Neal...I have to know about Neal."

John knew he had to tell her. "Do you remember in the doctor's office, the day he died? Remember how happy he was showing off how he could sit up."

Jane listened carefully, nodding, happiness filling her heart as she recalled that moment.

"Well, that's how he is. He rejoices at being with God."

"Ohhhhh," cried Jane, sinking her face into John's chest. Her baby was safe and happy with God. With sobs of joy she thanked the Lord.

John held her tight in his arms until she quieted down. He was now ready to make her feel wonderful. Holding her tight, he rolled back and forth saying over and over, "You look so good. You smell so good. You feel so good."

Unprepared for such an emotional outburst she yelled, "Stop it. We're going to fall onto the floor."

He stopped. "I just wanted to make you feel good."

"I wouldn't feel good crashing onto the floor. It'd make me angry."

Reminded of their private playfulness, he looked down at her breasts. Then he caressed them, lingering on each erect nipple. "I've never known you to be so angry," he murmured.

"Oooooo," she cooed, squirming in pleasure.

"I remember this skirt. As I recall, I only have to undo this button here and then this one." His fingers worked the buttons free. "You never knew how excited I'd get wondering what you had on underneath."

He lifted the skirt off her legs, revealing the final part of Jane's special transformation. "Oh what gorgeous tap pants." With his hands back on her breast he admired the revelation. Slowly his hand progressed down her tummy and over the silky fabric of the tap pants. His lips trailed kisses across her cheek. His wet tongue slowly worked its way in and around her ear. He blew a deep steady breath of warm air in her moist ear. Jane squirmed wildly. "You know what I've always enjoyed about tap pants. They're so silky smooth to touch on the outside and they're so easy for my hands to get inside."

Jane heard little of this—she was in another world. "Oh my," she gasped, as he began to rub her moist body.

"Do you know what I miss..."

Chapter 19

Stirring from her night's sleep, Jane reached for John and found only sleep-warm sheets. Heartbroken, she realized he was gone. Opening her eyes, she was greeted by bright sunshine. It had been his eleventh visit in the past nineteen years. Each one lasted no longer than a day—sort of like a one-night stand, she kidded herself. She had tried to fight off sleep, but once again had failed.

Going to the window, she looked at the sparkling blanket of new snow. Only a few hours earlier, before going to bed, she had stood there with John, his arms wrapped around her as they had watched the snow fall. The scene was New England rustic, clean and innocent.

Enchanted by her thoughts, she hadn't noticed the paper taped to an upper windowpane. Now she pulled it from the window and found it to be a poem from John, titled, "Angel in the Snow." Thrilled, she began to read it.

"From the bedroom window I gaze at freshly fallen snow.
It looks as if God has come to make all things pure below."

She paused, reflecting on the scene he must have been describing. Remembering the fun they had making their snow angels during the height of last night's snow storm, she looked down to the left. At first she saw only a solitary angel, but then, upon greater scrutiny, she saw the faint outline of two snow-covered angels.

Compelled by a sudden urge, she got dressed. She must make another angel next to John's. Though the years had slowed her step, love still guided Jane with the enthusiasm of a young woman.

Outside, the crisp wintry air bit her cheeks. It was a chill she hadn't noticed last night when her heart was afire as she frolicked in the snow with her love. Making her way to John's angel, she stood beside it. Not daring to fall straight back like she used to, she gingerly dropped to her seat and leaned back into the snow. Little wisps of frozen breath formed and evaporated as she looked up at the crystal clear, blue sky. Carefully she patted the snow, an important step in her creation of the perfect angel. Then, slowly moving her arms and legs, she created the sweep of the wings. With a rocking motion of her head, she was finished.

Now came the hard part. Her doctor had warned her not to exert herself; after all, she didn't have her youthful agility. Getting up without ruining the angel would be a challenge, but she managed to get to her feet with only a minimal amount of damage to it. Bending over, she brushed the angel's wings back to perfection, then stepped back to admire their snow angels. Her look of satisfaction soon turned to tears of sadness. She knew she wouldn't live long enough to see John again—at least not in this world. But with another thought, her face came alive with a big grin. She scooped up a handful of snow and looked around, wanting to see John. Seeing no one, she looked up at the sky. With a loud shout, she threw the snow high in the air. "I still make better angels than you, John Avery." Laughing to herself, she skipped back inside.

Jane hurried to finish her breakfast of tea, toast, and raspberry jam before Mary and her family arrived.

She had cleaned up and was applying lotion to her hands when the doorbell chimed. Opening the door, she had to brace herself for the exuberant charge of her eleven-year-old granddaughter Betsy. "Grandma, Grandma!" Betsy shrieked, giving Jane an almost crushing hug.

"Betsy, for heaven's sake don't bowl your grandmother over," Mary said.

Mary's husband, Ted, stood by the door coaxing their twelve-year-old son, Tucker, to get out of the snow. "Hi Jane. How are you feeling?"

"Wonderful, now that you and my grandchildren are here. Come in out of the cold and I'll fix you a cup of hot tea."

"I'll be in shortly. First, I'm going to have Tucker use up some of his energy by shoveling your walk."

"Are you feeling okay this morning, Mother?" Mary asked, as she watched Jane's slow shuffle to the kitchen. "You seem overly tired."

"I'm fine. I just don't have the energy I used to."

"Your cheeks are red. You haven't been outside making snow angels, have you?" Looking out the window, Mary checked the usual spot. Seeing the images in the snow, she turned back. "Mother. You *know* you shouldn't do that."

"Mary, I've been making snow angels every year I've lived in this house. And I'm not about to stop now."

"Oh, Mother." Ever the worrier of the family, Mary took her mother's hand. "What am I going to do with you? You've always been so independent." Then patting her mother's hand, she added, "I guess that's one of the things I admire most about you."

Over tea, Jane's eyes wandered around the familiar kitchen. Memories lurked everywhere. Her eyes came to rest on her intent looking, serious daughter. "You know, Mary, it won't be long before I go to be with your daddy and Neal."

"Mother, please don't talk like that. You're going to have many more good years with us here before you go off to be with Daddy."

"As long as God wills," Jane murmured.

"Why don't you go up and take a nap for awhile? I'll be here all weekend, so we'll have plenty of time to talk." Jane hesitated. "*Please.*"

In her room, Jane went to the window and smiled. The angels were how they should be, side by side. Remembering John's poem, she picked up the paper and sat in her rocker.

After Tucker and Betsy finished organizing their things, they were ready to explore. Going to their grandmother's room, they saw her sitting by the window. "Can we come in, Grandma?"

"Of course, my darlings. I love it when the two of you visit me."

Betsy was struck with concern when she saw tears on her grandmother's face. "Why are you crying, Grandma?"

"It's okay, princess. They're happy tears. I was reading a poem your grandpa wrote me."

Meanwhile the hyper Tucker was busy looking out the window. "Hey, who made the snow angels? That looks like fun. I think I'll make some."

"I made one of them," Jane said proudly, getting up.

"You did?" Betsy went to the window.

Tucker was staring down at the snow angels. "Who made the other one?"

"Your grandpa."

"Come on, Grandma. You can't fool me. Grandpa died before I was even born."

"That's true, Tucker." Jane turned and looked toward the hallway. "If you two can keep a secret, I'll tell you something very special." Both kids nodded. In a low voice Jane said to them, "Your grandpa comes to visit me sometimes. He was here last night. He's a very special man."

"Which angel did he make?" asked Betsy, authenticating Jane's startling revelation by the innocence of her question.

"Which one do you think? He always claimed he made the best angels."

Betsy stared, taking her time, giving her decision serious consideration. "I think the one on the left is better."

"No, I think it's the one on the right," countered Tucker.

Jane looked from one grandchild to the other as they anxiously awaited her answer. "His is the angel on the left. He makes a good angel for someone who'd be seventy-six years old. Don't you agree?" The kids swapped looks. Betsy's expression showed more belief than her brother's. "Would you like to hear the poem he wrote me?"

"Can we?" exclaimed Betsy.

The pragmatic Tucker asked, "When did Grandpa write it?"

"I don't know. I discovered it this morning taped to the window. So maybe he wrote it very recently."

The children sat at the foot of her rocker while Jane got out her glasses, Tucker found it difficult to sit still until his sister admonished him with a poke to the ribs. Jane grinned at the familiar Avery gesture. "The poem's titled 'Angel in the Snow'."

"From the bedroom window I gaze at freshly fallen snow.
It looks as if God has come to make all things pure below.
With clear blue sky and bright sunlight,
The snow sparkles like diamonds scattered everywhere in sight.
The swings in the yard look frozen in time.
Waiting for our grandchildren come the springtime.
With my wife at my side I hear her say,
'This is a wonderful opportunity to go out and play.'
Holding her close I brush my hand through now silvered hair.
Then we bundle up to go out in the cold fresh air.
Slowly we take a walk down the snow field of a street.
The dry powdery snow almost flying from our feet.

Then to our backyard still hand in hand we go.
To our special spot where we make angels in the snow.
Lying down we move our arms and legs in slow rotation.
Carefully stepping away, we stand to admire our creation.
As usual she insists hers is better and looks more real.
I tell her she's wrong 'cause I know what's ideal.
To prove her point she throws snow in my face.
Then with a scream of laughter she runs as I give chase.
Later she lies down on our bed for a rest.
Still laughing and so proud that she is the best.
I get under the comforter to lie at her side.
We laugh as I reminisce about things we confide.

With endless enthusiasm she talks of things yet to do.
When she closes her eyes I kiss her and whisper, 'I do love you.'
She just smiles and slowly falls asleep in my arms.
I'll always treasure how she expresses her love-charms.
God has blessed me with a lover and best friend for life.
Silently I leave the bed for the window, not wanting to disturb my wife.
Seeing the angels in the snow, I smile knowing the truth.
She always made better angels in the snow, even in our youth.
I glance back at her still in a peaceful sleep that so endears.
Looking as lovely as ever after all these years.
Thank you God for making my life fuller than anyone could know.
For the life I share with this angel in the snow."

The room remained silent. A radiator hissed and a pipe clanked somewhere in the old house. "That was so nice," Betsy said.

"I agree. Your grandpa never concerned himself with good poetic form. He only tried to express what he felt inside. And this poem, 'Angel in the Snow,' is his finest accomplishment." She reached down and caressed her grandchildren's downy-soft cheeks.

Tucker broke the silence, obviously thrilled with the idea. "Did you *really* throw snow in Grandpa's face?"

"Yup. Every time."

"What happened then?" Betsy asked eagerly.

"According to your grandpa, I screamed in laughter and ran away from him."

"Did he catch you?"

"I'd let him. He'd lift me in his arms as I pretended to struggle and yell to get free. Do you know what he'd do then?" The kids' faces turned eager. "He'd lay me down in the snow and start kissing me."

After a moment, Tucker asked, "Why would he do that?"

With a look of pure disgust, Betsy said, "Because he loved her, stupid."

Jane didn't think Betsy's crude directness was appropriate, but she was right. "Yes, he really did love me."

She wandered back in time, the children momentarily forgotten. They stared at her as she reminisced, smiling often. When she spoke again, she said, "I don't know which I enjoyed more, throwing snow in his face or him kissing me."

The room was quiet again. The rocker creaked. Jane pulled her shawl tighter.

Tucker, now in the spirit of things, asked, "What else did Grandpa do?"

Jane looked at them, seeing a little of John in each of them. "He did a lot of special things. Your grandpa was a very special man." Looking at their rapt faces, she thought about what would interest them. "Did you know we could pass thoughts to each other without talking?"

"No way," Tucker said.

"Shush up, Tucker," Betsy said. "How, Grandma? How did you do it?"

With a conspiratorial grin, Jane's eyes darted from Betsy to Tucker. "I've never told your mother this story, so it'll have to be another secret. Okay?" They nodded eagerly. "I think your grandpa could do it as soon as he met me, but I didn't believe him. It wasn't until we were married that I could do it." The kids were spellbound. "What we did was press our foreheads together and concentrate really hard. It was as simple as that."

Betsy sighed, a wistful look on her face. "I wish Grandpa was here so I could see you do it." Tears started to fill her eyes.

"I know your grandpa wishes he could have met the two of you. I tell him all about both of you and everything you're doing. I show him all your pictures. He loves to see the smiles on your faces. He used to say that people who smiled shared their happiness with others. That made him very happy."

"Do you think I'll be able to find someone as special as Grandpa to marry me when I grow up?"

"I certainly hope so, princess. I was thirty years old when I met your grandpa and he was forty. So you both have plenty of time to find the person God wants you to marry. I often wonder what God would have done if John hadn't caught me that day I stumbled. I'm sure He would have found some other way for us to meet. You know what's really strange? I didn't even see your grandpa approach me on the sidewalk. It was as if he came out of nowhere."

"Wow!" exclaimed Tucker. "Do you think Grandpa was an alien from outer space, with supernatural powers?"

"No, darling," Jane said, chuckling. "But he was a very wonderful man, and we had a deep love for each other."

Tucker had reached his limit of inactivity. Fidgeting, he stood up. "I'm going out to make some snow angels." He looked out the window. "I also want to follow Grandpa's tracks to see where he went. Maybe I can find his secret landing and takeoff spot."

"Wait for me," Betsy said, running out of the room after him.

After lunch, Ted took the children tobogganing, while Mary stayed behind to spend time with her mother.

Sitting at the kitchen table, Mary discussed with her mother the latest developments at ADOPTIONS FOR LIFE. She had taken over as executive director three years ago, but her mother still liked to be kept up to date.

"Do you think you'll have the magazine put together for the printer by the end of this month?" Jane asked.

For the past ten years, ADOPTIONS FOR LIFE had published a semi-annual magazine. It focused on the mothers who had lived at the homes, with updates on some of the six hundred babies who had been born at one of the facilities. The magazine's original intent was to be an in-house information piece, but it soon expanded. It was informing women around New England of the goodness in the choice of adoption.

"I don't think we'll have any problem with this issue. We have some really great articles planned. We're going to write about baby Caitlin and how she's now married and expecting twins. Isn't it amazing, Mother?" Mary paused and made closer eye contact with her mother. "The babies you helped save during your first years are now having babies of their own."

Jane smiled as she thought about Caitlin's birth mother. Back in the early years she had come to know all the mothers so well.

"Then," continued Mary, "we're going to write about the meeting David had with his birth mother last month. I'm going to make follow-up calls to both of them this week, so I can explore the lingering dynamics of their reunion."

Jane nodded her approval. Mary was carrying on her work, and that filled Jane with a special kind of warmth. "I also want to include this year's 'To My Little Baby' Christmas letter."

"That will be nice," Jane agreed. For eleven years now, without fail, a woman had sent the Newton home an unsigned letter. "I wish I knew who she was so I could pass it on to her child. Although," Jane mused, a strand of hair in her fingers, "Maybe I'm better off not knowing. This way I can believe it's a letter every child is receiving from their birth mother. I think she really expresses the sorrow and hope a woman continues to feel after giving up a baby. It seems no matter how long it's been they still feel the need to justify their decision."

Mary nodded and Jane continued. "It sounds like you'll have a good cross section for women to think about. But no matter what we do, it's still a tough decision for a woman to make."

Mary reached across the table and took her mother's hand. "But for some women it's been made easier, thanks to you. I know we're doing the right thing."

Jane looked at her firstborn, her eyes full of pride. "I only hope it's not too much for you right now. After all, you have a busy family to look after. There are times I wonder if you've only taken it over to please me."

"Mother, you must know my commitment is real. How could I be your daughter and not share your vision? Besides, with Ted being a full professor now, it's easier for me to schedule my time."

Jane had her doubts, but nonetheless her pride in Mary was boundless. "Life's funny," she said wistfully. "I bet you never dreamed your long-haired rock star would become part of the Establishment."

"I've always believed in him, Mother. Patty was the doubter. Speaking of my wandering sister, have you heard from her?"

"She called two nights ago to say her foot was fully healed. She sounded frustrated."

"About?"

"No matter how much time and energy she puts into the UN's Sudan relief effort it's never enough. The starvation and dying goes on."

"Has she decided on a date to come home?"

"In about six months she'll be home to stay."

"It's about time. Eight years working all over the world is enough. I hope she's not still in love with that guy. What's his name?"

"You know his name is Kevin Burke. Yes, she still loves him."

"I can't imagine what's gotten into her. For years she's said she'd find a handsome young doctor. So who does she fall for? A reckless Australian bush pilot."

"Now Mary," Jane said, tolerance in her voice, "he's not reckless."

"Of course he is. The only reason Patty knows him is because she was a passenger in the plane he crashed. She was lucky to get away with only her left foot broken."

"It wasn't his fault, darling. The plane had a clogged fuel line. If it wasn't for Kevin's skill they would never have landed safely." Mary looked unconvinced. "There were some important doctors on that plane...and didn't he carry Patty over a mile to safety?"

"A hero," Mary scoffed.

"Now Mary, be fair. Remember how people judged your Ted without really knowing him. It took you to see him for who he really was."

"That was different. This guy is taking advantage of a lonely, pretty, young woman. Patty told me about the lightweight clothes she was wearing. I bet by the time he finished carrying her he knew her body better than she did."

"I'm sure he acted properly," Jane insisted.

"How can you stick up for this guy? Can't you see she's letting him make a fool of her? She's been away from civilization too long. How about all that baloney about his friend, the jewel smuggler. How beautiful a multi-carat diamond and emerald necklace would look around her beautiful neck. Pa...leeeze."

"I thought it was romantic. Your father would probably have done something similar."

"Mother, don't be naive. Can't you recognize a line when it's handed to you? All this stuff about her beautiful neck, her gorgeous green eyes, how scrumptious she looks. Then to give her three carrots dangling from a string."

"Patty loved it. And she said that, from the way she laughs when she's with him, she knows God's telling her he's the one. She's so happy with him."

Sitting back in her chair, reminiscing, Mary said, "She's such a tomboy; she's probably had to settle for anyone who's willing to put up with her. I swear she scared all her old boyfriends away, the way she'd pounce and tickle them." The thought of her younger sister's roughhouse antics ruffled Mary's highly developed dignity.

"You're right about Kevin having his hands full. She challenged him to a home run derby."

"You mean she found another sucker?"

"He should have known something was up when she came out with her bat, glove, and a bucket of baseballs. They were each allowed twenty-seven swings, and she beat him four zip. Patty said her curve was really breaking."

"Knowing Patty, I bet her brush back pitch was working too." Mary smiled thinking about her sister. Getting up, she reheated water for more tea. The talking had made them both thirsty and conversation was so much more insightful over tea. Hadn't her father always said that?

"You don't think she's actually thinking of marrying him, do you?"

223

she asked, sitting down again.

Jane twisted a strand of hair. Her daughter could see her mind turning over. "Well," she began, "I wasn't supposed to tell you this, but on Friday he's going to surprise her and ask her to marry him. He knows where Patty will be at a certain time and he's going to sky write, MARRY ME, PATTY T."

"*What?*" Mary bolted up as though she had just sat on a tack. "How do you know all this if it's going to be a surprise?"

"Well," Jane said, with a tinge of guilt, "he called me to ask permission for her hand."

"He called you? Now I've heard everything."

"He's been calling me ever since the plane crash. When he's lonely and can't reach her he calls and we talk about Patty."

"What a weasel. A phony weasel. Working on you to get to Patty."

"I don't think so. Ted used to call me and we'd talk about you."

This was a day for surprises for Mary. "*My* Ted? Called you? When?"

"When he was on tour traveling around the country with his band. Back when you were in college. The nights you were in the library studying."

Truly surprised, Mary murmured, "He never told me. Never. I wonder what else he's never told me," she said, her tone now facetious. "Wait till I get my hands on him." Without skipping a beat she added, "Why didn't you or Patty tell me?"

"It wasn't a secret, but it wasn't our place. So I asked Patty not to tell you. Kevin has told her he calls me. Can't you see she wants to have a marriage like you and Ted have?"

Mary seemed genuinely surprised. "She certainly has a funny way of showing it," she mumbled. Quickly dropping that thought she said, "But Mother, he isn't even a Catholic."

"No, he's not," Jane said, looking down at the table, thinking to herself. "It's true," she said quietly. "He was always right."

Bewildered, Mary asked, "What's true? Who was right?"

Jane looked up at her daughter. "Your father. At night we used to talk in bed about you and Patty. We'd try to figure out which one of you had our different characteristics. Your father thought you had his physical attributes, and my intellectual and emotional ones, while Patty looked like me and acted like him."

"So what made you think of that?"

"You should know that it's not important what religion a person is. What is important is listening to God. On my wedding night your father asked me if I would have married him if he weren't a Catholic. I told him no. Yet he said he would have married me. Can't you see it's not being a Catholic that makes a person special?"

"But what if they have children? What'll they do about their religious education?"

"I don't know. They'll have to work that out between themselves. God loves us all, no matter what religion we are. If two Catholics happen to marry, like you and Ted, so be it. But if it happens to be a Catholic and non-Catholic getting married like Patty and Kevin, then that's good, too."

Chapter 20

After dinner that evening, Betsy went to her grandmother's room. "Grandma, may I come in and talk with you?"

"Why of course you may, Betsy." Jane put down her book, fluffed the extra pillow next to her, and patted the bed. "Climb up here and get under the covers where it's nice and warm."

Betsy kicked her shoes off, climbed up on the bed, and snuggled against her grandmother's cozy, long flannel nightgown. "Now, what do you want to talk about?" Jane asked, wrapping an arm around Betsy's shoulder.

"Will you tell me more about Grandpa?"

"Ah. My favorite subject. What would you like to know about him?"

"Oh, I don't know. There's so much I don't know about him. And when you were telling me and Tucker about him this morning, it was as if, for the first time, he became real to me. Maybe it was the way you looked when you were talking about him."

Jane gave a nervous laugh. "Goodness me. How did I look?"

"Oh, Grandma. You had the prettiest smile."

"Why thank you, darling. A woman can never get enough of that kind of flattery. Especially at my age."

"You're always pretty, Grandma. But when you were reading the poem and talking about Grandpa your eyes were so bright they twinkled. Did Grandpa make your eyes twinkle when you were with him?"

"I can't imagine my eyes twinkling. It must have been from my tears. But your grandpa always loved my eyes. I certainly hope they twinkled for him."

"Is that what love does? How will I know when I'm in love with the man I should marry?"

"Oh my. Such difficult questions." Jane eyed the ceiling in thought. "Love is so many things. It's a very special feeling that you have about someone. When you're young, things like their looks, their money, or the gifts they give may seem important. They're nice, but you'll find as time goes on they won't matter much. Real love is about respect. How you respect yourself and the person you love when you're with them and when you're apart.

"It usually starts off with simple things like communication, caring, sharing, and trusting. Someday there'll be someone who really cares about you, and whom you care about, too. You'll begin trusting each other and you'll start sharing more of yourselves. Then one day you'll discover you can't wait to share every special moment and thought with him. That's why communication is so important; it brings you so close to the other person."

"When Daddy's at work, he calls Mommy every afternoon," Betsy offered.

Jane reached over and wiggled her finger in Betsy's stomach. "That's a sign they love each other." Giggles filled the room.

"But with marriage there's so much more about love. It's very difficult to live with another person. Think about the times you and Tucker argue. A person can get upset like that with their spouse. So love also has to be about giving, sacrificing, compromising, and the desire to make it work no matter what. It's easy to give to the other person when things are going well. But when you're upset, it takes a special effort. That's why compromising and sacrificing are so important. You both have to always do it fairly so no one has to be the loser.

"But most of all in a marriage, I think it's about always believing your partner is the one God intended for you to be married to for the rest of your life. If you ever find you have any doubts about that person before you decide to get married, then it's probably God's way of warning you he may not be right for you."

"How did you know God wanted you to marry Grandpa?"

"When I first met your grandpa, I had no idea he was the right man for me. It took me a long time before I understood God's message. I thought your grandpa acted goofy and wasn't very impressive. But he wasn't goofy; he just saw a lot of humor in life. He never tried to impress me by pretending to be someone he wasn't.

"With your grandpa it was different. He knew he was in love with me almost from the day we met. I finally realized what God was trying to tell me when I was walking on a beach thinking about your grandpa and I saw the most beautiful rainbow I'd ever seen in my life. I had never known such serenity until that moment, when I realized your grandpa was the right man for me."

"What does serenity mean?" asked Betsy. "It sounds very special."

"It is. It's a wonderful, dignified feeling of calmness or tranquillity you have about yourself. Will you promise me you'll accept nothing less than the feeling of serenity before you decide to get married?"

"I will, Grandma. I promise."

"Don't expect it to happen the moment you meet him. It takes time for the friendship to build along with the trust, caring, respect, and touching that will grow into love. But I want you to be very careful with the touching. Did you know I was a virgin until my wedding night? It was something I believed in very strongly. I know it's very special to God and it was special to your grandpa also."

Jane stopped talking to take some deep breaths. The episodes of shortness of breath were coming more frequently. Looking over at her bureau, she gazed at the family portrait taken shortly before John's death. She hoped she'd live long enough to see her dearest little Patty safely home and married.

"Are you okay, Grandma?"

"Of course I am, princess. I just needed to take one of my oxygen breaks." With a big smile, Jane rubbed her fingers under Betsy's warm chin. "Let me get back to telling you about your grandpa. He wasn't a virgin when I met him. Fifteen years before we met, he had gone out with a woman for over three years. He had expected to marry her, but they weren't right for each other. During the year before we got married, your grandpa knew how I felt about remaining a virgin and he respected and honored my wish."

"I'm going to remain a virgin also. Then I'll marry someone as nice as Grandpa."

"Unfortunately nothing can guarantee you'll marry the right person. But if you can remain a virgin until you're married, it'd be very nice, and it'd make God very happy. And with all the diseases still being transmitted these days from sexual contact, like AIDS and syphilis, it's a smart thing to do.

"Always remember it's important to make sure you only do things that are right for you. Don't let anyone force you to do anything you don't want to. Your grandpa never forced me to do anything I didn't want to do."

Jane let out a short chuckle as she reminisced how she got to know John. Fleeting thoughts of his numerous antics and bizarre behavior crossed her mind. "He was satisfied with acting silly and being a constant embarrassment. I wasn't used to his humor, but as time went on, and I got to know him, I realized how much he made me laugh, especially when he gave me his weird look."

"You mean this look?" With that Betsy made the exact replica of John's, with the half smile, the big dimple, and the winking eye.

"Oh no. Not *you* too." Jane leaned over and gave Betsy a big loving hug. "That's exactly what he did. How did you know?"

"Mommy told me about how Grandpa would do it. Only Mommy and I know how to do it. Daddy and Tucker can't."

"Your grandpa would be really happy to know that you're able to carry on the tradition. He laughed so hard when he saw your mother do it for the first time. It was right before your Aunt Patty was born. It's interesting, Patty never could do it, either."

"Will you tell Grandpa I can do it when you see him again?" Betsy spoke as though this was a certainty. Jane could see that she was a believer.

"Of course I will." But Jane knew deep in her heart that she wouldn't live long enough to see John on earth again.

"That reminds me. Did you see the karate outfit I left on your bed?"

"You left that for me? I thought it was there by mistake."

"No, it's for you. Your grandpa told me it'd be a good idea for you to have it. I'm too old for that kind of stuff now."

Betsy looked up at Jane. "I can't believe it. Grandpa was actually here last night?"

"He certainly was. It was his eleventh visit in the nineteen years since he died. In fact, he lay right here where I am now."

Betsy's face displayed wonder. "How long does he stay? And how does he get here?"

"I don't know how he gets here. He won't tell me. And he leaves when I fall asleep."

"Wow, what do you and Grandpa do?"

"We have a very special time here by ourselves. We spend most of it talking. While we talk, we touch and hold each other. That's what I miss most about your grandpa, holding on to him. When I was younger, we'd get silly and play wrestle each other. And we'd always have a very special time when we made love like we did last night. He's such a gentle man and he knows the reactions of my body so well. But you're much too young to go any further about that."

Jane paused and thought about making love with her husband. A tear trickled down her cheek. "Before he'd leave, we'd lie on the bed with my head resting on his chest. I'd listen to the strong rhythmic beat of his heart while he played with my hair. After awhile, I'd become so relaxed and too tired to talk any more. Then that dreaded moment would come. I'd fall asleep and he'd disappear. How I wish I could have stayed awake forever."

Betsy watched as her grandmother wiped away her tears. "I'm sorry, Grandma. I didn't mean to make you cry."

Jane leaned over and gave the child a reassuring and comforting hug. Reassuring to Betsy, but comforting for herself. "Don't worry about these tears. They're happy ones."

Releasing Betsy, she said in a happier, upbeat voice. "Did I ever tell you why I started taking karate? It goes back to our early days when we'd wrestle. We were never rough, we'd just grab at each other. We'd end up rolling around on the bed or floor tickling each other.

"I always tried to make him admit I'd won, but he was so much stronger and heavier than I, so he usually kept on tickling. It'd drive me crazy. He enjoyed it when he could get me to admit I was angry at him."

"What happened then?"

Unconsciously Jane glanced down at her breasts to check her nipples. Realizing what had happened, she blushed. The child's innocence required an answer. "Why don't we just say I had to show him how angry I was and leave it at that."

Betsy smiled. The evasive answer was sufficient.

"Getting back to my karate. One day while we were downstairs in the living room he was teasing me about something. Your mother and Patty were at school at the time. Patty was probably around your age when it happened. I became really agitated at him, so I grabbed hold of him and flipped him. He hit the floor with a really hard thud. Your grandpa never complained. He just rolled on the floor moaning in laughter, 'Okay, you win.'

"It wasn't until over an hour later your grandpa finally admitted he'd better go to the hospital because he thought his arm was broken."

"You broke Grandpa's arm?" screamed Betsy.

Jane tried to hold back laughter, but failed. "I'm afraid so. But it was an accident. I didn't mean to hurt him. He just got me so mad he deserved it. I felt really bad when I saw him come out of the emergency room with the cast on."

Betsy laughed, admiring her grandmother's abilities. Jane felt a little guilty laughing at her husband's expense. "We shouldn't be laughing; your grandpa might not think it was very funny."

They both stopped, but the silence was short-lived, as Jane burst into laughter again. "We women have to stick together and do what's right, don't we?"

"That's right," replied Betsy. "Sometimes you've got to do what you've got to do, no matter who gets hurt."

Jane wondered if her message of women's strength and independence had gotten through *too* well for this soon to-be-blossoming young woman. She decided to keep Betsy from getting too carried away and let her comment drop. "Do you know what amazed your grandpa about our wrestling? After all these years we've determined that we're tied in who won the most wrestling contests. But pretty soon I'm going to change all that."

Jane looked around as if she expected someone to be listening and leaned closer to Betsy. "Do you know what I'm going to do?" she said in a soft whisper. "The day I die won't be a sad day for me, because the first thing I'm going to do if I go to heaven is flip your grandpa. I won't break his arm or hurt him, but he'll land with such a loud thud he won't know which end is up. Seeing me standing over him, he'll know once and for all who's the real boss. I bet he'll just laugh and moan something like, 'That's how I like my women, tough'."

Betsy couldn't smile; the thought of her grandmother dying was too painful. With tears in her eyes she grabbed her grandmother and said, "Oh Grandma, I don't want you to die."

But Jane had come to terms with the fact that her death was drawing near. "Everybody has to die sometime, Betsy. My heart is getting weaker all the time, so I know my time is coming soon. Don't you worry though, I'll be with God and your grandpa."

"But I want to always see you and have you tell me about Grandpa."

Jane ran the back of her fingers along Betsy's cheek. "Your mother can tell you about him." She gently eased Betsy's soft brown hair away from her wet eyes. "Remember, he was her father and she used to do lots of things with him."

"But I want to know him the way you knew him. With you, I'11 know he still exists."

Feeling Betsy's pending loss, Jane bent over and kissed her forehead. "Oh, Betsy, he'll always exist and so will I. Do you know what you can do for me which may help you feel better?" Jane leaned forward and pulled an old, worn-out pillow from behind her. "When I die will you take care of this pillow? It was your grandpa's and it's very special."

The pillow squished flat when Jane wrapped her arms around it and hugged it. "Do you remember how I told you that we could pass thoughts to each other by touching our heads together? I think your grandpa can pass sensations to me when I lie with my head on this pillow. It has to be true because of what he could do before he died."

Betsy looked at the crumpled pillow, wondering how it could be so special.

"When your grandpa was alive there were times I'd lie here and watch him sleep. Sometimes I'd get silly and want to have fun by influencing his thoughts. So I'd put my head against his and remind him that, as a woman, I was better than he was and deserved to be treated with more respect. But your grandfather always got even with me. He knew he could do something to drive me uncontrollably crazy.

"He had the ability to transmit sensations. First I'd feel soft touches to my ears like warm breaths. The tingling vibrations would go all the way to the center of my brain. Then I'd hear his voice whisper, 'Dum, Dum, De, Dum, Dum.' The sensation of it all would send shivers up my spine. But that wasn't enough for him. In the end, the worst thing would happen. I'd get a tickling sensation going up or down my ribs, or around my neck under my chin, or up and down the inside of my thighs. It would happen where I was least prepared for it. It was impossible to stop it. I'd writhe on the bed unsuccessfully trying to protect myself until I'd finally cry out, 'Stop it! I can't stand it'. And then, just like that it'd go away."

Betsy was spellbound. "But if you knew Grandpa was going to do that, why would you keep giving him those thoughts?"

Jane lay there on the bed remembering those days. Her face glowed by the time her memories were fresh in her mind. "I don't really know for sure. He'd look so peaceful lying there...and I guess I wanted to have some fun. I wanted the attention. To have him make me laugh."

Looking at Betsy, Jane's smile turned into a chuckle. "I just liked the things he'd do to me."

"I never knew you were such a troublemaker, Grandma."

"It's your grandpa. He brought it out in me."

"I think my mommy likes it when Daddy tickles her, even though she denies it."

Jane smiled, thinking back to how Mary laughed as a child when she was tickled. "I'm sure she does. Let me finish telling you why this pillow is special. One night about two weeks after your grandpa died I was alone in bed. The house was silent and the room was very dark. I was thinking about him, and for some reason that silly mood returned. As I lay with my head resting on this pillow, I told your grandpa that just because he wasn't with me any longer he still had to treat me with respect."

Jane gave Betsy a serious look, and with her voice dripping with suspense, she said, "Do you know what happened?"

Betsy felt a chill run up her spine and pulled the covers up to her chin. She shook her head and waited.

"I felt the sensation of warm breaths in my ear. And then that silly 'Dum, Dum, De, Dum, Dum' rang in my ear. My body convulsed as I prepared for the attack. Then it happened."

Betsy pulled the covers to her eyes.

"The tickle attack. It was under my chin. It drove me absolutely crazy until I yelled, 'Stop it! I can't stand it'. And then it was gone."

"Wow!" exclaimed Betsy. "That must have been so scary. I'd have turned the lights on and been too afraid to fall asleep."

"That's exactly what I did. I even went into Mary's and Patty's rooms to make sure they were all right. It doesn't happen every time I have those thoughts. So I don't know when to expect it. More than once though, your mother or Patty came into my room and asked if everything was all right."

"I'd have been too scared to do it again," said Betsy.

Jane lay hugging and admiring the pillow with the warmest smile. "But it lets me know that he's still there, listening to me."

"Marriage sounds like so much fun. I can't wait until I get married."

"Believe me it's not always fun. If it was, there wouldn't be so many divorces. Things happen that you don't expect, and married people start getting upset and mad at one another. The problems can get worse and worse until they reach the point where the married couple becomes unable to resolve them. Your grandfather and I were very concerned about making our marriage work. So the day we decided to get married, we created something that we thought would help us focus on resolving any problems we might have.

"We called it our I'M MAD. ARE YOU MAD? envelope. We each wrote a separate, two-minute spoken answer to six subjects and sealed them in separate envelopes. The subjects were:

1. When I first knew I was in love with you.
2. It was the happiest moment in my childhood.
3. How I enjoy you touching me in a special way.
4. It was the funniest thing I ever saw you do.
5. It will be the nicest moment of our wedding day.
6. We'll tell our grandchildren.

"Then each of us signed a contract stating we agreed to use this method to help us resolve any mutual disagreement. If either person didn't agree to follow this method, then they weren't living in high honor. We put those envelopes and the contract in a larger envelope along with a single die and a two-minute egg timer.

"The plan was, whenever one of us became upset with the other, we'd say, 'I'm mad. Are you mad?' which meant we were to get out our envelope. We'd empty the contents, and the person who had become mad first would roll the die. That person then had to think of and speak about the subject matching the number rolled for two minutes as shown by the egg timer. When that person was done, the other person would roll the die and talk for two minutes about the subject matching their die's number.

"We figured it'd help us feel better about each other, which would then allow us to discuss and resolve our problem. If the person refused to talk about that subject, then their envelope for that number would be opened. I'll admit we used the die many times to help us resolve our arguments. But I'm proud to say we never had to open any of the envelopes. They've remained sealed since that day in October 1989.

"The I'M MAD envelope is in a large box in my closet. The box has JOHN LOVES JANE in big letters written on the top. Betsy, I'll tell your mother I want you to have that box and whatever's inside of it. Maybe by having those things it'll help you know that we exist."

Betsy leaned over and gave her tired grandmother a big hug. "Can I really, Grandma? I'll treasure everything in it forever."

"I have only one condition," Jane warned. "You have to promise you won't open the sealed envelopes until you're at least nineteen. I don't know what your grandpa wrote, but you're much too young to read what I wrote. There's an additional envelope in there that I'm especially worried about. Your Aunt Patty was conceived on the island of St. Martin. We had a wonderfully passionate vacation there. After we came home your grandfather added an UPDATED VERSION #3. I can't believe how thick the contents of the envelope is."

Jane hung her head in silence. Looking at John's pillow, she hugged it tightly. "It's not fair," she said to the pillow. "We were only allowed to give two minute answers."

A moment later she turned to Betsy. "There are two dice in the envelope now. The white one is a good one, but be careful of the blue one. I discovered that your grandfather managed to obtain a loaded die, which causes the number three to come up an unusual number of times. I always had to keep an eye on him. He liked to do things like that."

Betsy had a new interest and couldn't wait to ask. "Grandma, can you tell me what you and Grandpa wanted to tell your grandchildren?"

"Okay, darling, but then you'll have to let me get some sleep." Jane shifted her position and sat up straighter. "We decided I would write about what to tell our granddaughters, while Grandpa wrote about what to tell our grandsons. Although your grandpa insisted that, no matter what, he'd always be there to let his daughters and granddaughters know what he felt was right for them.

"He said he'd tell his grandsons about all the experiences he had had while growing up. To be there to help them survive and learn from life's experiences in the school of hard knocks."

Betsy laughed. "School of hard knocks, that sounds funny."

"That's Grandpa for you. But I wanted to talk to my granddaughters before they had bad experiences. To tell them about important things like love and marriage. Just like we did tonight."

"But you only have one granddaughter."

"I didn't know that thirty-five years ago. I had hoped to have five children, and they would have given me lots of grandchildren. However, you may not be the only one for long. Your Aunt Patty has met a very nice man named Kevin and they're falling in love. Just like your parents, Patty and Kevin have a very special love for each other.

"If they get married, as I hope they do, they'll probably have children. And if they have any daughters I'll have to depend on you to tell them everything I've told you tonight."

"I'll tell them, Grandma, I promise. Don't you worry. I'm going to remember tonight for the rest of my life."

Her grandmother gave a big stretch and yawn. "But now I'm much too tired to talk any more."

"Okay Grandma, I'll let you go to sleep and I promise you, I'll wait until I'm nineteen before I look at the envelopes." Betsy's eyes beamed. Kissing her grandmother goodnight, she got out from under the covers. "Thank you for telling me about Grandpa."

At the doorway, Betsy turned back. "Grandma, tomorrow after we come home from Mass can you show me what's in your JOHN LOVES JANE box. I'd like to know why everything in it is so special to you. Just the two of us again."

Her grandmother smiled. "Of course we can. I'd enjoy it very much."

"Oh, Grandma," Betsy said, running back to the bed. "I love you so very much." Jumping onto the bed, Betsy scrambled to her grandmother's arms and gave her a long, tight hug.

Chapter 21

It had been a long day for Patty, arriving home from Geneva, Switzerland with Kevin two days ahead of schedule. Excited talk and laughter had filled the Avery house, but exhaustion had crept in with the late afternoon shadows. Tomorrow the two had an early flight to New York where Patty would give a speech about refugee hunger to the UN, then back home to prepare for a November wedding.

It was easy for Jane to see first hand the love between the two as Kevin covered his fiancée with an afghan. His smile broadened every time he looked at her. "She's so peaceful. So different from when she's awake."

Kevin ran his fingers through Patty's cropped hair. The look on his face reminded Jane of John. Patty's hair, while practical for Africa, wasn't an attractive style, but Kevin didn't seem to mind. "The moment I saw her at the airport," Kevin said, "I knew I had to meet her. I paid a pilot two hundred dollars to switch flights with me. It was like I heard a voice saying 'She's the one.'"

Jane gave him a knowing smile. "I'm grateful you were there for her on that fateful flight. I understand you plan to continue conducting photo tours in Kenya."

"Yes. It's a great way to combine my flying and photography skills.

Unfortunately it'll take me away from Patty for long periods. So I'm going to investigate doing something similar in Canada or Greenland."

"Greenland. Now there's a place Patty would enjoy. She loves the snow." Jane twirled a lock of her silver hair. "Her father did, too. In fact being an Avery *meant* you loved the snow. Genetics, I guess. She loved to toboggan down a hill called Death Hill. Being the adventurous one, she'd always sit in front with her father behind her. Mary, like me, hid behind John. What a ride. Really got the adrenaline flowing."

"I can imagine. Patty told me about that hill. I also heard about your family puddle days."

"Oh my, not our puddle days."

"The way Patty tells it, it sounded like a lot of fun."

"I hope she told you it was her father's idea. The kids adored his wacky ways. John always understood how to play at a child's level."

Kevin looked at Patty and lightly ran his finger across her lower lip. He smiled when she grimaced and did it again.

"Stop it," she moaned, trying to hide her lips in her mouth.

"It's time to get up. We're all going to bed now." Not responding, he did it again.

Breaking free from Kevin, Patty sat up. "You can be such a noudge."

At the guest room, door Patty kissed Kevin goodnight, then she followed her mother to her old bedroom. "It's so good to be home, Mother."

Jane ran the back of her fingers along her daughter's cheek like she used to do. "I can't believe you're so grown up. You're not my little girl anymore."

"Oh, Mother." Patty wrapped her arms around Jane. "Don't be silly, I'll always be your little girl."

Kissing her, Patty asked, "Do you like him, Mother?"

"Yes. Very much." Jane's eyes beamed for her daughter.

"I keep wondering...you know..." Her mother's eyebrows knitted, "... if Daddy would have liked him."

Jane's eyebrows straightened, her face relaxed. "I know your father would have given his blessing."

Patty's bare legs slid between the crisp, clean sheets. Emitting a luxurious sigh, she stretched her limbs and then went limp. The sheet's clean, fresh scent was intoxicating. An immense grin formed when she looked at the wall. As a ten-year-old, she and her father picked out new wallpaper—dancing bears, wearing pick or blue tutus and matching bonnets. Turning to the night table, she admired the vase full of dandelions. Her mother had arranged it special as a welcome home. She reached for a dandelion and rubbed its soft petals against her chin. Closing her eyes, she reminisced while continuing to brush her face with the flower. Then laying it on the sheet beside her, she reached over and turned off the light.

In the master bedroom, Jane, lying in bed, was filled with contentment. Her baby, in love with a nice man, was safe at home. Despite Jane's failing health, she could see the goodness around her. Tomorrow Mary and her family would arrive for the week. Everything was finally in order. Saying her prayers, she drifted off to sleep.

Jane looked around the private hospital room. She had asked the hospital chaplain on his way out to tell Mary and Ted to come back in. Patty and Kevin had left for the airport when Mary and her family arrived and found her in bed gasping for breath. Admitted to the hospital for observation, She neglected to tell anyone of her recurring chest pains.

Jane convinced her daughter she'd only be resting, so Mary agreed to an arrangement of shared shifts. Ted would stay the afternoon, while Mary looked after the kids.

Later, while Ted sat engrossed in his book, the pressure in Jane's chest returned. Ignoring her discomfort, she closed her eyes and prayed to prepare her soul. She was ready. During her lifetime of devotion to God, she had learned it was His will and not hers.

The extreme pain suddenly vanished. Overcome with a feeling of tranquillity, she sensed someone looking at her. Opening her eyes, she was startled to see John standing at the foot of her bed. But he was different this time; he hadn't aged as in all his other visits. He was even wearing his ridiculous shorts and purple jersey.

"John. How did you get in here with those shorts? You look just the way you did the day we met." She looked over at Ted who was reading his book, oblivious to what was going on.

"What am I going to do, John? I'm sorry, but I'm so weak. It's been such a struggle to breathe. I can't go on anymore."

"Don't worry, dear. Everything's going to be fine. I'm taking you home." He approached her, pulled back the sheet and lifted her frail body in his arms, then turned toward the door. "Are you ready?"

"John, they won't let you. Where are you—stop. Stop!"

Speechless, Jane stared at the mirror on the wall. Tears flowed from her eyes.

"You're so beautiful," John told her, as he looked in the mirror. There they could see Jane, looking just the way she had the day they were married, in her wedding gown. Turning to the bed, Jane saw an old woman with her eyes closed. Wrapping her arms tighter around John, she kissed his cheek. "I'm ready. You can take me home now."

The warm summer sun felt good as John carried her down the hospital steps. "I want to walk with you," she said. "Let me down. Please."

Hand in hand they walked and talked like old comfortable friends. Passing a flower shop, John said, "Wait here. I'll be right back."

She was more pleased than surprised when he emerged with a short stemmed pink rose. "You remembered," she declared, thoroughly charmed. "It's exactly like the one you gave me the day we met."

Slipping his hand inside her gown just above her breast, he pinned the rose. "For my snow angel."

"Ew, you're so good at that."

"At what? Pinning on the rose or slipping my hand in your gown?"

"Both." Jane had a gleam in her eye—a temptress's gleam. "Can you get me a daisy?"

"Why a daisy?"

"Please?"

Going back in the store, he emerged a minute later with a lovely blue daisy. It had long, soft blue petals, and a golden yellow center. He handed it to her and she put it to her nose. She began to walk. "I've

241

always wondered if you really were the right man for me."

She pulled a petal off and threw it in the air. "He loves me." With an over-the-shoulder smile, she continued to entice him. "He loves me not."

"Whatever happened to the timid woman I used to know? You know, the one who never wanted to bring attention to herself?"

"He loves me...." Leaving a trail of petals tossed in the air she told him, "In over sixty-five years of life and thirty-five of them married to you, I've come to know what's important."

Then, pulling off the last petal, Jane sang loud enough for the whole world to hear. "He loves me!" The last petal went flying from one hand and the stem from the other. Leaping into John's arms, she clung to him, arms around his neck, feet dancing in the air. "I knew it! I've always known it. You love me."

At the house, Betsy and Tucker were arguing whether or not Betsy could run for class president next year. They would both be returning to middle school, Tucker in the eighth grade, Betsy in the seventh. Tucker's argument contended that only eighth graders should run. "I can see it now. A wimpy girl trying to push around eighth grade boys for votes."

This was Tucker's fatal mistake. Enraged, Betsy grabbed her brother's right arm and turned into his body, shifting her weight she pulled him toward her. Her four months of karate worked perfectly. Tucker went flying, landing hard on the floor.

Flabbergasted, Tucker thought his sister had only learned to yell "hut" while making funny moves. Now he found himself lying on the floor with his little sister standing over him smiling. Even worse than the embarrassment was the physical pain shooting through his body.

Having heard the thud, their mother came running. "What happened?"

Triumphantly, Betsy announced, "I flipped Tucker to prove to him that I can run for school president."

Mary glared at her daughter. "Betsy, didn't they teach you never to flip a person unless you had to? You could have hurt him."

"Yes, Mother," Betsy confessed, barely hiding an impish grin.

"But Grandma flipped Grandpa when he deserved it."

Mary's glare darkened. "Did she also tell you she broke his arm?"

Betsy lowered her head, wishing she hadn't brought up that defense. "Yes, she did."

"Tucker, I'm sure you were partially at fault. I hope you learned something in the way you treated your sister. I certainly don't want you going through life learning lessons in the school of hard knocks. The two of you have to find a civilized way to settle your disputes."

Betsy started hopping like crazy. "But it's okay....But it's okay," she exclaimed, hands shaking by her face. "Grandpa will be there to help him. Grandma told me last winter."

"Now, Betsy, I don't know what your grandmother told you. And as much as I love and admire her, I find it hard to believe that she really thinks Grandpa is actually watching over Tucker."

"I know he is," Betsy proclaimed. Her feet were planted on the floor now. "I can prove it. Remember how Tucker acted funny going to soccer camp last week? How he combed his hair and wanted his special shorts cleaned?"

"Yes, he was acting a little peculiar. Is there something I should know?"

"No," Tucker yelled, his face reddening.

"Yes, there is," Betsy said gleefully. "And her name is Carol. On Friday, he was playing defense, and she ran by him and scored a goal. She was about to do it again when he tripped her. You should have seen the fire in Carol's eyes as she got up yelling at him."

"Is that true, Tucker?"

"No," he mumbled, to the carpet. "It was an accident."

Shaking her head at her mother, Betsy continued her persecution. "Uh uh, he's fibbing. The best part came in the second half; they were both going for the ball. Carol kicked Tucker on the side of his shins really hard. She just smiled as Tucker rolled on the ground, curled up in pain.

"They were both taken out of the game. Tucker couldn't play because of his injured leg and Carol was ejected for unsportsman-like conduct. They spent the rest of the game sitting next to each other. By the end of the game they were playing and laughing with each other. Why else would Tucker and Carol be friends if it wasn't for Grandpa?"

"That's a very interesting story, but I'm sure your grandpa had nothing to do with it."

Defiantly, Betsy stood tall and firm before her mother. "It *was* because of Grandpa," she yelled. "Grandma said that Grandpa told her that, no matter what, he'd be there for his daughters and grandchildren. Why don't you believe me? I bet it's because of Grandpa Aunt Patty's going to marry Kevin."

"Now, Betsy, you're being ridiculous. I...." At that moment she remembered—she remembered an event she could never understand. Absently turning from her children, Mary walked back to the kitchen. She thought of her graduation day. She had gone alone to her father's grave to talk to him. To tell him everything about the graduation ceremony. That's when it happened. That's when she decided to go to Notre Dame instead of Wellesley. Daddy must have known. He knew she'd meet Ted at Notre Dame. He must have guided her.

With their mother back in the kitchen, Tucker and Betsy soon decided on a new way to settle their arguments. Feeling just a bit silly, they tentatively got in position to put their foreheads together.

Jane finally pulled away from the passionate kiss. Rubbing her nose against John's, she hoped to elicit the truth to a nagging mystery. "Tell me," she purred, "where did you really come from when you caught me? I know no one was near me before I fell."

John gave her his silly look and laughed. "What does it matter?"

Jane chewed on that for a while. "I guess it doesn't. Actually that mystery has always been part of what makes you so special." They walked on. "Remember how you used to dart from one side to the other, looking at me from every angle? Aggravating the heck out of me?" Then she moved to his right. "How do I look from this angle?" Then she moved to his left. "Or this one? How do my legs look?"

"Can't tell. Your gown's covering them."

"I'll fix that." She lifted the hem, revealing her shapely calves. In a teaser's mood now, she continued to raise the hem to her knees. When the hem reached her thighs, she asked, "Still wondering if they're flabby?"

"Please, that's far enough. Don't you realize we're in public?" He looked around nervously, as if he expected people to be able to see them.

The hem dropping brought a look of relief to John's face. She hugged him and said, "Just wanted to be sure that you liked the whole package." After a pause, she said, "I don't know why I should be the one worrying about public displays with you wearing those shorts. It's bad enough they only go an inch below your crotch, but in spots the cloth is threadbare. I know it's your underwear showing through."

"Is that so? Good thing I don't wear colored underwear." John chuckled. "Except there was the time I put Mary's red sweatshirt in the wash and ended up with pink underwear."

"Mmmm. I remember. You were so cute in pink. I waited until spring to bleach them white again."

"That must be why you choked on the ice cream the day we met."

"John Avery. Whatever are you talking about?"

"I remember how you looked at my shorts."

He hadn't lost his touch; Jane's face was bright red. "I'm impressed," she admitted. "You really did notice everything."

They stopped at the end of their front walk and admired their house. John shook one of the white picket-fence posts. "Still strong. We built a firm foundation. Same as we did with our marriage." He felt it unnecessary to mention how he had replaced some posts one spring when Jane and the kids were visiting her mother.

"Yes, we made a very good and lasting foundation, John." Jane didn't feel the need to mention that she had replaced some posts a few years back.

Scooping Jane into his arms, John carried her up the walk to the door. As they walked into the house, they could hear their grandchildren. At the living room, John stopped and looked. Betsy and Tucker were on their hands and knees, heads together, arguing about the right way to do it.

"I can see Grandma and Grandpa," Betsy yelled. "He's carrying her and she's so young and in her wedding gown."

"Wow, this is neat. I see them, too."

Lifting their heads, they looked at the hallway. "Hey, nobody's there." Tucker bolted for the hallway followed by Betsy. Tucker looked around scratching his head, then he said, "Let's go back and touch heads. Maybe we can see them again."

As soon as their heads touched, Betsy announced. "There they are. They're waving to us."

"But they're heading for the stairs." Silently they watched as their grandpa carried his bride up the stairs and disappeared into the bedroom. Excited now, Tucker cried, "Let's go up to the bedroom."

But Betsy was much more insistent. "No. Let's go tell Mommy."

In the bedroom, John set his wife down and looked around. "We've spent a lot of years in this house and in this room."

"The best years of my life," Jane replied.

He walked over to the crucifix hanging on the wall. "I remember seeing this crucifix hanging on the wall by your bed the day we met." Turning to Jane, John looked at her with the broadest smile.

John's smile was contagious—Jane began grinning. "What is it?"

For the longest time, John just smiled at her. Finally he said, "Every memory I have of you brings me to happiness."

"You're so silly," she said, wrapping him in her arms, "and sweet." Hugging him tightly, Jane closed her eyes and bit her lower lip, her face became flushed. In a soft, breaking voice she said, "You make me happy, too."

They stood there hugging, their bodies gently swaying—dancing to the music in their hearts.

Looking down at the floor, John said, "My basket of palm leaves."

"Our palms," Jane said, releasing him. "Ever since I've known you I've added my palms to your basket."

"You're right, they're our palms. I was seven years old when I heard the Bible story about how people laid palms at the feet of Jesus as he entered Jerusalem. I decided that day to save all my palms. I wanted a path to honor Jesus as he entered my room. My mother wove me this reed basket so I'd have something special to keep them in."

They looked deep into each other's eyes. "And Jesus has come to this house many times."

"We have truly been blessed, haven't we?" John gazed around the room soaking in the memories. His eyes fixed on something new, a frame hung between two windows. He approached it and admired what he saw. It was his "Angel in the Snow" poem. Just below the last line, taped to the glass was a familiar bow of white satin ribbon with red stitched lettering.

"When did you decide to hang these?"

"Last winter. Betsy thought they were too important to keep in my JOHN LOVES JANE box."

From the bottom corner of the frame he pulled out a small heart and read what he had written long ago. I LOVE YOU BECAUSE YOU LET ME KNOW THAT I MATTER TO YOU. Then he read what she had written around the edge. KNOWING I MATTER TO YOU JOHN, I LIVE IN SERENITY.

"Why did you save this one?"

Jane thought for a moment, her eyes twinkling. "I've saved them all. But with this one I know it was God who chose you for me."

Jane slipped her hands behind his neck. Dragging her nails across his skin, she purred, "Speaking of my apartment, you know I've always fantasized about the time we first undressed for each other. I was sure timid that day. Do you know how I *should* have done it?"

John simply stared. She released his neck and stepped back. Lifting her hem to her knees, she kicked off her shoes. Barefoot she began gliding around the room, her fluid movements as graceful as any of her dreams. With her back to him, she gave an over-the-shoulder smile. The smile, come-hither and coquettish, had its own allure. Her hips swayed, a kind of hula, as her hand slowly reached behind and delicately tugged on the zipper.

John remained transfixed as the zipper lowered—exposing her creamy flesh. Hypnotically, she paraded to a far corner, gown in hand and dropped it. Feeling like a high-spirited lioness, she approached him. In total control, she hooked her thumbs into the waist of her half-slip. With a seductive wriggle, it dropped to her knees. Bending forward, she cooed, "I thought you were an eye man. How come you're not looking at my eyes?"

John had no snappy comeback. When he untied his tongue, the best he could offer was, "I can't help but enjoy the whole package."

Clad only in scant blue panties and lace bra, she sauntered to the gown and deposited the slip. With her rose in hand, she turned. She slowly lifted her arms and tucked the rose behind her ear. "Seen enough? Or would you like more?"

John, his eyes glazed over, managed to mumble something incoherent. Jane ran her hands over her breasts before reaching in back to unfasten her bra. As her breasts spilled out, John shuddered. When her thumbs hooked into the waist of her panties, she heard her husband's panting. Tantalizingly slow, she bumped her hips from side to side until the panties were nestled in a soft pile around her ankles. Stepping out with her eyes deep in his, she stretched her arms up. Still in the hula mode, she turned a teasingly slow circle. All the while she craned her neck over her shoulder to keep eye contact.

"I can't take any more," John groaned at the rapturous display. "You're the most gorgeous woman I could ever imagine." He pulled his jersey over his head. After unbuttoning his shorts, he unzipped them.

"Oooh," Jane cooed, seeing them fall to his ankles. "That's the part I like the best." She managed not to giggle as he did his little hokey pokey, something he'd perfected after years of dancing with his daughters at parties.

Embracing him, she nestled her head on his chest. "It's not a gorgeous body, but it's a good body. You're the only man I've ever wanted to be with." Jane's tongue found his ear and wetly swam in and out. He shuddered. "You know," she murmured, her voice an erotic buzz, "we've never resolved the deadlock over our wrestling matches."

"You can be sure I haven't forgotten."

"How's your arm?"

"So you were lucky once."

Eyes locked, they climbed into bed.

Downstairs Betsy and Tucker careened into the kitchen. Their mother was just taking a batch of chocolate-chip cookies out of the oven. "Mommy, Mommy," the girl cried, jumping high with excitement. "We just saw Grandma and Grandpa. They went upstairs to Grandma's room. She was wearing her wedding gown."

"Don't be silly, precious. You know Grandma's in the hospital."

"It's true! Let's go upstairs and see them," Tucker said, heading for the stairs.

"No you don't, young man. Besides, where are your manners? If they went in their bedroom, they'd expect some privacy."

"Darn." Slumping his head, Tucker dragged himself back in the room.

"Why don't you sit down while these cookies cool and tell me what you think happened."

By the time the kids had finished relating their story about what they had seen, and their secrets with their grandmother, they were breathless. Tucker reached for a cookie. "It's true, Mom. Every word."

"Even the stuff about putting heads together, I suppose?"

"Every word," Betsy repeated.

Mary's mind drifted back as she watched Tucker, then Betsy munch on a cookie. She went back to a bedtime routine her father had with her. Tucking her in at night, he'd put his head against hers and say, "I know what you're thinking. Oh my gosh, I'll have to tell your mommy that." He always had a silly first answer when she asked him what she was thinking. He'd say things like, "Your teddy bear had peanut butter for lunch," or, "You feed your peas to the plants." His silliness would give her fits of giggles. Her mother would get mad at him for getting her laughing so.

"You know something?" Mary finally said. "I think your grandpa used to read my thoughts when he put me to bed."

"Boy, this is neat!" Tucker said.

"Then it *is* true," Betsy exclaimed. "Did Grandpa do it with Aunt Patty, too?"

Mary nodded, her mind still back in childhood. Many things became clearer for her. Feelings she had thought were simply emotional longings, crystallized now. It must not have been her imagination that he had squeezed her hand in the hospital after she told him good-bye.

"I still think he's an alien from outer space even though I never did find his landing spot last winter."

Mary wiped at a tear. "No, dear, he was a real man, a very special man. But he *was* a little strange. Take those shorts he used to wear. Your grandma used to tell him that if he wore those terrible shorts outside the police would arrest him. 'With my beautiful legs?' he'd say."

"Why didn't Grandma just throw them away like you do with some of our old clothes?"

249

"Oh, no. She'd never do that. They reminded her too much of the day they met."

Mary glanced out at a garden as she crunched on a cookie. The cookies helped take her back. The black-eyed Susans swayed gently in the breeze. She remembered and smiled. Daddy used to take her and Patty out to cut flowers for their mother. They used to cut enough lilacs to fill vases in every room. She remembered her parents and their special love. Like early one morning she went into their room and her mother was asleep covered with lilac blossoms. Daddy denied having anything to do with it, saying an angel must have sprinkled them on her.

Memories flooded back to her. The nostalgia was so deep, she wanted to drown in it. This house was full of love. Mary's thoughts turned to her sister and her coming marriage. She needed her now, to talk to her about Daddy and their lives together in this house.

Betsy's voice interrupted her reverie. "I'm going out to the butterfly bushes. There should be some pretty butterflies flying around."

Before Mary could respond, the phone's jangle brought her to her feet. Thoughts of her mother at the hospital hurried her to the phone.

"Hi Ted," she said, after hearing her husband's voice, "how's Mother doing?" Instantly, Mary's face turned ashen with horror. The children gazed at their mother—stone-still, eyes riveted. Silence filled the old house.

Mary closed her eyes trying to hold back the tears streaming down her cheeks.

From upstairs a loud thud reverberated throughout the house.

"It's Grandma!" exclaimed Betsy, running for the stairs. "She just flipped Grandpa."